It had b  **re.**

His trip back t[...] see
if he'd gotten [...] had
forgotten him.

She'd passed with flying colors.

His results were still pending. But right now it looked
as if he'd get a big fat F.

He'd give his speech when they dedicated the high
school football field to Carter. And he'd stay for Amy.
But apparently the author had been right—a man
couldn't go home again.

Dear Reader,

I love Door County, Wisconsin. The combination of beautiful beaches, wonderful parks full of hiking trails and rocky lakeshores, and the little shops that cater to tourists is irresistible. It was the site of one of our few family vacations when I was a child, and I've been there a number of times as an adult. So it was probably inevitable that Door County would be the setting of one of my books.

When Kendall came to me, I knew her bed-and-breakfast and her cherry orchard were in Door County. But her story resonated beyond its location. It's a story of redemption, of righting old wrongs, and finally getting a chance to realize the most secret dreams of the heart. Who wouldn't want a chance for a "do-over"? Kendall and Gabe get that chance, and I loved watching their story unfold.

Kendall's brother George and his girlfriend, Amy, also have to face the past—and they struggle with it. It's not an easy thing to do, just as it's not easy to let some secrets go. But the secrets in Sturgeon Falls, Wisconsin, have been covered up for too long.

I hope you enjoy Kendall and Gabe, Amy and George and *Small-Town Secrets*. And I hope that some day, you can visit the wonderful Door County. It's no secret that it's one of the most beautiful parts of Wisconsin.

I love to hear from my readers. E-mail me at mwatson1004@hotmail.com or visit my Web site, www.margaretwatson.com.

Margaret Watson

SMALL-TOWN SECRETS
Margaret Watson

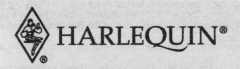

HARLEQUIN®

TORONTO • NEW YORK • LONDON
AMSTERDAM • PARIS • SYDNEY • HAMBURG
STOCKHOLM • ATHENS • TOKYO • MILAN • MADRID
PRAGUE • WARSAW • BUDAPEST • AUCKLAND

ISBN-13: 978-0-373-71371-4
ISBN-10:   0-373-71371-1

SMALL-TOWN SECRETS

Copyright © 2006 by Margaret Watson.

This edition published by arrangement with Harlequin Books S.A.

® and TM are trademarks of the publisher. Trademarks indicated with
® are registered in the United States Patent and Trademark Office, the
Canadian Trade Marks Office and in other countries.

www.eHarlequin.com

Printed in U.S.A.

ABOUT THE AUTHOR

Margaret Watson has always made up stories in her head. When she started actually writing them down, she realized that she'd found exactly what she wanted to do with the rest of her life. Fifteen years after staring at that first blank page, she's written eighteen books for Silhouette and Harlequin Books. When she's not writing or spending time with her husband and three daughters (and menagerie of animals), she practices veterinary medicine in Chicago, which has inspired wonderful characters and interesting stories for her books.

Books by Margaret Watson

HARLEQUIN SUPERROMANCE

Don't miss any of our special offers. Write to us at the following address for information on our newest releases.

Harlequin Reader Service
U.S.: 3010 Walden Ave., P.O. Box 1325, Buffalo, NY 14269
Canadian: P.O. Box 609, Fort Erie, Ont. L2A 5X3

This is for Kathy Watson, the sister of my heart, who shared her favorite parts of Door County with me.

CHAPTER ONE

Wednesday afternoon

HE'D THOUGHT he was ready for this.

The years away should have inoculated him against the emotions surfacing now—loss, pain, guilt and the familiar edgy tension that Kendall Van Allen had always inspired. He thought he'd dumped the baggage he'd been carrying when he left Sturgeon Falls seven years earlier.

He thought he'd gotten on with his life.

He was wrong.

Gabe rolled his BMW to a stop on the smooth driveway and studied Van Allen House. The fresh coat of creamy yellow paint, the green and rose of the contrasting trim and the flowers massed around the house all glowed in the sunlight. The house had certainly changed.

Had Kendall changed as much?

Would she welcome him? Or merely tolerate him?

Maybe he should have stayed away from her. The dedication committee had made the reservation, but he could have declined. Maybe he should have booked himself into one of the other B and B's. Sometimes old wounds were better left alone.

No. He got out of the car and shut the door. He'd run away seven years ago, and he'd regretted it ever since. He was done with running away. The dedication of the high-school football stadium to Kendall's late husband, Carter, had brought him back to Sturgeon Falls, but that wasn't the only thing that was going to happen this weekend.

Kendall would need his help. Even though she didn't know it yet.

THE DOOR KNOCKER SOUNDED just as Kendall was pulling on her black slacks. Shoving her feet into her image-enhancing Bruno Magli pumps, she finger-combed her short hair and then buttoned her blouse as she hurried down the stairs. The guest the dedication committee had booked into her bed-and-breakfast was right on time.

The tall, lean figure of a man was visible through the frosted-glass panels in the front door. Kendall took a deep breath, checked one last time to make sure all the buttons on her blouse were done up, plastered a smile on her face and opened the door.

"Welcome to Van Allen House," she said to her prospective guest's back. He was looking out over the ex-pansive front lawn, hands in the pockets of his elegant charcoal slacks, apparently studying the formal garden.

Then he turned to face her. "Very nice, Kendall. You've done a lot of work. It doesn't look like the same place."

The shock of recognition hit her like a blow. Even

after seven years, his black hair and blue eyes, his sensual mouth and beautiful face were unmistakable. Her smile vanished. "Gabe?"

"Hello, Kendall."

Her hand curled around the door. "What are you doing here?"

"I have a reservation. Compliments of the dedication committee."

"*You're* my guest?"

"In the flesh."

She itched to shut the door in his face. But the bill for the hot-water heater she'd just replaced still sat on the desk in her office. Even though she wanted nothing to do with Gabe Townsend or the memories that clung to him like stubborn cobwebs, she stepped aside and opened the door wider. "Come in."

He strolled into the foyer, his curious gaze registering everything, from the slightly threadbare rug on the floor to the faint depression in the plaster left by her daughter's soccer ball to the pictures of ancestral Van Allens that lined the wall alongside the stairs.

She closed the door a little harder than necessary. "Why did you come here? What do you want?"

He dropped his leather suitcase. "Other than a room? A 'hello, Gabe' would be nice. 'Welcome back to Sturgeon Falls' would be even nicer."

"If you came to Sturgeon Falls looking for a welcome from me, you're out of your mind," she said, moving to the small office she'd set up in a closet beneath the stairs. "There's nothing here for you."

"The committee made the reservation," he said. "Maybe they thought it would be nostalgic."

"I'm not much for nostalgia." She studied him, noticing the confident way he held himself, registering his assumption that he belonged. "I didn't think you were, either."

He shrugged. "That's what this dedication is all about, isn't it? Old memories? Looking at the past through rose-colored glasses?"

"I don't want to look at the past at all."

"No choice this time," he said lightly. "You're coming to the ceremony, aren't you?" He set his credit card on her desk.

"Of course I am. The girls are thrilled about the whole stupid thing. They've been talking about it for weeks." Dragging her gaze away from his long, elegant fingers, she swiped Gabe's card through the reader so hard it flew out of her hand. She grabbed it and slapped it back down on the desk.

"Let's cut to the chase, Gabe. I know I'm not the only bed-and-breakfast in town with a vacancy on a Wednesday this early in June. You could have stayed somewhere else. Why here?"

She couldn't read his expression. His eyes were just as inscrutable as they'd always been.

"Staying at your B and B is business. And when I'm doing business, I like to keep it in the family," he said.

"I'm not part of your family."

"I'm Jenna's godfather. Doesn't that count?"

"I assumed you'd forgotten."

Gabe held her gaze. "I take my obligations seriously."

"We're not one of your obligations, Gabe. We never have been. I thought I'd made that clear a long time ago."

"Obligation or not, I'm here for the dedication. When the committee suggested I stay here, as ill-advised as they may have been, I agreed. Why spend their money anywhere else?"

"I've put the past behind me. You should have, too."

He watched her for a long moment. "If you'd put the past behind you, Kendall, you wouldn't be telling me to find another place to stay."

Kendall took a deep breath, let it out slowly and then nodded. "You're right. Business is business. You can be sure I won't forget again." She was an adult now, a successful businesswoman. His money was as good as anyone else's. Pride wouldn't pay for a new hot-water heater. She completed the paperwork and smiled stiffly.

"Let me show you the main floor before I take you upstairs to your room. This is the dining room…"

Before she could continue, he asked, "Is that coffee on the buffet?"

"Yes. Would you like a cup?"

"Please."

She poured two mugs and absently added cream to both before handing one to Gabe. He stared at it.

"You remembered how I like my coffee."

"I wasn't thinking." She forced herself to relax the tight grip on her own mug as she set it on the table. "I made it like mine."

He took a sip, never taking his eyes off her. "It's been a long time, Kendall. What have you been up to?"

She stirred her coffee, watching the dark liquid lighten as it mixed with the cream. "Raising my daughters. Running the B and B. Living. What about you?"

"I keep busy. My company demands a lot of time."

Gabe wasn't any more eager to share his life story than she was. The swallow she took burned a path all the way to her stomach. "Now that we have the pleasantries out of the way, I'll show you your room."

She pushed away from the table, picking up a key attached to a laminated plastic business card on her way up the stairs. Gabe was close behind her. She turned to the right when they reached the second floor and opened a white-painted wooden door.

"This room has an updated bath and a view of the backyard and the beach," she said in her best tour-guide voice as she gestured toward the window. "Will it be all right?"

"It'll be fine," he said without looking.

She stepped back, but Gabe made no effort to go in. "Kendall…"

"Breakfast is from 7:00 until 9:00 a.m.," she said. "I lock the front door each night at nine, but your room key will unlock it. The living room is a common area for everyone who's staying in the house, so please make yourself comfortable. Is there anything else I can get for you?"

"Not a thing."

She gave him a tight, impersonal smile. "Then, I'll see you at breakfast tomorrow."

He didn't move as she headed back down the stairs.

Pausing, she picked up the two abandoned mugs, carried them into the kitchen and emptied them into the sink. Like old dreams, the coffee swirled down the drain and disappeared.

A HALF HOUR LATER, Gabe walked into the living room again. Kendall was nowhere in sight. He wasn't surprised.

Maybe she wasn't avoiding him deliberately. But she wasn't going to hang around, waiting to talk to him, either.

Running a bed-and-breakfast must be hard work, and Gabe was guessing that Kendall did it on her own. She'd always thrown herself completely into every job she'd undertaken, no matter how large or small it was.

And now she had an extra incentive for keeping busy. Being occupied and unavailable was much more graceful than simply telling Gabe to get lost.

He hadn't expected a warm welcome. She'd made it clear seven years earlier that she wanted nothing to do with him. He couldn't blame her. After all, as she'd pointed out at the time, he'd killed her husband.

The car crash had been an accident. The judge had *ruled* it an accident caused by icy roads and a snowstorm. But that didn't change the facts. It was Gabe's car. The police told her it had been going too fast. They told her Gabe had been driving. And Carter was dead.

Leaving her a widow with two young daughters and very little money.

Gabe poured himself a fresh mug of coffee from the thermos he found in the dining room and stared out the window as he sipped. The back lawn of Kendall's home sloped gently down to a secluded private beach on Green Bay. As a major Midwestern tourist destination, Door County, Wisconsin, was host to a tangle of traffic jams, packed beaches and crowded shops every summer from June until September. But even though Sturgeon Falls was at the epicenter, Van Allen House was a calm oasis.

Kendall had clearly worked hard to cultivate that image.

Gabe gazed out at the Adirondack chairs on the grass by the edge of the beach, with matching tables set between them. On one side stretched the dense pine forest of a county park, on the other was the family cherry orchard.

The house itself combined family heirlooms and modern comfort. The rich cherry wood of the spool bed in his room had been polished by generations of Van Allens. Downstairs, the hardwood floors were covered by vivid oriental rugs, and the formality of the ornate mantel over the living-room fireplace was offset by comfortable overstuffed chairs and couches.

He saw Kendall's hand in all of it.

The dazed young widow he remembered, who'd stood next to her husband's grave clutching the hands of her two young daughters, had vanished completely. She'd been replaced by the cool, confident professional who'd opened her door to him that morning.

The door to the kitchen swung open and Kendall came through, holding a stack of plates. When she saw him, her hesitation was so brief that most people wouldn't have noticed.

Gabe did.

He'd always noticed everything about her.

"Gabe. Is everything all right in your room?"

"Yes." He gestured around the dining room. "You've done a nice job with the house. It's beautiful."

The plates clattered as she set them on the buffet. "Thank you. I had good bones to work with."

She pulled a handful of silverware out of the pocket of her apron and arranged it in a wooden caddy next to the plates. He noticed that she'd changed her clothes. Instead of her expensive shoes and the dressy blouse, she wore a T-shirt, cutoffs and sandals. Her short blond hair looked as if she'd run her hands through it more than once. When she realized he was looking at her, she smoothed her hands over the faded blue apron she had on.

"Was there something you needed?"

She'd be surprised at what he needed. "Nothing at all. I'm just on my way out."

She couldn't quite disguise the flicker of relief in her dark amber eyes, although she tried. He set the coffee mug on the table with a sharp crack. "I'll see you later."

"I'll be here."

The weariness he thought he heard in her voice was probably just his imagination. When he paused and looked back, she'd already disappeared.

Time to deal with another piece of his past. Amy Mitchell had different claims on him than Kendall had, but they were almost as strong. At first, they'd been part of a debt of honor. But over the years, Amy had become a friend.

Climbing into his car, Gabe drove away from the seclusion of the estate and turned onto hectic County Road B. Merging into a steady stream of cars and trucks, he headed toward Amy's house on the outskirts of town.

He stopped in front of a tidy white house that was surrounded by a picket fence, and smiled. If anyone was defined by a white-picket fence, it was Amy.

A woman with dark, curly hair knelt in front of a flower bed, digging in the sandy soil, a flat of colorful snapdragons on the grass beside her. She turned when she heard the car door and sat back on her heels, pushing her hair out of her eyes. "Hi, Gabe," she said.

He walked through the arbor that arched over the sidewalk and sat on her front steps. "Hello, Amy."

"I wondered when you'd show up. Are you here to make sure I don't back down?" she asked.

"You're not going to back down. You know you have to tell George."

She placed a plant in the spot she'd prepared and pressed the dirt around it. "What happened is in the past."

Gabe eased back against the stairs, the angled edges of the wood uncomfortable against his back. "No, it's not. I think you know that, Amy."

"George asked me once who Tommy's father was. I told him it didn't matter, that it was in the past and Tommy's father wasn't a part of his life. He accepted that."

"Really?"

"George loves me. And I love him."

"That's why you need to tell him."

Amy dug another hole, the dirt flying through her hands. "I promised I'd tell him, and I will. You didn't need to come to Sturgeon Falls for the big show."

"I had to be here anyway. And since I'm the one who's pushing you, it's only fair I help you through this."

She flopped back onto the grass and sighed. "I'm sorry I'm being snotty," she said. "I know how hard it was for you to come back."

Honesty compelled him to admit that if it hadn't been for the dedication, he might not have come. "All the same, now that I'm here, I'll stay until you get this resolved with George." He hesitated. "And maybe I can help Kendall, too. She's going to be devastated."

"I know." Amy dashed a hand across her eyes and Gabe saw tears glistening there. "I really screwed up, didn't I?"

"You were seventeen," Gabe said gently. "Making mistakes is part of growing up."

"But some of us screw up worse than others."

Gabe held her gaze. "At least you didn't kill anyone."

"That was an accident," Amy said, her voice sharp.

"Accident or not, Carter's still dead." He forced the crash and its aftermath out of his mind. "So let's not use the words *screw up*, okay? You made a mistake."

Amy smiled through her tears. "I'm still making mistakes when it comes to men, aren't I? Of all the men in the world, I had to fall for Kendall Van Allen's brother."

"Your heart doesn't always listen to your head when it comes to love," Gabe said, his mouth twisting. "I'm the last person to give advice on relationships."

"What about Helen, back in Milwaukee?"

"What about her?"

"She sounds very nice."

Gabe sighed. "She is, but I broke it off before I came up here. There was no spark between us. It wasn't fair to her."

Amy's expression softened. "Oh, George and I definitely spark."

"You can't let a secret poison your relationship."

"I know you're right," she said. She brushed the dirt off her hands and moved the snapdragons into the shade. "I told myself it didn't matter, but the truth elbows its way between us whenever we're together. I can hardly bear to look at him right now." She wrapped her arms around her knees. "I'm so scared."

"But you're going to do it anyway. You've always been gutsy, Amy."

She rolled her eyes. "Right. That's why you have to hold my hand now."

"You don't really need me," Gabe replied. "I'm just here for moral support."

Amy reached out to touch him, looked at her dirt-stained hands and drew away. "You've been a real support all these years. "Carter was lucky he had you as a friend."

"It went both ways," Gabe answered. "Carter was a good friend to me, too."

"Was he?"

"He was the brother I didn't have. We didn't always agree, but we were still there for each other."

Amy dropped another snapdragon into a hole and pushed some dirt around it. "Does Kendall know you're in town?"

"Yes. I'm staying at her bed-and-breakfast."

"Oh, Gabe. Why did you do that? If Kendall finds out you're involved with this, that you've kept in touch with me, you'll spoil any chance you might have with her."

Gabe gave Amy a smile that was devoid of humor. "I gave up any chance I had with Kendall some time ago."

"Is she the same woman she was when you left?"

"I have no idea. She didn't exactly welcome me with open arms."

"I'll wait until you leave Sturgeon Falls to tell George. Kendall will never have to know that you knew all along."

"I'm not leaving, Amy. It's time to put these secrets in the past."

"You're willing to risk a relationship with her?"

"I have no relationship with Kendall. You know that. She wants nothing to do with me."

"But you'd be good together."

As Amy studied him, Gabe felt his nerves jump beneath his skin. He didn't want anyone seeing that deeply inside him. He didn't want anyone to know him that well. "You're a hopeless romantic, Amy."

"I'm not the one who's carrying a torch."

"I am *not* carrying a torch for her." He closed his eyes, blotting out the memories. "And you're getting off the subject."

"I worry about you, Gabe. I want you to be happy. As happy as I am with George. Except for…"

Gabe pounced on the chance to change the subject. He stood and pulled Amy to her feet. "I'm glad you found someone who makes you happy," he said. "And I know you're worried. But if George Krippner is half the man I think he is, he's not going to reject you because of something that happened long ago."

"I guess we'll find out, won't we? He's very close to his sister." Amy brushed her hands against her cutoffs and walked into the house with Gabe behind her. "I have no idea how I'm going to tell him. I hope he'll realize I'm a different person than the child I used to be. But if he doesn't?" She turned on the faucet at the kitchen sink, and Gabe saw she was still fighting tears. "Well, I guess that's my punishment for sleeping with a married man. I can't make this right until I tell George what I did. Until I tell him that Tommy's father is Carter Van Allen."

CHAPTER TWO

Wednesday evening

"Hi, Mom."

The screen door slammed. Kendall dropped the lettuce she'd been rinsing off and swung around to face her ten-year-old daughter. "Shelby. Where have you been?"

A sheepish look crept across the child's face. "I was supposed to make the salad for dinner tonight, wasn't I?"

"Yes, you were. I expected you home forty-five minutes ago. I called Bertie and sent him into the orchard to look for you. I was getting worried."

"I was helping him in the orchard," she said, dancing into the kitchen. "And now I have a new friend."

Kendall's irritation melted away. "You've known Bertie your whole life. He can't be a new friend." Kendall leaned against the sink, crossing her arms and trying hard to hide a smile. She never could resist Shelby's enthusiasm.

Shelby giggled. "You're being silly, Mom. Bertie's not my new friend. He's my *old* friend."

"Then who's your new friend?"

"Her name is Elena. Her family is working here for the cherry season and she's my age. When she saw me and Bertie cleaning the crates, she came over and helped, too."

"Does she go to school with you?"

"No. She wanted to go to school when they got here last week, but her mother said not to bother."

"That's too bad," Kendall said. "A week in school is never a waste." She'd have to talk to Elena's parents. Kendall offered bonuses to workers who enrolled their children in the local school.

"I told her she could be in fifth grade with me next year," Shelby said.

"I'm glad you made a new friend, sweetheart," Kendall said gently. "Now, how about making the salad?"

"Okay." Shelby jumped onto a stool by the sink and began washing the lettuce. "You know what's so neat about Elena, Mom?"

"What's so neat about Elena?"

"She lives in Florida in the winter! Can you believe that?"

"Florida. That's exciting."

"It would be so cool to live in Florida. Elena said they live close to the ocean. They could go to the beach every day, if they wanted."

"Elena's parents have to work hard, Shel. I don't think she goes to the beach every day."

Shelby's eyes shone. "But she goes sometimes. She told me. She said she found a big seashell, much bigger than the stupid tiny ones in Green Bay."

"Maybe someday we can go," Kendall answered. Her heart felt tight in her chest. A trip to Florida, to look for seashells, was one of Shelby's dreams. Kendall hoped they could afford it before her girls were too old to look for shells.

Shelby turned to face her mother as she prepared a cucumber. Ribbons of green peel scattered across the floor. "I bet I could find a Junonia or a Lion's Paw if we went to Florida. There are so many shells on the beach that you have to step on them."

"That's hard to imagine." Kendall turned Shelby back to the sink, then bent to pick up the vegetable peel.

"Sanibel Island has the best," Shelby confided. "That's what my book says."

"Then that's where we'll go, if we go to Florida." Kendall stirred spaghetti sauce on the stove and checked the bubbling pot of pasta while Shelby finished the salad. "Shel, could you go find Jenna and ask her to set the table, please?"

"Okay." Shelby jumped down from her stool, dropped the salad bowl on the table and ran through the swinging door.

Kendall smiled as Shelby took off, then picked up the remaining cucumber peel and put it in the compost bucket. She'd work on the "cleaning up after yourself" lesson once Shelby had mastered "come home when you're supposed to."

A few minutes later, Jenna appeared, her head buried in a book. She stopped just inside the kitchen door, apparently lost in the story.

Kendall smiled. "What are you reading, sweetie?"

The eight-year-old looked up with a start. "Hi, Mom." She held up the book. "The new Harry Potter."

"Again?" Kendall tweaked her nose. "Haven't you memorized that one by now?"

"It's so good, I could read it every day."

"How about you stop reading long enough to set the table and eat dinner?"

"Okay." Jenna reluctantly put the book on the counter, and headed for the table.

Kendall began to scoop spaghetti into bowls, but stopped at the sound of Shelby's voice from the other room. "Is Shelby talking on the phone?"

Jenna shook her head and set a fork by her place. "She's talking to some man."

Kendall's hand tightened on the spoon. "Mr. Smith?" she asked, hoping it was her *other* guest.

"Nope. I never saw him before."

The pasta cooker clanked on the countertop as Kendall set it down. But before she could call her daughter in, the door burst open.

"Mom!" Shelby cried. "Why didn't you tell me Uncle Gabe was here?"

Uncle Gabe? Kendall's eyes narrowed. What had Gabe said to her? There was no way Shelby would remember him. She'd only been three the last time she'd seen him.

Gabe stood in the doorway, watching Shelby with a bemused expression on his face. In spite of herself, Kendall softened. Her older daughter's exuberance charmed both friends and strangers.

Kendall touched Shelby's hair. "Go and wash up for dinner, honey."

"Can Uncle Gabe have dinner with us?" Shelby asked. "Please? You always make too much spaghetti."

"Gabe is probably getting ready to go out to dinner."

"Are you?" Shelby demanded. "Are you going out?"

"No. I just came down to get a glass of water."

"See, Mom? He *can* have dinner with us."

Trapped, Kendall searched for an excuse. Gabe could have smoothed the awkward moment by saying he had plans, she thought with a glimmer of anger. But he just stood there, watching.

Shelby jumped up and down. "Pl*eeea*se, Mom. I want him to eat with us."

Kendall couldn't refuse without sounding like an ogre. "Fine." She gave Gabe a tight smile. "Please join us."

"Thank you." He glanced at the counter, saw the steaming bowl of pasta and sauce. "Can I do anything to help?"

"Just have a seat. Shelby, show Gabe where to sit."

"This way, Uncle Gabe." Shelby tugged him toward the table.

Kendall frowned. She needed to talk to Shelby, instill in her a respect for the boundaries between the three of them and their guests.

But Shelby didn't think of Gabe as a guest.

Encouraged, apparently, by Gabe identifying himself as Uncle Gabe. *Unbelievable.*

Kendall sat and bowed her head while the girls said grace. Afterward, she passed the spaghetti to Gabe.

He served himself, and then turned to Jenna, who sat watching him with wide brown eyes. "You must be Jenna," he said.

She nodded cautiously.

"I saw you reading a book. What was it?"

"Harry Potter," Jenna answered, perking up.

Gabe nodded. "I like the Harry Potter books. Who's your favorite character?"

"Harry Potter, of course. But I like Hermione, too. I wish I could go to Hogwarts."

Gabe smiled. "Which house would you want to be in?"

Jenna's fork clattered to the table and she beamed at Gabe. "Gryffindor, of course. That's the best one."

Jenna, her normally reserved, quiet daughter, chattered to Gabe about Harry Potter for the rest of the meal. Kendall was grudgingly impressed by his knowledge of the books and by his patience with her daughter. He gave her his full attention.

Shelby, meanwhile, glowered on the other side of the table, clearly upset by her sister's appropriation of the spotlight. Finally, unable to take it any longer, Shelby interrupted the conversation.

"I love the Harry Potter books, too."

Gabe shot her a quick glance full of understanding. "I bet you used to read them to Jenna, didn't you?"

Shelby nodded hard. "Before she could even read. If I hadn't read them to her, she wouldn't know anything about Harry Potter."

"I would, too," Jenna said, turning on Shelby. "I know lots more about them than you do."

"Do not. I was just reading one today."

"That was my book," Jenna said. "I saw it was missing. Where is it?"

"It's right there on the counter."

Jenna slid out of her chair and ran to get it. Kendall silently acknowledged Gabe's skillful handling of her girls. "Let's talk about something else, Shelby. How was school today?"

Before she could answer, Jenna yelled, "It is not on the counter. Where's my book?"

"Girls." Kendall didn't raise her voice, but both girls immediately quieted. "Jenna, come sit down and finish your dinner. We'll worry about the book later. Shelby, stop teasing your sister."

The girls stabbed at the last of their noodles. "We apologize for disrupting your dinner," Kendall said to Gabe, mortified.

He gave her a smile. "If I wanted a boring meal, I wouldn't have accepted your invitation."

Kendall's hands tightened around the napkin in her lap. She looked over at the girls, who'd finished eating and now watched their mother and Gabe with bright curiosity. "Shelby, Jenna, would you clear the table, please? And after that, go get started on your homework."

She waited until they were out of the kitchen, then turned on him. "I didn't think you'd stoop that low, Gabe. To use my daughters."

"I didn't," he said. "Shelby said hello and introduced herself. Should I have ignored her?"

Kendall swallowed an angry retort. Impulsive, reckless Shelby was definitely her father's child. It was both the source of her charm and the reason she got into trouble so often.

Just as it had been with Carter.

"You didn't have to tell her you were her uncle Gabe."

He raised an eyebrow. "That's what she used to call me."

"She wouldn't have remembered." Kendall pressed her lips together, holding back sharper words. Shelby and Jenna were in the next room.

"She said she remembered that silly game of airplane we used to play."

In her mind's eye, Kendall saw a younger, smiling Gabe twirling a laughing child in circles through the air. In the months after Carter had died, Shelby had asked about her uncle Gabe more than once.

"I don't want them to remember!" Kendall leaned toward Gabe. "Do you know how hard it was for them after Carter died?" she demanded. "Shelby asked me every night when he was coming home. I found one of Carter's shirts in her bed. She told me it smelled like her daddy."

Kendall pushed her plate away from her and threw her napkin on the table.

"Jenna was only a baby, but she became a fussy, clinging child. It was so hard, but we got through it.

They're happy now. You're going to bring back all that pain."

"For Shelby and Jenna? Or for you?" Gabe stared at her until she looked away. "I'm not trying to hurt any of you. I'd just like to get to know Carter's girls."

"There are good reasons I want you to stay away from them," she said. She stared at the checkered pattern on the tablecloth, not seeing the design. "There are things I don't want them to know about their father."

"Do you think I'd tell them anything ugly about Carter? Anything that would hurt them or their memories? Is that what you think of me?"

She blushed. "I'm sorry," she said gruffly. "That wasn't fair."

"No, Kendall. It wasn't." His hand hovered above hers, touched her lightly. She snatched her hand away, shocked at the spark that leaped through her.

Gabe didn't seem to notice. "Carter was my best friend," he said, his voice quiet. "Jenna is my god-daughter. It was wrong of me to stay away for so long. You shut me out after he died, and I understand why, but I'd like to be in the girls' lives."

"That's not going to happen, Gabe." She stood and stared out the window, watching the sun splash red and pink smears as it sank below Green Bay. It had been a struggle to get her life back on track after Carter died, and Gabe wasn't going to derail it now. "I won't tell you to stay away from them while you're here, but I'm not opening that painful chapter again."

Gabe was silent behind her. When she turned, she forced herself to meet his gaze. "Do you understand?"

"I do, Kendall. But maybe the girls need some of those memories."

"They have plenty. I've told them lots of stories—the ones I want them to hear. Are you going to tellthem about the times you and Carter got drunk? Or about the times you were arrested for drag racing down County B? Or the times you went to the casino in Green Bay and lost a whole paycheck playing blackjack? Are those the memories you're going to share with the girls?"

"I can tell them what he was like when he was their age." He paused. "I see a lot of Carter in Shelby. And Jenna, too, for that matter. She's as passionate about those Harry Potter books as he was about the orchard."

She turned back to the window. "You can tell them all the stories you want about Carter's childhood between now and next Wednesday. But after that?" She wrapped her arms around herself as she stared at the sunset. "There's just too much baggage for all of us to try and pick up where you and Carter left off."

He came up behind her, and her skin prickled. "That was a long time ago." His voice was a low murmur in the quiet kitchen. "There doesn't have to be baggage."

Before she could answer, his attention snapped to the window. "Someone's hiding behind the house."

Disoriented by the abrupt shift in Gabe's tone, Kendall peered out the window. "I don't see anyone."

"Over there to the left. Near the orchard."

Kendall strained to see through the darkness. Two

darker shadows detached themselves from the shadows cast by the trees. She watched the two figures move toward the house.

"Do you know them?"

"I have no idea. I can't see who they are."

Gabe stood by the screen door, watching as they got closer. As if he was putting himself between Kendall and any trouble. She went to move him out of the way, but he didn't budge.

As the pair got closer, Kendall could see that the two were a young woman and a girl. The woman's long black hair hung down her back in a ponytail, and she wore loose pants and an old T-shirt. The girl wore shorts and a red blouse.

"The woman must be one of the laborers from the orchard," Kendall said to Gabe in a low voice.

"Do your employees come here often?"

"Never."

The pair stopped at the foot of the stairs. Kendall could see that the child clutched something against her chest. The woman murmured in Spanish to the girl, then let go of her hand.

"Is Shelby here?" the child said in a low voice.

"Yes, she is. Are you a friend of hers?" Kendall asked.

"My name is Elena Montoya." The girl climbed the stairs. "She left this book in the orchard."

Elena's hand tightened around the book, then she extended it. It was the Harry Potter that Shelby had taken from Jenna. Kendall unlatched the screen. "Please, come in."

The girl turned to her mother, and the woman nodded. Kendall motioned for the girl's mother to come in, as well. The woman hesitated before stepping into the kitchen after her daughter.

"Just a moment," she said. Shelby was bent over a sheet of paper at the dining-room table. "Shel," she called. "There's someone here to see you."

Shelby bounced up from the table. "Who?"

"Your friend Elena."

"Really?" She dashed into the kitchen. "Hi, Elena."

As Kendall and Jenna followed, Kendall saw Elena hand Shelby the book. Elena's gaze lingered on it, then her mother spoke to her sharply. She grabbed her daughter's hand and pulled her close.

She was afraid she'd get in trouble, Kendall realized.

"Thank you very much for bringing back Shelby's book," Kendall said to Elena. "That was very thoughtful of you." She repeated the thanks to Elena's mother in Spanish.

The mother relaxed a little before edging toward the door. "Thanks, Elena," Shelby said. She grinned. "My sister was mad because I couldn't find it."

Jenna darted forward and snatched the book from Shelby's hand.

"We had cake for dessert, Mrs. Montoya," Kendall said to Elena's mother. "Would you and Elena like to stay and have a piece?"

Elena turned to her mother and pleaded with her to say yes. Her mother shook her head.

Elena's shoulders drooped. "We have to go home."

"How about if you take some with you?" Kendall suggested. She cut a large piece, put it on a paper plate and covered it. "There you go."

"Thank you very much," Elena said. "I'll see you later, Shelby."

"You bet," Shelby said.

As Elena and her mother walked back toward the orchard, Kendall was aware of Gabe standing next to her, watching them until they disappeared into the shadows.

"Do you have outside lights on this side of the house?" he asked.

"There's one on the porch." She switched it on.

He frowned. "I'm talking about floodlights, mounted on the second floor. Something bright that will illuminate your yard."

"Don't you think that's overkill for Sturgeon Falls?"

"There's no such thing as overkill. You're a woman living alone with two children."

"We've never had a problem. I haven't thought about security lights."

"You should."

Kendall shrugged. "Maybe." Want them or not, they were a luxury and would have to wait in line behind a long list of necessities.

Kendall turned to Shelby and Jenna, who were still bickering about the book. "Girls, is your homework done?"

"Almost," Shelby said.

"Why don't you finish it so you can take your baths and read for a while."

When both girls had skipped out of the room, she turned to Gabe. "I'm glad you joined us for dinner. I'll see you in the morning," she said. "At breakfast."

A smile teased the corners of his mouth. "You're glad I could join you? It's a good thing the girls aren't here. I wouldn't want them to hear their mother tell such a whopper." He glanced at the sink. "Are you sure you don't want help with the dishes before I leave?"

"I'm positive," she said firmly. "But thank you for offering."

She waited until he was out of the room, until she heard his footsteps on the stairs, before she turned back to the dishes. She wouldn't be able to relax until Gabe was out of her house. And out of her life.

CHAPTER THREE

Wednesday night

THE SCENT OF a night-blooming flower was floating through his room when Gabe jerked awake from a restless sleep. As he lay in bed, inhaling a long-forgotten memory, a small scraping sound drifted through his open window from the backyard.

He eased out of bed and looked out the window. Moonlight bathed the lawn, waves lapped gently against the sand and Gabe couldn't see a thing that didn't belong.

Then he heard another noise. A thump.

As if someone was trying to get in the back door.

He wrenched open the bedroom door and ran down the stairs. A tiny lamp threw a narrow band of light along his path. Another night-light illuminated the hall. It was still too dark to see the kitchen door, however. Gabe swore as he banged into it.

If there was an intruder, he'd be scared away by now, Gabe thought with disgust. Pushing the swinging door open, he hurried into the kitchen and toward the back door.

He didn't see a thing. Just as he opened the door to go outside, light flooded the kitchen.

"What's going on?"

Gabe swung around and saw Kendall standing in the doorway in low-riding boxers and a faded shirt. His pulse quickened.

"What's wrong?" she asked sharply. Her boxers were a faint blue-and-green plaid and her T-shirt announced, My Job Is So Secret, Even I Don't Know What I Do.

He dragged his attention away from Kendall and stepped outside. "I'm not sure. I heard something."

"It was probably a raccoon. They try to get into the garbage cans."

"This didn't sound like a raccoon." He scanned the yard and let his eyes adjust to the darkness. Nothing moved. Nothing looked out of place.

"Turn on the porch light," he said as he moved down the steps.

The single lamp barely illuminated the area beyond the stairs. He examined the door, looking for signs of tampering, but he didn't see a thing. The window next to the door appeared to be undisturbed.

"The raccoons are sitting in the orchard, laughing at you." Kendall stepped onto the porch.

He spared her a quick glance. "What if it wasn't raccoons?"

"What else would it be? Everyone in town knows us." She leaned against the porch railing. "They know there's nothing worth stealing in this house."

"This is the summer, Kendall. There are lots of tourists in Sturgeon Falls. All they see is a big house on a bigger piece of land."

"Are you trying to give me the creeps?" she asked.

"Yes." He looked up from his examination of the damp ground near the house. "I want you to take your safety and your daughters' a little more seriously."

She stood straighter and narrowed her eyes at him. "I take my daughters' safety very seriously."

When he reached the cellar doors that opened out at an angle from the house, he stopped. There were marks in the mud, as if someone had tried to open the doors and lost his footing. The doors were locked together, but there was some give in them. When he pulled on one of the doors and then let it drop, it made the thumping sound he'd heard through his bedroom window.

Kendall squatted next to him. "Those marks weren't there earlier," she said, studying them.

"Someone tried to get into the cellar."

Ignoring Kendall's sudden gasp, Gabe tugged at the doors, making sure the lock would hold. Then he stood up.

"I'll get a better look in the morning, when it's light. There's not much more I can do now."

Kendall was still staring at the marks in the mud, as if she couldn't believe what he'd said. At his words, she stood up. "There's nothing more you need to do," she said, her voice low-pitched in the darkness. "I'm glad you heard the door rattling and came down here. You probably scared the guy away. But the police can take it from here."

"This is my business, Kendall."

"It's not your business." Her eyes flared. "It's *my* business and I'll take care of it."

She wrapped her arms around herself again, and he saw goose bumps on her arms. When she shivered, he put his hand against the small of her back and steered her toward the house.

"You're cold. We don't need to stand out here."

She stepped away from his hand and hurried up the steps ahead of him. Her legs in the loose boxers were smooth and white in the dim light.

Kendall waited until he was in the house, then she shut and locked the door. "I mean it," she said, turning to face him. "This has nothing to do with you. It's not your business."

An involuntary smile curved his mouth. "I meant it's my *business*. I own a security company. We install security systems."

"Oh." Surprise flickered over her face. "I didn't realize you'd—"

"You didn't realize I'd become a model citizen?"

She flushed. "That's not what I meant. I had no idea you owned a business. Especially a security company."

"Why not? It was a perfect fit." He smiled again. "Carter and I were quite the hackers in our younger years. Didn't he tell you?"

"There were a lot of things Carter didn't tell me."

Gabe thought of Amy, in her little house on the other side of town, agonizing over what and when to tell George about her son. "Carter wasn't perfect. None of us was."

A ghost of sadness flickered over Kendall's face, and Gabe longed to touch her. Kendall stepped out of his reach.

She walked over to the stove, picked up the kettle and filled it with water. "Thank you for coming downstairs, Gabe," she said. Her voice was a low murmur in the quiet room. "I'm glad you heard the noise and scared whoever it was off. But I'm not going to keep you up any longer."

Gabe leaned against the kitchen counter, watching her. Her back was stiff and ramrod straight, and she stood at the stove with her arms wrapped around herself.

"I'll keep you company until the water is heated. I could use a cup of that instant coffee I noticed in the dining room," he said.

She spun around. "Just go to bed. Please. I don't need or want company."

He took a step closer, then another. "Are you sure?"

"I'm positive."

Her eyes were enormous, and he could see a faint sprinkling of freckles across her nose. Before he could think, he reached out and skimmed his finger across them. "You still don't remember to use your sunscreen when you work in the orchard, did you?" he murmured.

She pulled away from his hand and slid sideways. "Go to bed."

The kettle started to whistle, and he watched as she poured the boiling water into a mug with a tea bag. "I'll wait for you," he said.

The spoon she had used clattered to the counter. "That's not necessary. I'm a big girl."

"I'm well aware of that."

She turned to face him, curling her toes under. Her feet were long and narrow and her toenails were painted bright red. "What's going on?" she asked quietly. "What are you doing here?"

"I'm here for the dedication ceremony."

"I mean, what are you doing in my kitchen at one in the morning?" She watched him steadily. "And don't tell me you're protecting me from the person who was trying to break into my house. He's long gone."

What *was* he doing? The quiet, softly lit kitchen was an oasis of intimacy. Kendall stood inches away from him, dressed only in a thin layer of worn cotton. She was so close that her scent drifted over him, fresh and herbal and full of memories.

He shook off the spell she'd cast on him and raised his eyebrows. "Waiting for a cup of instant coffee."

She held his gaze for a moment longer, then she brushed past him. Reaching into a cabinet, she set a mug on the counter with a snap. "You drink too much coffee. Make sure you turn off the lights before you come upstairs," she said. She pushed through the swinging door without another look.

Gabe listened to her footsteps on the stairs. She moved quickly, as if she was anxious to get back to her bed. Anxious to get away from him.

It had been a mistake to stay here. A mistake to think either of them could ignore their shared past.

His trip back to Sturgeon Falls had been a test to see if he'd gotten over Kendall. And to see if Kendall had forgotten him.

She'd passed her part of the test with flying colors.

The results were still pending on his part of the test. But right now it was looking like a big fat F.

He was here and he'd play the hand he'd dealt himself. He'd give his speech, when they dedicated the high-school football field to Carter. And he'd stay for Amy. But apparently the author had been right—a man couldn't go home again.

Leaving the unused mug on the counter, Gabe checked the back door one more time, turned off the lights and walked back up the stairs to his room.

KENDALL CLIMBED out of bed earlier than usual the following morning. The predawn sky was midnight blue. The moon had sunk below the horizon and the sun hadn't yet begun to rise. She threw on worn jeans and an old sweatshirt and headed down to the kitchen to begin baking.

Her eyes felt gritty, as if sand had blown into her face. It had taken a long time to get to sleep after she'd gone back to bed, and her restless night had been punctuated by vivid, disturbing dreams.

All starring Gabe Townsend. The unsettling emotions they'd evoked—longing, regret and guilt—had lingered, too, making it impossible to sleep.

So she'd bake. The feel of the dough beneath her hands, the scent of cinnamon, butter and vanilla, would soothe her. It would remind her of her priorities, of the realities of her life.

She mixed batter for a coffee cake, then made a batch of apple-raisin muffins. By the time she slid the muffin pans into the oven, the sky was beginning to lighten.

At seven-thirty she woke the girls, and twenty minutes later they were sitting at the kitchen table, eating breakfast. She listened for the sound of Gabe's footsteps on the stairs, hoping he'd come down while Jenna and Shelby were still home. Then she could serve him in the dining room and stay in the kitchen while her daughters ate. She knew it was the coward's way out. She didn't like hiding behind her children. But right now, she was too tired to deal with Gabe.

And she wanted no repeat of the disturbing flash of heat that had swept over her the night before, as Gabe stood close to her in the kitchen.

The girls finished their oatmeal, gathered their lunch boxes and backpacks and ran out the door to wait for the bus. After they climbed onboard, Kendall headed back to the house to clean up.

A few minutes later, someone knocked on the kitchen door and she looked up to see her brother, George, waving at her through the window. Kendall hurried to unlock the door.

"Hey, Kenny," George said, giving her a hug.

Kendall gave him a peck on the cheek. "Hi, George. What are you doing here?" she asked.

George sniffed the air. "I was on my way to school

when I smelled your cinnamon coffee cake. My car turned off the highway all by itself."

She poured a cup of coffee and cut him a slice of the still-warm cake. "What's up?"

George closed his eyes as he ate. "Yum. Heaven. What a way to start the day," he said. Then he opened his eyes and grinned at her. "You think you could teach Amy to make your coffee cake?"

Kendall sat down, a smile blooming on her face. "Are you trying to tell me something, George?"

Her brother fumbled in his pocket and pulled out a small box. Flipping it open, he showed her a diamond engagement ring.

She flew out of her chair and hugged him. "It's gorgeous. I'm so happy for you." She leaned back, studying his glowing face, smiling back. "I really like Amy."

"I love her, Ken." He shook his head. "I can't believe it. I wasn't looking for anyone. But then I had Tommy in my first-grade class, I met Amy and *wham*. It was all over."

"So when are you popping the question?" Kendall asked, grabbing a cup of coffee and sitting down.

"I'm not sure. I have to set the scene just right." George got a faraway look in his eyes. "You know, a candlelight dinner, wine, flowers, the whole nine yards. And I'm hoping Tommy can spend the night with a friend."

"I can't believe my baby brother is getting married."

"Hey, don't jinx me. I haven't asked her yet."

Kendall rolled her eyes. "As if there's a chance she'd say no." Kendall reached for his hand, squeezed it. "How are things with Tommy?"

George's expression softened. "A lot better. He's a great kid. He was a little standoffish at first, but Amy said he was jealous of me. She hasn't dated much, and I'm the first guy who really took her attention away from Tommy. But we're cool now. I'm crazy about him."

Kendall heard footsteps on the stairs. "There's one of my guests. I have to get breakfast together for him."

He reached for another piece of coffee cake, then hesitated. "You have someone besides that Smith guy staying here?"

"Yes, I have two guests, but Dylan and Gabe certainly aren't going to eat all that."

"Gabe?" George frowned as he dropped another slice of cake on his plate. "Not Gabe Townsend?"

Kendall turned and stared at him. "Yes, it's Gabe Townsend. I didn't realize you knew he was in town."

"I heard he was giving a speech at the dedication." George shoveled food into his mouth and avoided his sister's eyes.

"What else, George?" she asked.

He shrugged. "I've heard rumors. That he's, you know, Tommy's father."

"Gabe? Tommy Mitchell's father? I don't think so. Gabe wouldn't run out on that kind of responsibility."

"He hasn't. He kept in touch with Amy."

"That doesn't mean he's Tommy's father."

George tilted his head and watched her. "Why are you standing up for the guy? Do you really know him that well?"

Why *was* she defending Gabe? "I knew him pretty well before he left town. Hasn't Amy told you who Tommy's father is?"

George looked at his plate. "No. But it's not important."

Before she could answer, the kitchen door swung open and Gabe walked into the room. "Good morning, Kendall."

"Good morning, Gabe." She looked from Gabe to her brother, wiping her hands on her apron. "Do you remember my brother, George Krippner?"

"Of course." Gabe nodded at George. "Hello, Krippner."

George nodded at Gabe but didn't say anything. The two men stared at each other longer than necessary, reminding Kendall of two dogs warily circling each other. The air in the kitchen suddenly seemed too thin, the oxygen sucked out of it by a sudden surge in testosterone.

Finally Gabe turned to Kendall. "There wasn't any coffee in the dining room. I just came in to get a cup."

"Here you go." Kendall poured coffee from the carafe sitting on the counter. As she handed it to Gabe, some of the coffee slopped out, scalding her fingers. She sucked on the burn as she herded Gabe toward the dining room. "Why don't you sit down and I'll bring you some breakfast. How would you like your eggs?"

Gabe took a sip. "Scrambled is fine," he said, keeping

his eyes on George. Almost as if he was warning George about something, Kendall thought, puzzled.

Then she shook her head. She didn't understand the posturing that went on between males. Apparently this was triggered by George's suspicions about Tommy Mitchell's paternity.

Before she could react, the door swung open again and her other guest wandered into the kitchen. "Hey, Kendall," Dylan Smith said. His dark blond hair looked as if he'd run his hand through the waves several times already this morning, his T-shirt was rumpled and his jeans hung low on his lean hips. "There's no coffee."

"Sorry, Dylan." Kendall poured another cup and handed it to him. "I'll get a pot in there right away. Have you met Gabe Townsend? He's in the room across the hall from you."

Dylan stuck out his hand. "Dylan Smith."

Gabe shook his hand. "Nice to meet you."

"You're here for the dedication of the football field, aren't you?" Dylan said. "You were Carter Van Allen's best friend."

"Yes," Gabe answered warily. "How did you know?"

"I'm an investigative reporter for the *Green Bay News-Gazette*," Dylan said. "I'm doing a piece on Carter Van Allen and his legacy in Sturgeon Falls."

"Really." Gabe set his cup on the counter. "Why would the Green Bay newspaper be interested in someone from Sturgeon Falls who died seven years ago?"

"The whole football-field thing," Dylan answered. "It's got everything—the golden boy who turned down a football scholarship to stay home and run the family orchard when his dad died. His marriage to his high-school sweetheart. His tragic death in a car crash, the dedication of a football field to him seven years later." Dylan looked over at Kendall. "Don't you think it's a great story?"

Kendall turned away and busied herself at the stove. Dylan was too adept at reading people's expressions.

"I've tried to convince him no one would want to read about it, but he's stubborn," she said lightly. "I guess he's going to have to learn that for himself." She cracked three eggs over the frying pan, adding a little milk and then scrambling the mixture together. "Do you want your usual this morning, Dylan?" she asked over her shoulder.

The dimple in his right cheek appeared. "I'm getting into a rut, aren't I?"

"You've only been here three days," she said, her voice dry. "I'd hardly call that a rut."

"Okay. I'll be back down in a half hour or so. Is that all right?" Dylan said.

"I'll have your breakfast ready then," Kendall promised.

Dylan turned to Gabe. "I have some questions I'd like to ask you. I'll catch up to you later."

As Dylan disappeared through the swinging door, Gabe asked, "Is he giving you a hard time?"

"Dylan? He asks a lot of questions, but I don't give him many answers." Her smile was forced. "So far, all he's gotten from the rest of the people he's talked to is

'Carter Van Allen—fabulous athlete and all-around good guy.'" She gave him a pointed look. "With any luck, that's all he'll get."

"Do you think I'm going to talk to him about Carter?"

"He doesn't give up very easily."

"Neither do I. I'm not going to tell secrets to a reporter."

"Then we won't have to worry about what he's going to write, will we?" She herded Gabe toward the door. "Have a seat in the dining room," she said. "I'll bring you juice and muffins while your eggs and bacon are cooking."

When the door had swung closed behind Gabe, Kendall turned to George. He was on his feet and heading for the door. "Have a good day, Ken," he said, bending down to kiss her cheek. He wasn't smiling anymore.

"You, too." She grabbed his hand. "You don't seriously think Gabe is Tommy's father, do you?"

He shrugged. "He kept in touch with Amy. She and Tommy go down to Milwaukee to see him. No one else in Sturgeon Falls has heard from him in seven years. You do the math."

The back door slammed and George ran down the stairs. A few moments later, she heard his car speed away.

Kendall glanced at the closed door to the dining room as she stirred Gabe's eggs and finished cooking his bacon. Would Gabe have left town, abandoning his son? She would have said no. Gabe had always had a strong sense of loyalty.

A sense of loyalty she'd both admired and hated.

Sliding the eggs onto a warmed plate, she added the bacon and some toast, and grabbed a dish of fresh strawberries. Then she put everything on a tray and backed her way through the swinging door and into the dining room.

Gabe was sprawled in a chair at the table, reading the newspaper. He looked up and folded the newspaper when she walked in.

"Does your brother stop here every morning?" he asked.

"No, just once in a while." She set the food down in front of him and started to move away.

Gabe reached for her, then dropped his hand. "What's wrong?" he asked.

"What was that all about in the kitchen?" she asked. "That stare-down with my brother."

"Stare-down? I have no idea what you're talking about."

"Don't you?" She got a visceral kick of satisfaction when he looked away. "Is this about Amy Mitchell?"

"Why would Amy be involved?"

"My brother is dating Amy. He's been seeing her for the past year."

"And?"

"You and Amy are friends." Kendall inwardly cringed. It sounded as if she was fishing for information.

Gabe didn't offer any. He looked at her for a moment, then nodded. "Yes, Amy is my friend. I hope your brother is good enough for her."

Kendall bristled. "The question is whether Amy is good enough for George," she retorted.

"I guess they have to be the ones to decide that."

"Yes, they do." She clutched the tray to her chest. "You'd better not interfere."

"Why would I do that? I want Amy to be happy. And all indications are that George makes her happy."

"Then I guess that makes George good enough for her, doesn't it?"

Gabe looked up at her. The combination of regret and sadness in his eyes startled her. "We'll find out."

CHAPTER FOUR

Thursday evening

AMY UNLOCKED the door and walked into her house, setting her purse on the kitchen table. Tommy barreled in behind her. "What's for dinner, Mom?" he asked.

She did a mental check of the contents of the refrigerator. "How about barbecued chicken?"

"Okay." Tommy dropped his bulging backpack on the kitchen floor and opened the refrigerator. "I'm starving."

He grabbed a carton of yogurt. "How come we don't have any cool snacks? Roger gets Pringles and Pop Rocks."

"Sorry, T. Yogurt is as cool as it gets around here." Amy stumbled over Tommy's backpack. "And pick up your stuff," she said a little more sharply than she'd intended.

"Jeez, Mom, you don't have to yell." Tommy gave her a dark look as he scooped up the folders and papers that had spilled out. "I wasn't going to leave it there."

Amy rubbed her forehead. The headache that had simmered all day had just kicked into high gear. "I didn't meant to yell," she said. "Just pick it all up, okay?"

Tommy dropped the pile of locker detritus on the kitchen table, grabbed his carton of yogurt and stalked into the living room. Moments later, Amy heard the sounds of a *Star Wars* video game.

Amy pressed her hands against her eyes and took slow, even breaths as she listened to the sound of virtual weapons blasting away. Okay, so it had been a rough day at the nursery. She should be able to laugh at the woman who'd tried to return a dead plant she'd purchased the year before, then had a tantrum when Amy refused to accept it. So what if she felt sick to her stomach every time she imagined talking to George about Tommy? That was no reason to take it out on her son.

She opened the freezer and pulled out a bag of French fries she'd hidden in the back, then switched on the oven and poured the fries onto a cookie sheet. Tonight, she and Tommy both needed comfort food.

TOMMY DRIED the dishes after dinner, chattering about what he'd done at school that day. French fries still cured a multitude of ills, Amy thought as she listened. If only all her problems were solved as easily. As they were finishing their cleanup, Amy heard a car pull into the driveway.

Tommy dashed to the door. "Hey, George," he called.

Amy's stomach tightened into a knot. She closed her eyes, breathed deeply, then wiped down the counter and arranged the dishcloth precisely over the sink as George walked into the kitchen.

"Tommy tells me there were French fries for dinner," he murmured against the nape of her neck. "Was the day that bad?"

Amy turned into his arms, smiling in spite of her anxiety. "Not anymore."

George bent his head to kiss her, and their lips clung together. Finally, aware of Tommy in the next room, Amy stepped back. "How are you tonight?"

"Much better now." He pulled her close for another kiss, laughing as she tried to wriggle away. "Don't you think Tommy is used to seeing us kissing by now?"

"It's not the kissing I'm worried about," she said, twisting away as he slid his hand over her rear end.

George grinned and rocked back on his heels, his light brown hair flopping over his forehead. "I can wait. But not for long."

"Me, neither," Amy whispered.

Leaning into the living room, she said to Tommy, "Turn off the game and get started on your homework."

Tommy rolled his eyes. "Mom, tomorrow is the last day of school. I don't have any homework."

"Okay, then get a book and read for a while."

He sighed loudly but switched off the video game and grabbed a Captain Underpants book that had been sitting on the end table.

"George and I will be in the backyard."

The adults stepped into Amy's yard, early-evening sunlight filtering through the leaves of the maple trees.

Making their way down a path that wove past hostas, coralbells and astilbe, they sat down on a swing that was tucked into a corner of the garden.

"Do you have anything going on this weekend?" she asked George, scooting closer to him.

He brought their joined hands to his mouth and kissed Amy's fingers. "I have to get my classroom cleaned out, but I should be done with that by Friday night." He waggled his eyebrows. "Did you have something in mind?"

Her stomach fluttered. "Oh, yeah," she whispered. "But it will have to wait. There's something I need to talk to you about."

George's foot, which had been gently pushing the swing, stilled. "What?" he asked. "Is something wrong?"

"I don't want to talk about it right now," she said. "Not with Tommy here."

George grabbed her upper arms. "Something *is* wrong. Are you sick? Is Tommy?"

"We're both fine," she reassured him, and his grip on her arms loosened. "It's just something we need to discuss and I don't want him to interrupt us."

He searched her eyes, then wrapped his arm around her shoulders and pulled her closer. "Okay. It just so happens there's something I want to discuss, too."

"Really? What?"

His eyes twinkled. "If I have to wait, so do you."

In spite of her anxiety, she felt herself responding. She'd fallen in lust with him the moment she'd met him

"I know what you want to 'discuss,'" she said, snuggling closer. "The same thing you always want to 'discuss.'"

"You think so?" He gave her a mysterious smile. "Wait and see." He nuzzled her neck as his hand touched her midriff. "What about *your* discussion? Are you going to give me a hint? Or do I have to tickle it out of you?"

She sprang from the swing and rubbed her hands on her shorts. "Not now."

George sat back. "What's going on, Amy? I haven't seen you this jumpy since our first date."

"You'd have been jumpy, too, if you were going out with your son's teacher," she said, trying to distract him.

"I *was* jumpy that night," he said. "I'd never slept with one of my former student's moms before."

"We didn't sleep together that night." It had been several weeks before they'd made love. Several long weeks.

"Yeah, but I wanted to." He stood up and pulled her into his arms. "You're trying to change the subject, but that's okay," he said into her neck. "I'm not going to give you any hints, either."

"I'll see if Tommy can sleep over at his friend David's house on Saturday," she said. "Then we'll have all night."

"I like the sound of that," George murmured.

So did she. But would George be interested in staying after what she had to tell him?

She was afraid to find out.

GABE LOWERED HIMSELF to the back steps of Van Allen House on Friday morning, his cell phone next to his ear. "Tomorrow. I'm going to tell him tomorrow night." Amy's voice caught on the final word.

"That's good, Amy," Gabe answered. "Do you need someone to watch Tommy?"

"No." Amy cleared her throat. "Tommy is going to have a sleepover at his friend's house. So George and I can hash it out by ourselves."

"What can I do to help?"

The silence on the phone lasted too long. "Nothing," Amy finally said. "I have to do this by myself. And don't you have stuff you have to do for the big ceremony?"

"I have to work on my speech, but I have plenty of time to finish it. Do you want to get together on Sunday?"

"I don't know." Amy's voice wavered. "It depends on what happens Saturday night."

"I'll call you Sunday."

Gabe snapped his cell phone shut and put it into his pocket. Then he stood and strode to the cellar door.

He hadn't seen any police at the house today. He wondered if Kendall had even called them. Squatting next to the door, he studied the smeared footprints.

They didn't look any different than they'd looked the night before. Or this morning. Clearly, Kendall's intruder hadn't been back.

He stood up and examined the back of the house. It would be easy enough to put floodlights on the wall.

The right fixtures would illuminate the backyard all the way to the water.

"What are you doing?" Kendall's voice came from the direction of the garage.

He turned to see her striding toward him, dressed in khaki cotton pants and a long-sleeved white shirt. The wind plastered the shirt to her body, highlighting her smooth muscles and flat abdomen. When he realized he was staring, Gabe looked away.

"I was checking to see if your intruder had come back." He gave the cellar doors a nudge with his shoe. "It doesn't look like it."

"I figured it was kids." She sat down on the step Gabe had just been sitting on and lifted her shirt to wipe sweat off her face. Then she removed her beaten-up work boots and padded over next to him in stocking feet. As she stared down at the smears in the dirt, he could smell the clean tang of her sweat and the scent of lemons and oranges he'd always associated with her.

"Just because they didn't come back doesn't mean it was kids," he said.

She looked annoyed. "It doesn't mean it was a crazed serial killer, either," she retorted. "Forget about it, Gabe. I have."

"I know. You didn't call the police, did you?"

"No, I didn't call the police. And I'm surprised you're pushing it." She bent down and peeled off one white sock. "When did you get to be such a law-abiding citizen?"

"When I grew up," he said, his voice neutral.

She stilled, her right leg propped on her left knee. Slowly she straightened, her face turning red. "I'm sorry. That was a terrible thing to say."

He picked up a pebble and threw it into the yard. "You always did speak your mind," he said. "I should be used to it by now."

"You bring out the worst in me, Gabe. But that's no excuse for rudeness."

He stared at the waves on the water, remembering a long-ago Fourth of July. "I used to think I brought out the best in you, Kendall."

She went still behind him. Finally she said, "I don't know what you're talking about."

He faced her. "Don't you?"

She wouldn't meet his eyes. "I need to get cleaned up before the girls get home."

He nodded at her clothes. "Working in the orchard?"

The tension in her shoulders eased as she shoved her blond hair, damp with sweat, off her face. "We have to get the nets over the trees, and the whole orchard needs to be irrigated. I was helping to haul the hoses."

"You don't have enough work to do in the house?" He kept his voice light.

She shrugged. "I like working in the orchard. That's where the Van Allen roots are."

"You're not a Van Allen," he said. "You just married one."

She narrowed her eyes. "My daughters are. The orchard belongs to them and I'm making sure it's still there when they're old enough to understand what it means."

"And you think hauling hoses yourself will ensure that?"

"I like doing physical work. Not that it's any of your business what I do." She made a show of glancing at her watch. "I have to go and get ready for the rest of my weekend guests. I'll see you later."

At the crunch of tires on the driveway, Kendall spun around. "Oh, no. It sounds as if they're here early."

Gabe stuck his head around the corner and saw Dylan Smith climb out of a small car. "It's just that reporter."

Her hand tightened on the doorknob. "He's probably going to come looking for you," she warned.

"I can handle him," he said.

She chewed on her lower lip.

"Trust me, Kendall."

"Can I?" Her voice was soft, almost as if she hadn't meant to say it out loud.

He didn't answer her immediately. He had been keeping secrets from her for years. "I know how to handle the press," he finally said. "He won't get anything out of me."

No, he saved all the secrets in his life for Kendall. But that was going to change this weekend.

KENDALL CAME DOWNSTAIRS a half hour later, dressed in her "successful businesswoman" clothes—the same outfit she'd worn when Gabe arrived. Smoothing her hands down her black slacks, she sped through the first floor, filling the coffeepot on the buffet in the dining room, straightening the magazines on the table in the living room and picking up a book that Jenna had left on the couch.

Gabe's battered leather briefcase sat next to the couch. He must have left it there that morning. She grabbed it and moved it to her office, where it would be safe and out of the way. The scent of leather drifted up, something she'd always associated with Gabe, and she abruptly left the room.

Memories were perilously close to the surface, and she shoved them down. She didn't want him in her head, messing up her thinking. Confusing her.

Gabe and Carter had graduated from high school fifteen years ago, and everyone remembered Carter as the star quarterback on the football team, the rich kid who could do no wrong. Even when he did.

She and Carter and Gabe had been friends all those years ago. Then she became Carter's wife, but still the three of them remained friends. Until the day Carter died.

Now those years were washed in the same golden, nostalgic glow that colored the high-school memories. No one wanted to look at the ugly truths that hid beneath them.

The hiss of the school-bus brakes drifted down the driveway, and Kendall hurried to the front door. Jenna and Shelby would be excited about the last day of school. They'd have stories to tell, and they'd be looking forward to the traditional "last day of school" chocolate-chip cookies she'd baked that morning.

The girls' animated voices announced their arrival. Kendall started down the steps, then stopped abruptly as her daughters rounded the bend in the driveway.

They were walking with Gabe, who was dressed in nylon soccer shorts, tank top and running shoes. Shelby danced around him, clearly regaling him with last-day-of-school stories. Jenna, always more serious, looked up at Gabe as she talked, and he bent his head to listen to her.

Gabe must have met their bus at the end of the driveway. As Kendall watched the three of them, a sharp claw of jealousy raked over her. The girls were *her* babies. *She* was the one who welcomed them home after school and listened to their stories.

This was perfectly normal, she told herself as she sank down on the top step. Jenna and Shelby had latched onto "Uncle Gabe" with the single-minded ferocity of children who hungered for a father figure. And Gabe was a link to the father neither of them remembered.

Even after a day, it was clear that Gabe was much better with the girls than their own father had been. Kendall closed her eyes to block the remembered pain. Carter had been a careless father, ignoring his daughters one day and lavishing expensive presents on them the next. But he'd rarely spent time with them. They'd been a drag on his social life and they'd taken his wife's time away from him.

No wonder they'd glommed on to Gabe.

Suddenly both girls dropped the papers in their hands and Shelby went running around the side of the house. Gabe scooped up the school things before they fluttered away and handed them to Jenna, who studied the rocks in the garden before selecting one to hold down the papers.

Then Shelby came running back, dribbling a soccer ball. She passed it to Gabe, who kicked it to Jenna.

Kendall stood up. Normally Jenna didn't play soccer with Shelby. Shelby was good, and she was merciless when she played against her younger sister. Kendall wanted to step in before the inevitable tears.

But Gabe was evening the odds.

Shelby tried to hip-check him and tumbled to the ground, laughing. Jenna ran with the ball, dribbling awkwardly, and then let loose with a huge kick. She spun around and threw her hands in the air, a huge grin on her face.

"I won! I beat you, Shel," she cried.

Shelby stood up, brushing herself off. "Did not. You cheated."

"I did not! You're just a sore loser."

"That's better than being a cheater," Shelby retorted.

Kendall started down the steps, determined to head off the fight that she knew was coming. But to her surprise, Gabe draped an arm around each girl's shoulders.

"Jenna kicked that ball fair and square," he said to Shelby. "Right?"

"Yeah, but it didn't…" Gabe gave Shelby a big wink. "Yeah," she finally said.

"So tell her she made a nice shot," Gabe suggested.

"Nice shot, Jen," Shelby said, trying to hide her smile behind a scowl.

"Shelby is a good soccer player. Right, Jenna?" he said to the younger girl.

"Yeah, but I beat her today," Jenna crowed.

"So tell Shelby that she played a good game," Gabe instructed her.

"Good game, Shel," Jenna said happily.

"Okay." He squeezed both girls' shoulders once more and let go of them. "If you want to work on that scissors move later, Shelby, I'll be happy to help you."

"Yeah?" Shelby eyed him. "No one on my team knows how to do that."

"Maybe you'll be the first," Gabe said.

"Cool." Shelby ran toward the door. "Hey, Mom, Gabe's going to teach me that cool scissors move."

Gabe looked up at Kendall, standing on the stairs, and flashed her a grin. His dark hair was disheveled and his blue eyes sparkled. Kendall felt as if a fist had just hit her chest.

She couldn't look away, and neither did Gabe. His grin faded as got closer, replaced by an intensity that made her throat tighten.

"I was out running when the school bus stopped," he said, his voice gravelly. He cleared his throat. "I hope you don't mind that I walked with them back to the house."

"Why would I mind?" She twisted her hands together behind her. "It's not like you're a stranger."

"You're protective of your girls. I don't want to overstep the boundaries."

"Shelby and Jenna like you," she said, the words heavy in her mouth. "They enjoy spending time with you. I'm not going to tell them to stay away from you."

"Thank you," he said, giving her another smile that made her heart race. "They're a lot of fun. So you don't mind if I teach Shelby that soccer move?"

"No, I don't mind. And thank you for helping Jenna."

"It's hard being the less athletic one."

Was he talking about himself and Carter? Gabe had been a decent athlete, but he hadn't been in Carter's class. She remembered wondering if it bothered Gabe.

He was standing too close to her, she realized suddenly. She'd backed up until she pressed against the front door, and he'd followed her. His scent surrounded her, mixed with the faint smell of pine that she remembered far too well.

"Well," she said brightly, fumbling behind her for the doorknob. "I better get those chocolate-chip cookies out for the girls. They're going to start yelling for them in a minute."

"Go ahead, Kendall, and take care of the girls. I'm not going anywhere."

CHAPTER FIVE

Friday afternoon

KENDALL POURED glasses of milk and put a plate of cookies on the table. As Shelby stuffed a cookie into her mouth, Kendall said, "Change your clothes before you play soccer with Gabe. Both of you. Okay?"

Both girls nodded, their mouths full. Kendall sat between them. "So how was the last day of school?"

They started talking at once, and Kendall relaxed. This was her real life. Sitting in her kitchen, talking to her daughters. Gabe Townsend was from a time that no longer existed. And any feelings she'd had for him back then were buried and forgotten.

When Jenna and Shelby eventually pushed away from the table and ran upstairs to change their clothes, Kendall walked out the back door. Gabe sat on the stairs, staring at a sailboat on Green Bay.

"What's going on with this football field, Kendall. Why are they dedicating it to Carter? And why now?"

"He was the star athlete," she said. "Remember? We won the football championship, and then he took us to the basketball and baseball playoffs."

"I remember." Gabe shifted on the steps and finally looked at her. "He was exceptional. But why now?"

Kendall rested her chin in her palm and watched the waves roll gently onto the shore. "I think it's money."

"Did they hit you up for a donation?" he asked.

"Not yet, but I think it's coming. I'm pretty sure they asked Carter's aunt Emily for money."

"Did she give them any?"

"I'm not sure. Aunt Emily never approved of Carter. She thought he was spoiled. But the Van Allen name is important to her, so she might have."

"And you think they're going to ask you next?"

She shrugged. "It's the only thing that makes sense to me." She leaned back against the step. "It's pretty clever, actually. Name the field for my late husband, then ask me for money to maintain it. It would be awkward and ungrateful to refuse, wouldn't it?"

"I know everyone on that committee. I didn't think they were that smart," he said.

"Never underestimate the cunning of a committee trying to raise money." She stood and dusted off the back of her shorts. "So I'm just waiting for them to approach me."

"You're going to tell them to go to hell, aren't you?"

She sighed, trying to ignore the anxiety that had lodged in her chest ever since she'd heard about the scheme. "I don't know what I'm going to do. The girls are excited that the high-school football field is going to be named for their father. And if I refuse to donate money, they're going to find out. You know how gossip is in small towns. How would I explain that to them?"

"Dammit, Kendall, why didn't you tell me this was going on? I might have been able to stop it."

"I appreciate the thought, but I need to figure this out on my own." With a mixture of regret and relief, she heard Shelby clattering through the kitchen. She'd enjoyed talking to Gabe like a friend. And she didn't like enjoying that. "Here's Shelby. Don't let her wear you out."

"We're not done talking about this," he warned her.

"Yes, Gabe. We are," she said.

He opened his mouth to answer her just as Shelby pushed through the door from the kitchen. "Can you show me that move now, Uncle Gabe?"

"In a minute. I need to finish talking to your mom. Why don't you start warming up?" When Shelby was dribbling her soccer ball around the yard, he turned back to Kendall. "I want to help you with this."

"Thank you, but I'm handling it."

He didn't want to let it go, but she held his gaze until he nodded. "All right, Kendall. We'll let it go for now. But don't think for a moment that I've forgotten."

As he ran down the steps, she couldn't help comparing Gabe to the young man she remembered from seven years ago. That Gabe had been skinny as a rail. This Gabe was still lean, but now his arms and legs were muscled and strong, his gait confident. He was a man, not a boy. And still far too attractive for her peace of mind.

God help her.

A HALF HOUR LATER, Gabe grinned as he watched Shelby execute the scissors move, faking one way and then cutting the other way. "Good job," he called. "I would have bitten."

Shelby's eyes sparkled as she dribbled the ball to him and stopped. "The girls on my team are going to be so jealous," she said.

"You're a good soccer player," he told her. "Tell me about your team."

Shelby chattered while they kicked the ball back and forth. When she halted in the middle of a sentence and went racing toward the orchard, Gabe stopped running and watched her. Then he saw the slight figure of a child step out of the shadow of one of the trees.

Shelby skidded to a stop and said something. When the other child nodded, Gabe saw the long black braid hanging down her back. A girl.

With a quick look behind her, the other girl started running alongside Shelby. Shelby passed her the ball, and the girl dribbled it up the field. Gabe's eyes narrowed. She was damn good.

"Uncle Gabe!" Shelby shouted. "This is Elena. She wants to play soccer with us."

Gabe recognized the girl. She'd come to the house to return Jenna's book on Wednesday night. "Great," he replied. "What do you want to do?"

Shelby grinned. "Me and Elena will play you."

The girls were good. And they worked together well. When they passed the ball around him, and Elena shot the ball into their makeshift goal, they slapped hands in the universal athletic high five, both of them smiling.

The next time they had to take the ball out of bounds, Elena whispered something to Shelby. Gabe saw Shelby's eyes widen. "You can do that?"

Elena nodded, a tiny smile on her face. Then she took the ball, stepped far out of bounds and ran toward the sidelines. Suddenly she was in the air, doing a flip throw. The ball landed far away from Gabe, who watched, dumbfounded, as Shelby scored an easy goal.

"That was so cool, Elena," Shelby yelled as she ran toward the other girl. "Can you teach me how to do that?"

"Sure." She gave Shelby a considering look. "You have to practice a lot, though."

"I will," Shelby said, jumping up and down. "I don't know anyone else who knows how to do that. I only saw it once before, at a tournament."

Gabe flopped to the ground. "Okay, you two win. You've worn me out."

Shelby dropped to the ground next to him, but Elena looked uncertainly toward the orchard. "I should go."

"Stay for a minute," Shelby urged. She scrambled to her feet. "I'll get us something to drink."

As Shelby ran toward the house, Gabe turned to the girl. "You're a very good soccer player, Elena." She shrugged, but he could see the pride in her eyes. "Do you play on a team?"

She shook her head. "We're not at home when the teams are playing. I play with my father and my brothers."

Of course she wouldn't be able to play on a team. *Way to go, Townsend.* "They must be pretty good, too."

"My father knows a lot about soccer. He taught all of us to play." Her eyes crinkled into a smile. "I'm better than my brothers, though."

"I bet you are." Gabe nodded toward the soccer ball. "You and Shelby played well together."

"Shelby's pretty good," Elena said.

Shelby came out with three glasses of lemonade and sat down beside Elena. "Can we do this again, Uncle Gabe?"

"Sure," he answered. "Whenever you want."

"You, too, Elena," Shelby said, her eyes shining with excitement. "Can you come back tomorrow?"

"Maybe. I'll ask my mother."

As the two girls chattered, Gabe took a long drink of lemonade. When he set his glass on the ground, he saw Jenna on the back porch with a book in her hand. He walked over to the porch and sat down next to her.

"Shelby and Elena are planning a soccer game for tomorrow," he said. "Do you want to play?"

"No," Jenna said. "I can't play soccer."

"You beat Shelby earlier."

She gave him a very grown-up look. "That's because you were helping me."

"I'll help you again. You can be on my side. It'll be you and me against Shelby and Elena."

Jenna shook her head. "No, thank you. I don't like soccer."

"What sport do you like?"

"I'm not good at sports," Jenna said.

"Who told you that?" Gabe demanded.

"No one told me that. I just know."

"I bet there's a sport you like, though."

Jenna shrugged. "I don't know."

"If you could play any sport, what would it be?"

"Maybe tennis." Jenna got a faraway look in her eyes. "I see kids playing tennis at the high school. It looks like fun."

"Have you ever tried tennis?" Gabe asked.

She shook her head. "No. I'm too young. I've only seen high school kids playing."

Kendall was kneeling on the beach, pulling out plants. Gabe wished she were closer. He wasn't sure how to handle this. "I could show you how to play tennis," he said cautiously. "If your mom said it was okay."

"Really?" Jenna had dropped her book, and she gave him a wide-eyed stare. "You can play tennis *and* soccer?"

"Knowing how to do something and being good at it are two different things," he said. "But I know enough tennis to show you how to play."

"I'll ask Mom." She jumped up and ran toward the beach. As Jenna spoke, Kendall turned around and looked at him, then said something to her daughter. The little girl dashed back to the house. "Mom said maybe," Jenna reported breathlessly. "She said she'd talk to you about it."

"Okay."

"She's right there," Jenna said, pointing toward the beach. "Maybe you could talk to her now."

"I don't know if I should interrupt her." Gabe watched Kendall kneeling in the sand. "She looks busy."

"It's okay to interrupt her. She doesn't like to pull the beach grass." Then she ran over to Shelby and Elena, calling out, "Uncle Gabe's going to teach me how to play tennis."

Kendall glanced over her shoulder at him, and Gabe wandered down to the beach. She had a pile of uprooted plants beside her. "What are you doing?" he asked.

"Another skirmish in the ongoing battle between me and the marram grass for control of the beach. If I don't pull this stuff out at least once a week, it gets away from me."

Gabe squatted next to her and grabbed one of the tough stalks. He was surprised how much strength it took to pull the thing out of the sand.

"What's going on, Gabe?" she asked quietly.

"I'm helping you pull out marram grass," he said.

"That's not what I mean and you know it. What's this about teaching Jenna how to play tennis?"

"That's all there is to it. I told her I could show her how to play. That's all."

Kendall rocked back on her heels, suspicion in her eyes. "Jenna's never expressed any interest in tennis."

"I didn't plant the suggestion that she might like tennis, if that's what you're suggesting."

"Jenna mentioned tennis all on her own?"

"Yes, she did. Do you think I'm using Jenna and Shelby to suck up to you?"

"You wouldn't be the first man to do that."

"When I'm interested in a woman, I tell her myself. I don't use her children to soften her up for me."

She pulled out another plant. "They're hungry for male attention. Be careful with them."

"I'm not going to hurt them."

"Not on purpose. But they'll be sad when you leave."

"I'll be sad to leave, too. But I can come back."

She didn't say anything, just yanked out another plant. Gabe wasn't surprised. He was discovering all over again how stubborn Kendall was.

"Why are you going out of your way to charm them?" she finally said.

"You think that's what I'm doing? Trying to charm them?" he asked, incredulous.

"Isn't it?"

"Have you really forgotten? I've never been charming. Carter was the charming one. I was the serious one."

"You're definitely charming my children," she said.

"You make that sound calculated and cold. I like your children, Kendall, and that's the way I'm treating them."

"Why are you taking so much trouble with them?"

"Jenna is my goddaughter," he said quietly. "I've never spent any time with her, never gotten to know her. It was wrong of me, and I want to change that. And Shelby is hard to resist. She reminds me so much of Carter."

Kendall glanced at Shelby, now running in circles with Elena, and her eyes softened. "She *is* just like Carter. It's both her strength and her weakness."

"She's very active."

"She loves soccer, and it's a great outlet for her energy. But she can't play soccer all day, every day."

Gabe turned to look at the girls, now kicking the soccer ball back and forth. They'd included Jenna, but her kicks were weak and off target compared to Shelby's and Elena's. "Have you ever thought about enrolling Shelby in an acting class? It's a different kind of energy, but she might enjoy it."

She gave him a wary look. "Did Shelby put you up to this?"

"Of course not." He glanced at Shelby. "She's mentioned it to you? That's interesting, because I've always thought Carter should have been an actor. He could take on any persona he wanted, and he was always completely believable. I used to think that was why he got into so much trouble. He'd put himself in a role, make up a story to go along with it and then forget he was just pretending."

"He said something once about how he was always running away from himself. Maybe if he'd had a chance to grow up, he would have figured out why."

He was surprised how much Kendall's words hurt. Standing up, he said, "Subtlety was never your strong suit, was it?"

She stood up, too. "I wasn't talking about you and the car accident."

"No? It sure sounded like it."

She sighed. "I was thinking about his parents. They didn't allow him to grow up. He was a spoiled, rich kid and a spoiled, rich adult, until he wasn't rich anymore.

Then he was a spoiled adult who acted like he was rich."

"He left you with a lot of debt, didn't he?"

She lifted her chin a fraction. "That really isn't any of your business," she said, her voice cool.

"Can you knock it off with your damn pride for a moment? I was there, remember? I know how Carter went through money. I know about his stupid investments."

"Then why didn't you stop him?" she burst out. "Why didn't you tell him they were stupid?"

Gabe rubbed the back of his neck. "Do you really think I could have? Do you think he would have listened?"

"He listened to you all the time. Every other sentence out of his mouth began with 'Gabe said.'"

"Whatever you've been thinking, you're wrong. I had very little influence over Carter."

"That's easy to say now, isn't it? When he's not around to challenge you. When he's not around to talk about how you were the one who came up with all the ideas."

"You're going to believe what you want to believe," Gabe said. "I know that. You always did."

"Are you saying that *Carter* was the one who got *you* into trouble?" Disbelief made her voice rise.

"Carter and I had a complicated relationship. Let's leave it at that." He looked at the girls, who were sprawled in the grass. "Can I teach Jenna how to play tennis?"

"I suppose so."

"You don't sound thrilled with the idea."

"Tennis lessons are expensive," she said. "If she likes it, she's going to want to continue after you leave."

"Why worry about that? She may not like the game at all."

"You're right." She sighed. "Go ahead and teach her, and I won't worry about later."

He took a chance and touched her arm. "That's a good policy in general, Kendall. Don't worry about what hasn't happened yet."

A car's tires crunched on the driveway, and Kendall sprang to her feet, brushing sand off her legs. "Oh, no! That's probably my other guests for the weekend, and I'm not dressed."

"I'll answer the door for you, if that would help," he said, hurrying toward the back of the house with her.

She glanced at his baggy nylon soccer shorts, faded tank top and beat-up running shoes. "That's not exactly the image I'm going for," she said.

"I'll let them in, show them where the coffee is and tell them to have a seat while you're changing your clothes."

She hesitated. "All right—and thank you. I'll be right down."

Gabe watched as she took the stairs two at a time, then smiled as he reached for the door. Kendall trusted him to deal with her guests.

It was a small thing. But it was a start.

One he meant to build on.

CHAPTER SIX

Friday evening

"I'LL GO WITH Jenna, Mom," Shelby said over the noise of the other diners. "To make sure she's okay."

"Thanks, Shelby," Kendall replied, biting the side of her mouth to keep from smiling. Earlier in the year Shelby had declared herself too old for McDonald's Play Place. But every time the three of them ate beneath the golden arches, Shelby found an excuse to clamber over the multicolored equipment and dive into the ball pit.

Kendall started to glance at her watch, then stopped herself. She didn't need to know what time it was. The girls could stay up a little later tonight. They were celebrating the last day of school, after all.

She'd left a note at the house, providing her cellphone number, in case any of her guests needed to speak with her. But her rooms were full and her No Vacancy sign was up, so she was free to relax and enjoy herself.

Jenna raced to their table for a drink of milk. "Uncle Gabe would have liked this," she said breathlessly.

"Uncle Gabe wouldn't fit in the Play Place."

Jenna giggled. "I know that. But he could have watched us. I bet he would have liked being with us."

"Probably," Kendall said, smoothing her hand over Jenna's hair.

Jenna glanced into the room that contained the play equipment. "Some kids' dads are in there," she said wistfully.

Kendall wrapped her arm around Jenna and pulled her close, her heart aching for her daughter. "I know you wish your daddy was here," she whispered. "I know you miss him. We all do." *Liar.* "Maybe we can come back here next week with Uncle George. Would you like that?"

"I guess."

"You always have fun with Uncle George, don't you?"

"He's hanging around with Tommy Mitchell." Jenna stepped on a plastic spoon and crunched it beneath her foot. "Tommy was bragging to me in school."

What was Kendall supposed to say? Her brother's impending marriage would mean he'd spend even less time with Jenna and Shelby. She was happy for George, but her daughters would miss him. "Uncle George is dating Tommy's mom," she said cautiously. "That's why he sees Tommy so much."

"Yeah?" Jenna gave her a speculative look. "Maybe you could date Uncle Gabe. Then he could do stuff with us."

Smart kids were both a blessing and a curse. "Uncle Gabe is just here for a few days, then he's going home,"

Kendall said, keeping her voice matter-of-fact. "But you can play with him whenever you want while he's here."

"Did he come here for Daddy's stadium?"

"Yes, he was Daddy's best friend, so he's going to make a speech."

Kendall could see Jenna mulling this over in her mind. "Did you know Uncle Gabe before?"

"Of course. He and your father spent a lot of time together." Time to change the subject. "Do you still want to play miniature golf tonight?"

"Yes! You brought the tickets, didn't you?"

"They're right here," Kendall answered, patting her purse. The local miniature-golf course passed out certificates for a free round to all students on the last day of school, and the girls were anxious to use theirs. "Why don't you tell Shelby it's time to go."

"Okay," Jenna said, running back into the Play Place.

Kendall finished her iced tea as the girls collected their shoes from the bin in the playroom and put them on. Jenna was saying something to Shelby, and Shelby looked impressed. When both girls finished with their shoes, they came barreling into the restaurant.

"Are you really going out with Uncle Gabe?" Shelby demanded excitedly, skidding to a stop in front of Kendall.

Kendall choked on the last of her iced tea. "What?" she sputtered.

"Jenna said you and Uncle Gabe were going on a date."

"Jenna, I said no such thing." Kendall frowned at her younger daughter. "Why would you say that to Shelby?"

"You said you used to know him, and that he was Daddy's friend. And you didn't say no when I asked you if you were dating him."

My God. What if she'd asked Gabe the same thing? "Jenna, Shelby, I'm *not* going out with Uncle Gabe. He's staying in our house because we rent out rooms to people. That's all."

"Oh." Jenna looked crushed.

"You're so stupid, Jenna," Shelby sneered. But she looked equally stricken. "Mom doesn't go out on dates."

"Shelby, don't call your sister stupid," Kendall said automatically. She cringed with embarrassment. Kendall had officially joined the ranks of the pathetic. Even her daughters recognized that she didn't have a social life. She stood up and grabbed her purse. "Do you girls want to go miniature golfing tonight, or not?"

"Yeah." Shelby kicked at a French fry on the floor.

"Me, too," Jenna said.

"Good. So do I."

THERE WAS A CROWD at the miniature-golf course, mostly kids from school and their parents. The scent of popcorn filled the evening air and moths fluttered beneath the bright lights that illuminated the greens. Intermittent shrieks from young golfers drowned out the sound of a waterfall on the first hole.

As Kendall waited in line to get their clubs, Shelby and Jenna darted through the crowd, stopping to talk to friends, laughing and acting silly. Kendall was keeping an eye on them and thinking about what she'd prepare for breakfast the following morning when someone grabbed her from behind and planted a kiss on her cheek.

When she spun around, her brother, George, was grinning at her. "You and the girls using your free tickets?"

"We are. What are you doing here? You just got out of school and away from kids."

"I brought Tommy and Amy and Tommy's friend David." He nodded toward the end of the line, where Amy stood with Tommy and another boy. "Tommy was hot to use his coupon."

"I'm impressed. Bringing Tommy *and* a friend? You've got it bad."

George winked. "Amy's watching David tonight. Tomorrow night, David's parents are watching Tommy. I have a big evening planned."

Kendall grabbed his arm. "You're asking her?"

"Yep. I officially go off the market." George beamed, touching the outline of the ring box in his pocket. It had already worn a white spot in the denim.

"How long have you been carrying that ring around?" she asked, slipping her arm through her brother's.

"A couple of weeks." He touched the box again. "Getting up my nerve, you know?"

"I don't think that's necessary. Amy adores you. It's obvious every time she looks at you."

"Yeah, well, the feeling is mutual." He cupped his hand over the box. "It's kind of overwhelming."

"Hasn't she been curious about that box you're carrying around?" Kendall teased.

"I usually leave it in the car when I'm with her. I forgot to take it out tonight."

"You'd better give it to her before it wears a hole in your jeans," Kendall said, hugging her brother and reaching up to kiss his cheek. "Congratulations, George."

"Thanks, Kenny." He glanced back at Amy, who was talking to the boys. "You want to play with us? The kids can hang together and you can have some adult company."

"I'd like that. I want to get to know Amy better."

"Yeah, she's anxious to really get to know you, too."

But when Kendall made her way back to where Amy waited in line with the two boys, Amy didn't seem excited to see Kendall. She looked shocked.

"Kendall is here with her girls, so I asked her to golf with us. That way the kids can keep each other entertained and we get some adult time," George said.

"Great," Amy said, her gaze darting from George to Kendall. "That'll be fun."

George bent down to answer a question from Tommy, and Amy let her gaze rest on the two of them for a moment. For just a moment, Kendall thought she saw grief and despair in Amy's eyes. Then the expression was gone and Amy gave her a tentative smile.

"How are you, Kendall? It's good to see you again."

"I'm fine, and it's good to see you, too. I've been telling George we need to get together. I wanted to thank you for helping out at the party." George had brought Amy and Tommy to Jenna's birthday party a couple of months earlier. "Every time I looked, you were cleaning up someone's mess or pouring lemonade for one of the kids."

"I had a good time. It was a fun party." Her voice softened. "Your orchards and your beach were beautiful."

"It's nice to have all that space when we're having a party."

Amy looked at her son. "I'm glad Tommy's birthday is in the summer. I can take the boys to a park or to the beach and let them run themselves ragged."

"It helps, doesn't it?" Kendall smiled companionably at Amy. "But that's the point of having an outdoors party. The kids can entertain themselves and the adults can sit back and watch them. I never got a chance to talk to you at Jenna's party."

Amy shrugged. "I like to keep busy."

"George didn't bring you to the party so you could work," Kendall replied. "You and George will have to come over for dinner one of these days."

"That would be great." Amy shifted her purse to her other shoulder. "But isn't this your busy season?"

"It is, but we try to have family time as often as we can. It gets so crazy during the summer." Kendall scanned the crowd for her daughters. When she saw them leaning on the fence, talking to a pair of girls who were already golfing, she turned back to Amy. "What all are you doing at Tilda's Garden these days?"

"I do a little bit of everything."

"I saw you when I bought my annuals, but you were

helping someone else and I didn't want to interrupt. What a great place to work."

Amy relaxed. "I love it there. Tilda's been wonderful to me. I started as a clerk, and now she's actually letting me design some small projects."

"Really? Tilda's supposed to come out and help me arrange a couple of new perennial beds at the house. I'll ask her to send you, instead."

Amy paled. "Oh, I couldn't ask you to do that. The Van Allen House gardens are one of Tilda's favorites projects."

Kendall laughed. "Every garden is one of Tilda's favorites. I know Tilda. She'll be thrilled to give you a chance."

"You've never seen my work. How do you know you'll like my ideas?"

Kendall's smile faded. Amy looked almost panic-stricken. "Hey, Amy, it's okay. We'll work together to figure out what I want. If Tilda trusts you, I'm sure you'll do a good job."

She elbowed her brother. "George, tell Amy I don't bite. I want her to design those new beds for the house."

"Great idea, Ken," George said. "Amy is amazing." He draped his arm over Amy's shoulder. "You should see what she's done with her own house."

"Maybe I'll drive by. Are your flower beds pretty well planted, Amy?"

Amy hesitated, and admitted that they were.

George tilted his head and looked down at Amy. "Is something wrong?" he asked, looking puzzled.

"I need to find the restroom," Amy murmured. She stepped away from his arm. "Could you keep an eye on Tommy and David?"

Without waiting for an answer, Amy hurried away. Kendall and George watched her disappear into the building. Tommy tugged at George's arm. "Me and David are going to talk to Jason," he said, pointing at a mass of kids milling around the area.

"Sure, buddy," George said, watching as the two boys ran toward their friend.

He turned back to Kendall. "Thanks for asking Amy to design your garden, Kenny. That will be good for her."

"I'm not sure Amy thinks so," Kendall replied. "She seemed almost scared by the idea."

"Amy? Scared to take on a project? No way." He shook his head decisively. "She's been bugging Tilda to let her do more work."

"She sure didn't act happy about it."

"She didn't, did she?" He scowled. "She's been jumpy lately. Do you think it's because of Townsend?"

"Gabe? Why would you think that?"

"You tell me." Anger flared in his eyes. "Remember our conversation the other morning?"

Kendall thought back. "You mean about Gabe being Tommy's father? I don't believe that," she said, remembering how Gabe had been with her girls. If he were Tommy's father, he wouldn't have walked away.

"She's been jumpy ever since he got here."

"Have you asked her what's wrong?"

George looked away. "Yeah. She wouldn't tell me."

Kendall kissed his cheek. "You and Amy don't need me hanging around tonight," she said. She spotted the girls, who were standing in front of the rental counter. "You spend time with Amy and Tommy and figure out what's wrong. I'll grab the girls and we'll stay out of your way."

As Kendall wove her way through the crowds, she spotted Amy walking toward her. Changing direction, she touched Amy's arm to get her attention. "My girls are getting restless," she told the other woman. "You and George and Tommy go ahead on your own." She smiled. "Why don't the three of you come over to my house for dinner on Sunday. We can talk without so many interruptions."

"Sunday?" Amy glanced back to where George stood. "I'll have to check and see what's on our schedule. Can I let you know?"

"Of course." Kendall smiled again. "You and George have a good time tomorrow night."

As she walked away, she felt Amy's gaze on her back. When she turned and waved, Amy looked as if she was going to cry. Kendall hesitated, but Amy headed toward George, disappearing into the crowd.

CHAPTER SEVEN

Saturday morning

"DYLAN, THIS REALLY ISN'T a good time," Kendall said, wiping sweat off her forehead with the back of her hand.

The reporter shoved his notebook into the back pocket of his jeans. "Let me help you," he said, grabbing the hose that she'd been dragging to an irrigation pipe.

Her foreman, Bertie, took it from Dylan with a suspicious look, then spit on the ground. "You trying to suck up to Mrs. Van Allen?" he asked.

Dylan smiled at the old man. "Nah, just trying to keep up with her." He turned to Kendall. "Why are you working out here in the orchard, anyway? The B and B has to keep you pretty busy."

"I enjoy working in the orchard," she said, tugging the hose over a root that projected from the ground. She handed it to Bertie, who attached it to the pipe, then wiped her hands on her jeans. "Don't you like to get your hands dirty once in a while?"

The reporter glanced at his hands. "Not really."

Kendall laughed. "I guess you're not a gardener, either, then."

"Nope. I'm a condo kind of guy."

"Your loss," she said lightly. She turned and headed back for another hose.

"Is working in the orchard the way you keep connected to Carter?" Dylan asked. "I gather he loved the orchard."

A rusty laugh rumbled in Bertie's throat and Kendall stopped dead. She turned around to face Dylan. "What is that supposed to mean?"

"That he loved the orchard?" Dylan shrugged. "It's pretty common knowledge in Sturgeon Falls."

She'd meant the "keeping connected to Carter" crack, but she wasn't going to pursue that. There was no reason to give Dylan Smith any more questions to ask. "Who have you been talking to in Sturgeon Falls?"

"Different people." His smile was charming. "You know a reporter doesn't reveal his sources."

"What's going on, Dylan? You said you were writing an article about the stadium being dedicated to Carter. A small human-interest story. So why are you digging around in Sturgeon Falls, asking people about my husband?"

"I didn't say it was a small story," he protested, his dimple flashing. "No reporter ever writes a small story."

"There isn't any big story about Carter. So what are you doing here?"

He shrugged, but didn't quite meet her eyes. "I was curious. The reporter's curse."

"Curious about the life of a man who died when he was twenty-five? That sounds like a pretty boring story."

"You never know what you might find."

Kendall yanked one of the hoses a little too hard and stumbled backward. "No, you don't." She brushed past the reporter. "It must be nice to have a job where you get paid even if you're wasting your time."

"Hey, Kendall, you need some help?" Gabe's hand circled her upper arm, tightened in warning. "That hose looks heavy."

She dropped the hose and found him standing close. "Where did you come from? I didn't hear you."

"You were too busy talking to Smith." Gabe turned to the foreman. "Hi, Bertie." The old man waved to him as he disappeared into the row of trees.

Gabe gave the reporter a polite smile that held no warmth. "You out here learning how an orchard runs?"

"Nope," Dylan replied. "I'm grilling Kendall about Carter."

"Really?" Gabe pulled the hose toward the waiting connection as if it weighed nothing. "Why is that?"

"For the article I'm writing." He picked up another hose and dragged it over. "About Carter Van Allen and the stadium dedication."

"If you want to know about Carter's high school days, I'm the person to ask. Carter and I were in the same class." With a slight shift, Gabe moved between Kendall and the reporter. "Kendall was a couple of years behind us."

Gabe was trying to protect her. More touched than she wanted to be, Kendall stepped beside him. "I told Dylan I'd answer his questions about Carter. I just don't have time right now. These irrigation hoses need to be moved this morning."

"No problem," Dylan said easily. "I'll catch you later. I'll be around all weekend."

He started to leave, then stopped and glanced at Gabe. "I do have some questions I'd like to ask you, as well."

"I'm sure I'll see you around," Gabe answered. "Since we're both staying in Kendall's house."

The reporter studied Gabe, glanced at Kendall, and then nodded. "Don't worry. I'll find you." His gaze flickered over Kendall again. "When it's more convenient."

Kendall felt the heat of Gabe's arm as they watched Dylan walk out of the orchard and head back to the house. "What's he really doing here?" Gabe asked, narrowing his eyes as he watched the reporter move off. "At your house, at the dedication. In Sturgeon Falls. The *Green Bay News-Gazette* can't be interested in Carter."

Gabe was still too close. Kendall picked up her hose again and dragged it until she was a safe distance away from him. "You know as much as I do." She dropped the equipment and brushed dirt off her hands. "Clearly there's more going on than a nice human-interest story."

"I'm going to do some checking on Smith. Find out if he's really from that Green Bay paper. See if I can figure out what he's doing here."

"I can do that myself, Gabe."

"I know you can. But you have your hands full." He

nodded at the tangle of hoses snaking around the cherry trees. "Trying to take care of the orchard and the house, and looking after the girls. Getting information is part of my job, and I'm good at it." He picked up a loop of hose and untangled it. "Let's play to our strengths here, Kendall. I'll check up on Smith. I do a lot of Internet research."

"It's not your problem." She could Google Dylan Smith as easily as Gabe could.

"My God, Kendall. Are you afraid you'd be indebted to me for such a tiny thing?" He stepped closer, looming over her. "Can't you take anything from me?"

"I don't want to put you out. You're a guest," she said, struggling to hold on to her composure.

He slapped his hand against a low-hanging branch of one of the trees, making the leaves flutter. "That's bull and you know it. I'm more than a guest in your house. I'm part of your past, and this is as much my problem as yours. I don't want him poking around in my life. Any more than you want him poking around in yours."

As much as she'd struggled to forget Gabe, to erase him from her memory bank, he *was* a part of her past and he always would be. Kendall sighed, slumping against the tree. "I should have told Dylan I wasn't interested in talking to him. I shouldn't have let him stay at the house. But I had to put in a new water heater last week, and I needed the business." She raised her hands in a "what was I supposed to do?" gesture. "Be careful what you wish for, right? I should have known that an open-ended booking was too good to be true."

Gabe stepped closer, hesitated, then reached for her upper arms and drew her close. His body was warm and he smelled familiar, as if the scent of Gabe had lingered in her subconscious all these years.

As he shifted against her, she felt hard muscle and sinew and determination. She stiffened, but he held her loosely, apparently intent only on comfort. "It'll be okay, Kenny," he murmured. "I'll find out everything there is to find out about Smith. I won't let him destroy any illusions about Carter."

"I don't have any illusions about Carter," she said, and eased away from him. She was surprised by how bereft that statement made her feel. "But the girls do. I don't want them reading a negative story about their father in the newspaper."

"Don't worry. They won't."

His voice was hard and filled with a ruthlessness that hadn't been there when he'd left town. Gabe had changed.

So had she.

Glancing at her watch, she put distance between them once more. "I have to get back to the house. Shelby has a soccer game in an hour."

He fell into step beside her. "That's why I came looking for you. Jenna wanted to know if I could give her a tennis lesson this morning."

She shoved her hands into her pockets. "I haven't had time to get her a tennis racquet."

"No problem. I was going to get her one, anyway." He gave her a sidelong glance. "Or would that be stepping on your pride again?"

She caught his gaze and held it a moment too long. In the sudden silence, her heart beat a little faster. "Pride is all I have," she said, bending to pick up a pruning clipper someone had left on the ground. "I got used to taking care of the girls myself the last seven years."

"You've been doing that for longer than that," he answered. "I know Carter wasn't a model father."

He stopped abruptly, and she wondered what else he'd almost said. "He was too young when Shelby was born."

"Carter would have always been too young…" He pressed his lips together and kept walking. Moments later, he stopped in front of the orchard maintenance building and nodded at the clipper. "Are you going to put that away?"

She tightened her grip on the tool. "Yes. You don't have to wait."

"I don't mind waiting for you, Kendall."

She glanced at him as she unlocked the door, but Gabe returned her gaze steadily. Slipping into the cool darkness, she hung the tool where it belonged, then locked the door behind her.

"So is it all right to give Jenna a tennis lesson this morning?" he asked.

"Yes," she said. "Go ahead and buy her a racquet."

"Thank you." His hand brushed hers, almost as if it was an accident. "What about a tennis court? Where would you suggest I go?"

"There are courts at Big Hill Park, where Shelby plays soccer. Why don't you take her there."

"So you can keep an eye on me?" he said, but there wasn't any heat in his voice. Just resignation.

"I don't need to keep an eye on you," she said more sharply than she'd intended. "If I didn't trust you with Jenna, I wouldn't let you teach her to play tennis."

"Thank you for that," he said.

She took a breath. "I thought maybe when you and Jenna were finished, you could watch Shelby play soccer." She gave him a sideways glance. "To nip any jealousy problems in the bud." Not because *she* wanted to spend time with him.

"The girls would fight over me?" He sounded astonished.

"Don't act so surprised. You've been showering them with attention. You don't think they're keeping track of how much time you spend with each of them?"

"Really? I had no idea." He looked bemused.

"You don't spend much time with kids, do you?"

"No, I don't." He shrugged. "Not many of my friends have children."

"What about Tommy Mitchell?"

She felt him tense beside her. "What about him?"

"I understand you're a friend of Amy's."

Gabe walked a few steps without answering. Finally he said, "What's that supposed to mean?"

"You said you didn't spend much time with kids. Doesn't Tommy count?"

After a long moment, he said, "Tommy is an only child. There aren't any jealousy problems."

So he acknowledged that he was Amy's friend.

Kendall itched to ask him more, to ask if George's suspicions about Tommy's paternity were true. But she kept her mouth shut. That wasn't any of her business.

And maybe she didn't really want to know. She'd told George that Gabe wasn't the kind of man who would abandon his child. Had she been wrong?

She walked a little faster. "You know where Big Hill Park is, don't you?"

"Vaguely. I'm sure I can find it."

She stepped onto the first step of the back porch, then turned to face him. "Jenna is very sensitive," she said quietly. "She doesn't have Shelby's tough skin."

"I know," he said. "I'll be careful with her."

She blew out a breath. "I know you will, Gabe. It's my job to worry."

"You're a good mother. Your girls are very lucky." He pulled out his cell phone and opened it. "It's ten o'clock now. If Shelby's game is in an hour, that should give us enough time for a lesson." He snapped the phone shut and slid it into his pocket. "I'll gather my stuff together and meet Jenna at my car."

"I'll get her ready." She watched the screen door shut behind Gabe and mulled over what had happened in the orchard. Instead of adversaries, for a little while she and Gabe had become allies. Some seismic shift had occurred.

She wasn't sure she was ready for the aftershocks it might produce.

"WHY DO WE HAVE to stop?" Jenna asked as Gabe dropped his racquet into his tennis bag and retrieved the last bright yellow ball.

"Because we've played enough for today. You don't want to be sore tomorrow."

Jenna frowned. "Why would I be sore?"

He looked at her, still swinging the racquet, dancing from foot to foot as he'd showed her. "Maybe you wouldn't. Maybe it's only adults who get sore." He dodged the edge of the racquet and steered her off the court. "I guess I should say we've played enough for today because *I* don't want to be sore tomorrow."

Jenna giggled. "Okay. Can we practice tomorrow?"

"We'll see." He nudged her toward the soccer field, where two teams of girls were running up and down the field. "Let's watch your sister play soccer."

"I'll tell her about my tennis lesson after she's done." Jenna gave him a triumphant look. "She doesn't know how to play tennis."

So Kendall had been right. They *were* keeping score. He'd have to be careful. "Which one is Shelby's team?"

"They have the blue shorts and yellow shirts." She hunched her shoulders. "Don't tell her, but I think her uniform is cool."

"Can I tell her *I* think her uniform is cool?"

"I guess so. Especially since you're not teaching her tennis."

"Okay." They were almost at the edge of the soccer field. Kendall was deep in conversation with another mother, but she glanced up as Gabe approached. She held his gaze for a heartbeat too long, then nodded and turned back to her conversation. Jenna ran off to talk to another girl her age, and Gabe stood on the sidelines, watching Shelby.

She ran down the field with the ball. A defender came close, and Shelby executed the scissors move he'd taught her. "Good job, Shelby," he yelled without thinking.

She glanced over and flashed him a huge grin.

The other parents glanced his way and smiled, and he relaxed. Apparently he hadn't broken any rules by yelling.

The back of his neck prickled, and he stepped away from the field. A casual sweep of the area revealed a man, presumably another parent, staring at him.

When he caught Gabe's eye, the man sauntered over. "Townsend? Is that you?" he asked.

Gabe nodded, trying to place him. The man's brown hair receded from his forehead and his watery blue eyes were prominent. "Jim Donaldson," he said, extending his hand. "We had history with Mrs. Segunda our senior year."

Gabe vaguely remembered a skinny, quiet kid with pop-bottle glasses and a bad case of acne. "Hi, Jim," he said, shaking hands. "It's been a while."

Donaldson's smile was thin. "You don't remember me. I kept a pretty low profile back then," he said.

Gabe frantically searched his memory. "You got contacts, didn't you?"

"Yeah, I did," Donaldson replied, some of the antagonism fading from his eyes.

"Amazing how they change your appearance, isn't it?" Gabe answered. "How have you been?"

"I'm good. My Sarah is on the soccer team." He gave Gabe an assessing look. "I didn't realize you were back in Sturgeon Falls."

"Just for a few days. I came for the dedication."

"Ah, yes. The dedication of the high school stadium to the deserving Carter Van Allen." The edgy antagonism in Donaldson's eyes flared again. "It's probably going to bring a lot of people out of the woodwork."

"Carter was my friend," Gabe said quietly. "Of course I'd come for the dedication."

"You always were a loyal guy, Townsend." Donaldson's mouth formed a tight line.

Gabe studied the other man. "Did you have a problem with Carter?"

"Carter Van Allen was a spoiled jerk of a rich kid," Donaldson retorted. "He always got everything he wanted. I can't imagine why they're dedicating the football field to him." He glanced at Kendall and his mouth twisted. "Oh, wait, I forgot. Money causes amnesia for a lot of folks."

"You think Kendall paid to have the stadium named for Carter?" Gabe asked.

Donaldson snorted. "Can you think of another reason to name it after him?"

"The committee didn't share their reasons with me." Gabe fixed the other man with a hard stare. "Look, Donaldson, I don't know what you have against Carter, but don't you think it's time to let it go? The guy is dead, for God's sake."

Donaldson smoothed his hand over his thinning hair. "Sorry," he muttered. "I get worked up every time I think about watching my kid play soccer in Carter Van Allen Stadium."

"Carter wasn't perfect, but then, were any of us?" Gabe held his gaze until the other man looked away. "I'd hate to have one of his daughters overhear something negative about her father." He waited a beat, but Donaldson didn't respond. "Do you understand me?"

Donaldson narrowed his eyes. "Still protecting him, Townsend?"

"No. I'm protecting his daughters." Gabe waited until Donaldson shrugged.

"I won't say anything to Shelby, if that's what you mean."

"That's a start."

Gabe felt Kendall next to him even before she spoke. "Sarah's playing great today, Jim," she said. "Did you see that last stop she made?"

"I missed it." He shot Gabe an indecipherable look. "I'd better go pay attention."

Donaldson walked away and Gabe shoved his hands into his pockets, pleasure buzzing through him. "Rescuing me, Kendall?"

"Jim doesn't make any secret of his feelings about Carter," she said, her gaze lingering on the other man.

"Isn't that a little awkward?"

She shrugged. "There are enough parents that we can

stay out of each other's way. His wife told me that Jim wanted to be the quarterback for the football team. He's always resented Carter for being so good."

"It was more than ten years ago. He needs to grow up."

"Some people never mature past the age of eighteen."

Carter had been one of them. "Isn't that the truth?" he muttered.

"Jim has been bad-mouthing Carter since high school," she said. "No one pays any attention to him anymore."

"I don't give a damn what he says about Carter. As long as he doesn't say it around Shelby or Jenna."

Kendall's fingers brushed his. "He's not a bad man, Gabe. He's just stuck in the past."

"Hell." Gabe shoved his hand through his hair. "Life is much less complicated in Milwaukee."

"Yep, that's what we're known for here in Sturgeon Falls—intrigue, danger and excitement," she said with a smile. It was the first genuine smile she'd given him since he'd arrived, and his heart caught in his throat.

"Thanks again for rescuing me," he said, trying to lighten his voice.

"Don't mention it," she said, equally lightly. "I'd better go ask Jenna about her tennis lesson."

Gabe watched as she walked away, wondering if their apparent truce was permanent.

Or if it would shatter after Amy's revelations to George tonight.

CHAPTER EIGHT

Saturday evening

THE DINNER DISHES were finished and Kendall sat on the back porch. Shelby, Jenna and Elena were playing hide-and-seek in the orchard. The sun filtered through the tall pines next to the beach, casting lacy shadows on the grass. Green Bay was calm, the waves lapping gently on the sand. A perfect evening.

Kendall had sat on this porch countless times over the past seven years, watching the girls play in the yard, on the beach or in the orchard. She'd always been alone. She'd liked it that way.

Tonight, as she listened to the children giggle and yell as they dodged between the cherry trees, she wondered where Gabe had gone. After they'd returned from the soccer game, he'd changed his clothes, gotten into his car and driven off. He still wasn't home.

No. He wasn't at her house. She stood up abruptly and dusted off the back of her shorts. What was wrong with her? This wasn't Gabe's home.

Clearly she had too much time on her hands, if she

could sit on her porch and wonder where Gabe had gone. She knelt in front of one of her flower beds, running her hands against the cool, damp soil as she tugged weeds from between the alyssum and salvia.

When had Gabe invaded her thoughts? And why had she let him?

The rich, earthy aroma of the soil mingled with the scents of the pine trees and the lake, triggering bittersweet memories. Gabe and Carter, laughing at some shared joke as Kendall planted flowers in one of the beds she'd created. Gabe standing next to Carter at their wedding, watching her, the scent of gardenias almost overpowering. That Fourth of July party on the beach, Kendall and Gabe swimming in chilly Green Bay, Gabe reaching for her in the water, his hands warm against her cold skin...

She grabbed the mound of weeds she'd pulled up and strode to the compost pile, tossing them into the box. If only memories were as easily discarded.

When she turned back toward the house, Gabe was sitting on the porch, in the spot she'd vacated. She faltered to a stop. Had he read her mind, known she was thinking about him? Or had she conjured him up from some vaguely remembered longing, some long-suppressed emotion?

Of course not. He was on her porch because it was a beautiful summer evening, and he'd heard the girls playing.

"Hi, Kendall," he said as she approached. "The kids sound as if they're having fun."

She eased onto the step below Gabe, taking care not to brush against him. "I can't believe they still have so much energy."

"I had a good time today," he said. "Giving Jenna a tennis lesson, watching Shelby play soccer."

"Jenna chattered all the way home about tennis." Considering her younger daughter's excitement, and her older daughter's barely concealed jealousy, she smiled at him. "To hear Jenna tell it, she'll be playing on the pro tour in a couple of years."

Gabe looked toward the orchard, where the girls could be heard and occasionally glimpsed. "I don't know about that, but she did seem to have a knack for the game. She's pretty analytical, isn't she?"

"How did you know that?" Kendall asked. She relaxed, forgetting her earlier discomfort.

He shrugged. "From watching her and listening to her these past few days. Tennis should be a good fit. It's all about analyzing angles and moves and being three steps ahead of yourself."

"Thanks for taking the time to teach her—and for figuring out what she would like. I've been trying to interest her in something physical, but she keeps saying she's not good at sports and doesn't like stupid games."

"Then I guess I'd better not tell her that tennis is a sport," he said.

"Probably not."

They sat in companionable silence as the sun moved closer to the horizon, painting the sky over Green Bay with streaks of pink and orange. Kendall strained to hear the girls, but their shouts were farther away and now she couldn't see them at all.

She stood up. "I'm going to rein them in. I don't like them in the orchard when it's getting dark. There are too many ways they could hurt themselves."

"Mind if I walk with you?" Gabe asked.

"Why? Don't you have anything better to do?" She glanced at him as they headed toward the shadowed trees. "It's Saturday night. You were gone all afternoon, and I expected you'd be gone tonight, too."

"Are you asking me where I was this afternoon?"

Yes. "Of course not. That's none of my business."

"I don't mind you asking, Kendall. Do you want me to tell you?"

"Not particularly." *Liar.*

She'd been lying a lot lately.

"Maybe I'll tell you anyway." They'd reached the orchard, and the deep shadows beneath the trees made Kendall think of Gabe's voice—mysterious, dark and dangerous.

Her steps slowed, and almost against her will, she turned to him. "All right, Gabe," she said in a husky whisper. "Where were you?"

Before he could answer, a piercing scream shattered the quiet of the evening. Kendall's stomach lurched. "Shelby! Jenna!" she shouted as she pivoted and ran toward the scream.

Gabe was right behind. In the gathering darkness, Kendall didn't see the tree root pushing out of the ground. Her foot caught and her ankle twisted. Gabe grabbed her arm and steadied her. As soon as she was moving again, he let her go.

"Shelby! Where are you?" Kendall yelled, her voice laced with panic.

"Over here, Mom." Shelby's voice was frightened, and Kendall darted between two trees, running faster.

Gabe held on to her again. "Take it easy," he panted.

She jerked her arm away. "One of my babies is hurt." She accelerated over the rough ground, stumbling, then catching herself. "Shelby! Jenna!" she hollered, frantic with fear.

"Hurry, Mom." Kendall swiveled and then saw the pink of Jenna's T-shirt through the trees.

Shelby and Jenna were crying when she reached them, and she pulled them into her arms. "Who's hurt?"

"Elena." Shelby wiped her nose. "She's over here."

Kendall let her daughters go and raced toward the child who was huddled on the ground nearby. "What happened?"

"We were running, and she tripped over something. There's a lot of blood." Shelby's voice quavered. "We told her to stay there and we'd get you."

"That was very smart, Shelby," Gabe said. Kendall had forgotten he was there.

When she reached Elena, the young girl was holding the hem of her shirt over her face. The white material was soaked in blood.

"Elena, do you remember me? I'm Shelby's mom," she said softly. "Can I see?"

The girl slowly lowered the shirt from her face. She

was bleeding profusely from a deep gash near her hairline.

"What did you cut it on?" Kendall asked.

"That." The girl pointed to a gnarled tree root. She touched the wound, and her hand came away covered with more blood.

Gabe thrust his shirt at Kendall. "Hold this over it," he said. "It's reasonably clean."

The T-shirt was warm from Gabe's body. Kendall pressed it against the cut on Elena's head and put her arm around the girl. "I think you're going to need to see a doctor," she said, her voice gentle. "Let's go find your parents."

"They're not home," she said. Kendall could hear the effort it took for Elena not to cry. "They go out on Saturday night."

There were a couple of bars the workers visited on the weekends. "Who's watching you?"

"My grandmother."

"Then let's get her."

"I'll go," Shelby said. "I know which house is theirs."

Before Kendall could answer, she'd gone racing through the trees. The light was fading fast, and Kendall lost track of her quickly. "Be careful, Shel," she yelled after her daughter. "Do you think you can stand up?" she asked the injured girl.

When Elena nodded, Kendall helped the girl stand up, then wrapped an arm around her shoulders. "Do you want to walk, or do you want me to carry you?"

Elena took a shaky step, then another, and stumbled. She caught herself and remained upright. "I can walk."

"Hold on, Elena. Maybe we better wait here for your grandmother," Kendall said, easing her to the ground. She sat down, drawing the child close and holding the shirt to the wound. Elena slumped against her.

Gabe crouched low. The dark hair curling over his bare chest was level with Kendall's eyes. She shifted her gaze to Elena and rearranged the makeshift bandage.

"Do you want me to pull my car to the edge of the orchard?" he asked. "We need to get her to an emergency room. I think she's in shock."

"Yes, but take my car. The keys are on a hook in the office beneath the stairs."

Gabe stood up. "Jenna, do you want to come with me and show me where the keys are?"

"Okay," she said. Kendall could hear the anxiety in her daughter's voice.

"Thanks, Gabe," Kendall murmured, and he nodded.

Holding out his hand for Jenna, he steered her around the trees. "You were very brave with Elena. You and Shelby made sure we got here right away."

His bare back was broader than it had been seven years ago, muscled and tan. Kendall watched him and Jenna until they disappeared into the gathering darkness, and then looked at the cut again. It was still oozing. "I think the bleeding is slowing down," she told Elena.

"Really?" The child reached up, touched the shirt and let her hand drop.

Kendall rocked her slowly as the orchard grew dark. Finally she heard the crunch of approaching footsteps.

"I brought Elena's brother," Shelby said breathlessly.

A boy of twelve or thirteen crouched in front of Elena and spoke to her in Spanish. Elena answered him in the same language. Kendall understood most of what they were saying, and she tightened her arm around the girl.

After calling her clumsy, Elena's brother grabbed her arm and tried to pull her to her feet. She had to come back to the house now, he said. There were probably some bandages in the bathroom, and anyway they didn't have money to go to the doctor. As he harangued his sister, tears slid down her cheeks.

Kendall put her hand on the boy's arm. "Elena needs stitches. We'll take her to the doctor," she said.

"She'll be fine," he said, glancing uneasily at the blood-soaked shirt. "My grandmother will take care of her. We don't go to the doctor much."

"It's okay," Kendall said gently. "I'll pay for it."

A mixture of shame and relief washed over the boy's face. "I guess that's all right," he muttered.

Elena was plastered to her side, crying softly, and Kendall stroked her hair. She'd seen the humiliation in Elena's eyes when her brother had been talking. "Here's my cell-phone number," she told the boy, reciting the digits. "Have your parents call me when they get home. If they don't have a phone, tell them to wake Bertie up."

"They have a cell phone," the boy assured her.

"I'm sorry you can't come with Elena," Kendall said,

actually not sorry at all. She suspected he would only continue to upset the girl by railing at her for her accident. "But you need to be there when your parents come home."

The boy nodded solemnly. "I'll wait up for them. I'll remember your phone number."

"Good." She stood up and eased Elena to her feet. "Can you walk?" she asked the girl.

"I think so."

Kendall kept her arm around the child, and they made their way out of the orchard. Shelby was uncharacteristically silent as she walked beside Elena.

As they approached the edge of the orchard, Kendall heard the unmistakable rumble of her car. The muffler needed to be replaced, but that, too, was on the list of luxuries—at least until it became an absolute necessity.

Gabe got out, and the car's headlights outlined his figure as he walked toward them. "Did Elena's grandmother know how to get hold of her parents?" Gabe asked.

"Her brother came to get her. He doesn't know where they are, and we can't wait for them," she said.

Gabe knelt in front of Elena. "You're scared, aren't you, sweetheart?" he said in a low, soothing voice.

When Elena nodded, he turned his head and brushed back his dark hair, showing her a thin white scar behind his ear. "I fell out of a tree in this orchard when I was about your age. I was bleeding a lot, too, but I got the cut stitched up and that's all that's left." He gave her a tiny smile. "When I was there, they gave the kids lollipops. What's your favorite flavor?"

"Grape," Elena said.

"Then let's go get you a grape sucker."

Ten minutes later, Kendall led Elena into the emergency room. The nurse at the admitting desk looked up and wrinkled her forehead. "Oh, my," she said. "What happened?"

"I tripped," Elena said.

"Why don't you and your mom sit down so I can get your name and some other information," the nurse said, reaching for her keyboard. "Name?"

"I'm not her mother," Kendall said.

The nurse looked up. "How are you related to her?"

"I'm not. Her parents work for me."

The nurse's gaze shifted from Kendall to Elena and comprehension filled her eyes. "She's a migrant?"

"Yes."

"Then she doesn't have insurance."

"I'll pay her bill," Kendall said.

"You could take her to the hospital in Green Bay. They have to treat everyone, insured or not."

"I'm not going to take her to Green Bay," Kendall said sharply. "She's bleeding and in shock."

The nurse shrugged. "It's up to you."

Kendall supplied the necessary information, then the nurse stood up. "You're lucky you came in early," she said. "We get pretty crowded later on Saturday nights." She turned to Elena. "Come on, dear. I'll take you back."

Elena pressed a little closer to Kendall. "I'm coming with her," she said.

"But..." The nurse glanced at her, then shrugged. "If you'd like to."

As they headed into the emergency room, Gabe walked in with Jenna and Shelby. The girls clung to his hands.

Gabe nodded to her. "We'll wait out here."

As Kendall and Elena walked through the swinging doors, Kendall heard Gabe say to her daughters, "Let's check out the vending machines."

THREE HOURS LATER, Kendall, Gabe, Shelby and Jenna walked into the house. Elena had been stitched up, treated for shock, given a tetanus shot and taken home. Kendall was uneasy about leaving her there, because her parents weren't back yet, but her three brothers assured Kendall they'd help their grandmother take care of Elena.

Shelby and Jenna were drooping, practically asleep on their feet. "Go and get ready for bed, girls," Kendall said, giving each of them a kiss. "You were both wonderful—finding me, keeping Elena calm, trying to make her feel better. I'm proud of you."

"Is Elena going to be okay, Mom?" Jenna asked.

"She's going to be just fine," Kendall said firmly. "She'll have a sore head for a few days, but that's all."

"Good." Jenna leaned against her mother's side, and even Shelby was subdued. "There was a lot of blood."

"I know that was scary for you. But she's not bleeding anymore, the cut has been taken care of and before you know it, she'll be playing with you again."

"Okay." Jenna smiled tentatively and headed up the stairs, followed by Shelby.

When they had disappeared around the corner and Kendall heard their door close, she slumped to the stairs, suddenly shaky. Dried blood was spattered on her clothes and now her hands trembled as she brushed at the dark spots. She was so cold.

"Kendall." Gabe knelt in front of her. "Go upstairs and change your clothes. I'll make you some tea."

"You don't need to do that," she said.

He sighed. "I know you can take care of yourself. I know it isn't my place to make you tea. But I'm really not in the mood tonight to listen to all that crap again. I'm going to make myself coffee anyway. I'll make you tea at the same time. All right?"

She struggled to her feet. "That's not what I meant. You've done so much tonight, I don't want to put you out."

He tucked a strand of hair behind her ear. "You're not putting me out. I'm heating the water anyway."

"Okay." She managed a smile. "Thank you. I'll be right down."

CHAPTER NINE

Saturday evening

TEN MINUTES LATER she walked into the kitchen, her face and hands scrubbed, wearing a clean shirt and a pair of baggy shorts. Gabe leaned against the counter, two mugs steaming gently beside him.

"Feel better?" he asked.

"Much." She gave him a weary smile as he handed her a mug of tea. "Thank you for all you did tonight."

"It wasn't much," he said. "But you're welcome."

"You did a huge amount." She took a sip. It was hot and too sweet and tasted wonderful. "You kept Shelby and Jenna calm and occupied so I could concentrate on Elena. You drove us all to the hospital." She looked away, disturbed by the softness in his eyes. The yearning. "I'd say you did a lot."

"You would have managed just fine by yourself," he said. He studied her in the subdued light. "Why did you insist on taking your car? Mine is bigger. It would have been more comfortable."

She had another sip of tea, letting the warmth seep

into her bones, then wrapped her hands around the mug. "I know what you're thinking, and you're wrong. I wasn't trying to prove I didn't need help. You have a nice car and I didn't want to get blood all over the upholstery."

"I didn't care about that."

"I know, Gabe, and that was sweet of you. But if upholstery had to be cleaned up afterward, it was going to be mine."

"I'm not sweet, Kendall." His eyes darkened. "I'm a lot of things, but sweet isn't one of them."

She set the mug on the counter with care. "You were with the girls."

"I wasn't talking about the girls."

As their eyes met, Kendall's heart began to race and she found it difficult to breathe. She gripped the counter. "Why did you come back, Gabe?"

"I couldn't stay away. And not just because of you." His gaze was as intimate as a touch. "I need to take care of some unfinished business before I can move on."

"Aren't you a little young to be having a midlife crisis?"

The old Gabe would have risen to the bait like a hungry bass. This Gabe gave her a wry grin. "Good comeback, Kenny. But you'll have to do better than that if you want to distract me."

"Don't call me Kenny," she said, her throat tightening at the nickname. Her brother, Carter and Gabe were the only ones who'd ever called her that.

"Why not? It suits you."

"Not anymore," she said, pushing away from the

counter. "I'm a different person than I was back then. I'm Kendall now."

"I think Kenny is hiding inside you, waiting to come out and play." He trailed his finger down her arm. "I catch a glimpse of her every now and then."

"Kenny grew up." She eased away. "She had to."

"Life isn't always fair."

"No one ever promised it would be. As my mother was always so fond of telling me, I've made my bed and now I'm lying in it."

"I think I like the grown-up Kenny better than the one I left behind," he murmured, crowding closer to her.

She smelled his skin, the wild scent she remembered all too well. His eyes had darkened until the blue almost disappeared. When he leaned closer to Kendall, her heart fluttered and her abdomen tightened with anticipation. She put her hands on his shoulders. *To push him away.*

"I can't do this, Gabe," she murmured.

"Do what?" He picked up one of her hands and kissed her palm.

"*This.* You and me. Together."

"I understand." He drew one of her fingers into his mouth, and she sucked in a breath.

"Good," she said, her voice tight. "I'm glad that's clear."

"Me, too." He swirled his tongue around her finger.

She trembled, unable to tear her gaze away from Gabe's as he drew her finger into his mouth and released it once again. Drew it in again. In and out. In and out.

"Let me go, Gabe!"

He kissed her palm one last time, then dropped her hand. "You can leave anytime, Kendall."

But she didn't move away, didn't retreat. "Carter will always be here," she said quietly. "Watching. Standing between us."

"Carter is gone. And he wasn't always between us," he said, brushing the pad of his thumb over her lips. "The Fourth of July. Remember that?"

Memories of the Fourth of July party and the scorching kiss they'd shared, suppressed for so long, burst into the open. "That was wrong," she whispered.

"It didn't feel wrong." He brushed a kiss over her mouth, his lips barely touching hers. Her body tensed, urging her to move closer. He drew away and looked into her eyes. "Did it feel wrong to you?"

"You know it didn't." When he bent closer again, she rested her hand on his chest. "But it was. I was engaged to Carter. I had no business kissing you."

"Then why did you?"

"I don't know." *She knew perfectly well why she'd kissed him.* The remembered need swelled inside her, mocking her claim she'd forgotten.

And the guilt followed, just as it always did.

"You're not engaged to Carter now."

"No. He's dead." She whirled away from him and braced her hands against the counter. Thinking of what had happened the night he'd died.

He put his hands on her shoulders, slid them down her arms. His fingers were callused, and she shivered as they rasped against her skin. "Seven years is a long time," he murmured. His breath stirred the hairs behind her ear, stirred the need that threatened to consume her.

"Not long enough," she said. It would never be enough to make her forget.

"Are you sure?" Slowly he turned her around. He cupped her face with his hands, brushing his thumbs across her cheeks.

Then he lowered his mouth to hers, stifling the protest she should have made. The taste of the coffee he'd been drinking was dark and potent in her mouth. But it couldn't distract her from the taste of Gabe himself, heady and intoxicating. A taste that triggered feelings she'd kept hidden all these years.

She shouldn't be kissing Gabe, but she couldn't tear herself away. His mouth moved over hers, tasting, teasing, nibbling at her lower lip. When she opened her mouth to him, he groaned and swept his tongue inside.

He pulled her tightly against him, running his hand down her back, pressing his hips into hers. But it wasn't necessary. His body fit hers as if they were the last two pieces of a puzzle, finally found.

"Kenny," he murmured, lifting his head. "Look at me."

She dragged her eyes open to find him staring at her. He smoothed the pad of his thumb over her cheeks, down her neck. "I want to watch you. I want you to watch me."

Slowly, deliberately, he moved his hands lower until he cupped her breasts. His thumbs rested lightly on her nipples, and beneath the T-shirt and the thin bra she wore, they tightened and swelled. She took a deep breath, pushing her breasts against his hand, but he didn't move.

His face was taut and flushed. "Can I touch you, Kenny?" he whispered. "Really touch you?"

"You already are," she said.

"That's not what I mean." His eyes glinted. "But it will do for now."

He moved his thumbs and heat flashed through her groin, prompting a tiny cry. He circled her nipples again, and she began to tremble.

"Do you remember?" he asked, his voice dark velvet. "I remember everything."

God help her, she did, too. She hadn't forgotten the passion that arced between them, the heat, the need, the arousal so strong it was almost painful. The same need, the same arousal that drummed in her blood tonight.

He bent his head, replacing his thumb with his mouth. Even through the layers of fabric, the sensation made her whimper with desire. She clutched his shoulders, afraid she would fall if she didn't hold on to him.

He focused on her mouth again, his kiss hungry and desperate. As if nothing existed but their mouths, their tongues, their bodies. As if the whole world had shrunk to this room, to the taste of Gabe, the feel of his hard body pressing against hers.

The juncture of her thighs throbbed and ached and swelled. Sexual need, suppressed for so long, burst free in a heated rush. Urgency swept through her, the need to join her body to his, to feel him moving inside her.

She reached for the button on his jeans, her fingers trembling.

"I never stopped wanting you," he said with a groan, kissing her neck, taking her mouth with wild abandon. "Never."

His words cut through the thick haze of arousal. My God. What was she doing?

Her hands dropped from his jeans and she eased away from his mouth. Gabe straightened and looked down at her, his arms still holding her tight.

"I can't do this," she whispered.

He stared down at her for a moment, then kissed her once more and stepped away, putting space between them. "I'm sorry."

"Me, too." She crossed her arms over her chest, holding herself tightly.

"We're a pair, aren't we?" He slid his thumb over her mouth again, then let his hand drop. "There's so much between us. So much history. So many secrets." He smiled grimly. "I forgot all of it when I touched you."

She had, too. But her memory had returned. "It's late, and we're both tired." She dredged up a smile. "It was an emotional night. That's all."

"You're right. We got lost in the moment." He brushed her hair away from her face with a shaking hand. "Just like at the Fourth of July party."

So neither of them was going to talk about that other night—the night Carter died. "I swore that day that it wouldn't happen again." *But it had. Even though they were both pretending it hadn't.*

"You were a good wife to Carter," he said quietly. "But he's gone, and you have to move on."

"I have moved on." She turned away from him and picked up her cup of tea. It was lukewarm.

"I know. You've made a life for yourself here, a successful, happy life. It takes a strong woman to build a life like this from the ashes Carter left behind." His hand hovered over her shoulder, finally touched her. "You've always been strong."

She forced herself to turn back to him. "We both know that's not true," she said. "If I had always been strong, I wouldn't have married Carter in the first place."

He cupped her head and gave her a bittersweet smile. "You're still painfully honest, aren't you?"

"I learned long ago that you can lie to everyone else, but it doesn't do any good to lie to yourself. The truth keeps nagging at you until you face it."

He slid his hands down her arms and took her hands. "A very strong woman," he murmured.

She held on to his hands and he tightened his grip. Then the chime of her cell phone broke the silence, and she moved away. When she answered the phone, a woman on the other end unleashed a torrent of Spanish.

"Wait," Kendall said in Spanish. "Slower. I can't understand you."

The woman took a deep breath and started over. It was Elena's mother, thanking her for taking the girl to the hospital. Her voice faltered as she told Kendall to take the money out of her paycheck.

"That's not necessary," Kendall said firmly. She didn't know where the money would come from, but Elena's parents had far less than she did. "It's already paid." She told the woman what the doctor had done, and how to care for Elena's stitches. "She has to go back in a week to get the stitches out. If you don't have a local doctor, I'll take you to my doctor's office, if you like."

The woman hesitated for so long that Kendall was sure she would refuse. Finally she said thank-you and hung up the phone.

"Elena's mother?" Gabe asked as she hung up.

"Yes."

"You told her you were going to pay the bill. I thought money was tight."

She shrugged. "I'll manage."

He nodded slowly. "You always will, won't you?"

As he stared at her, she swayed toward him. But before she could make a huge mistake, she heard the front door open. One of her guests was out late.

By the time the door to the kitchen swung open, she was far away from Gabe, sipping her cool tea. Dylan walked into the room, then stopped when he saw her.

His gaze went from her to Gabe, and she saw curiosity and questions in his eyes. "Sorry," he said with a grin. "I didn't mean to interrupt."

Dylan had been drinking. He wasn't drunk, but he was pronouncing his words just a little too carefully. "You're not interrupting anything. I was having a cup of tea. Did you need something?"

"Not a thing," he said, his voice breezy. But she could see the wheels turning in his head. "What are you two doing up so late?"

"Same thing as you, Smith. I just got home and came in for some coffee," Gabe said smoothly. "You want some?" He lifted the kettle of warm water.

"No, thanks," Dylan answered. "I was looking for a glass of water."

"Here you go," Kendall said, filling a glass. "Were you out working on your story tonight?"

Dylan took a long drink. "I was doing what everyone does in Door County on a Saturday night. I was at a bar."

"Did you find a good one?" she asked, trying to be a good hostess.

"The Blue Door," he answered.

"Really?" she asked, her voice light. "I wouldn't have thought that was your kind of bar."

He shrugged. "I was talking to some people there. I lost track of the time." He didn't quite meet her eyes as he put the glass on the counter. "I'll get out of your way. See you in the morning."

The door swung gently behind Dylan, and Kendall listened to his footsteps as he headed into the dining room, paused, then continued into the living room. What was he doing?

"What's the Blue Door?" Gabe asked.

"It's a bar in Sturgeon Falls," she said. "It's one of the places the migrants go to drink. In fact, I've never heard of anyone but migrants going there."

"Maybe he didn't know that."

"It would have been pretty easy to figure out when he walked in and heard everyone speaking Spanish," she retorted. "I wonder who he was talking to."

"You think he was trying to dig up more dirt on Carter?" Gabe asked.

She rinsed out her teacup and put it in the dishwasher. "Who better to question than people who might have worked for Carter back then?"

Gabe leaned against the counter. "Carter spent a lot of time in that orchard," he acknowledged. "If I was looking for information, I'd go to his employees."

"Dylan Smith isn't writing any human-interest story about the dedication," she said, her voice grim. "He's asking too many unrelated questions. He's too slick and charming. Too sneaky. I want to know what he's up to."

"Me, too." Gabe's voice was equally grim. "Maybe I'll drive to Green Bay on Monday and talk to his editor."

"I think that's a good idea." She snapped the dishwasher closed. "I'll see you in the morning."

"Don't go just yet, Kendall."

"Why not?"

"Smith hasn't gone upstairs. He probably couldn't see anything in the dim light in here, but you don't want to walk right past him. He nodded at her T-shirt, still damp from his mouth.

Instinctively she cupped her hands over the damp spots. Gabe's eyes darkened and he moved a step closer.

The sound of Dylan's footsteps on the stairs broke the spell. She dropped her hands. "Good night, Gabe."

"'Night, Kenny. Sleep well."

His voice was soft in the shadowy kitchen, and she hesitated as she looked at him. When he didn't move, she pushed through the swinging door. "You, too, Gabe."

"Pleasant dreams."

Her hand tightened on the door at his whispered words. Oh, she'd dream tonight. But she didn't think her dreams would be particularly restful.

CHAPTER TEN

Saturday evening

AMY SMOOTHED the swirling burgundy fabric of her dress over her thighs and glanced around the living room. Candles flickered on the end tables and on top of the television, giving everything in the room a golden glow. She'd made lasagna, George's favorite, and the aroma of tomatoes, spices and cheese drifted out of the kitchen. A bottle of red wine was open and sat breathing on the kitchen counter.

The romantic setting was missing only George. She glanced at the clock. He'd be here any minute. George never kept her waiting.

She walked into the kitchen to check on the lasagna. The cheese on top was bubbly and beginning to brown—it was almost done. As she closed the oven door, she heard the crunch of tires on her gravel driveway.

Amy bit her lip, fighting a swell of panic. This was the right thing to do. She couldn't think about a future with George until she'd told him the truth.

She opened the front door just as George stepped onto

the porch. "Yum," he said. "You look good enough to eat."

He swept her into his arms, kissing her. His hand roamed restlessly over her back. Finally he lifted his head. "Is Tommy at David's?"

Amy nodded. "Gabe took him to buy some video games for the big sleepover tonight, then dropped him off at David's house."

George frowned. "I would have taken Tommy to buy video games. What was Townsend doing over here?"

"Helping me out. I wanted to have plenty of time to get ready," she said, reaching up to kiss him again.

His eyes heated as he slid his hands up and down her sides. "I guess I should thank Townsend, then. You're gorgeous." He kissed her again. "Breathtaking."

He pulled her closer and deepened the kiss, and need surged through Amy. It would be so easy to let George sweep her into the bedroom, so easy to lose herself in their lovemaking. To delay telling him about Tommy.

When she felt herself pressing against him, kissing him with desperation, she eased away. "I made dinner," she said breathlessly.

"There's only one thing I want right now," George said, nuzzling her neck.

Brushing her mouth over his cheek, trying not to give in to the need racing through her, she murmured, "The lasagna will burn if I don't take it out of the oven."

He leaned back and smiled down at her. "Lasagna, huh? This is a very tough choice."

She nipped at his lower lip, then stepped away. "Poor baby. Come and pour the wine while I serve dinner." She turned to walk toward the kitchen, and George grabbed her from behind and pulled her against him. His hands brushed her breasts, then he kissed her below the ear. "Anticipation is good," he murmured. "You can think about all the things we're going to do after dinner."

Amy closed her eyes, her stomach knotting. "I will be." She leaned against him for another moment, absorbing his heat and his scent. Then reluctantly she pulled away.

While the baking dish cooled on the counter, she set the table and lit the candles. George handed her a glass of wine, and she took a too-big gulp. When she started to cough, George took the glass from her hand and patted her on the back.

"Take it easy," he said, pouring her a drink of water. "We've got all night to enjoy the wine."

She forced a smile as she brought dinner to the table. They talked off and on as they ate, and gradually she realized that George was as nervous as she was. "What's wrong, sweetheart?" she asked, her sense of dread coiling tighter. He'd said he had something he wanted to talk about, too. What would put that tension in his eyes?

He pushed away his half-eaten lasagna. "Let's go into the living room."

George put his wine on the coffee table as they sat on the couch. When he turned to her, his eyes were serious and uncertain.

"Wait, George," she said, her heart pounding against her chest. "Don't say anything. Let me go first."

"Nothing's more important than this," he murmured. He brushed his hand over her cheek, lightly covered her mouth. "I love you, Amy. You're my heart, my soul, my world." He fumbled in his pocket and brought out a black velvet box. "Will you marry me?"

"Oh, George." The diamonds glittered in the candlelight, and tears prickled in her eyes. "It's beautiful."

"Can I take that as a yes?" He licked his lips, and she saw his hand tremble.

"I love you, George. I want to say yes. But I can't. Not yet." She took a deep breath. "I told you there was something we needed to talk about. Ask me again after we're finished talking."

He looked down at the diamond ring and slowly closed the box. "I knew something was wrong," he said in a low voice.

"It's not you, sweetheart. It's me."

His mouth twisted. "That line is older than you are."

"Stop it, George." She grabbed his hands and the black velvet box tumbled to the couch. "There's nothing wrong between us. I love you. Nothing will change that." She held on to his hands tightly. "I can't marry you until I tell you about Tommy." She swallowed. "About who his father is."

The tension in George's face dissipated. "It's okay, Amy. I know Townsend is Tommy's father."

"Did someone tell you that?"

"No one had to tell me. It's obvious. He spends time

with you and Tommy. The kid adores Townsend." He shrugged. "It wasn't that tough to figure it out."

Amy closed her eyes, praying for the right words. "I wish it was that simple," she said. "I wish Gabe was Tommy's father. But he's not."

"He isn't?" He looked puzzled. "Then what's he doing hanging around?"

"It's complicated. Gabe's been a good friend to me and Tommy."

"Are you saying you used to date him?"

"No." She nervously folded the skirt of her dress with hands that shook. "No, Gabe and I never dated."

His eyes narrowed. "Does he know who Tommy's father is?"

"Yes. He knows."

George jumped up. "You told him but you haven't told me?"

"I didn't tell him. He already knew." Amy grabbed at George's hand and pulled him back to the couch. She moistened her lips as she gripped his hand.

"This is so hard to say," she whispered. "I've never told anyone who Tommy's father is. Gabe is the only one who knows. I never intended to tell anyone else."

"What made you change your mind?"

She twined their fingers together. "I love you, George. I didn't want my secret to come between us. And I know you love me. Two people who are thinking about spending their lives together shouldn't have secrets like this."

George's eyes warmed in the candlelight. "Okay, Amy. Who is Tommy's father?"

She swallowed and hung on to George's hand still more tightly. "Carter Van Allen. Your sister's husband."

He stared at her blankly. Then, as her words sank in, he let go of her fingers and sprang from the couch. "What?"

"Carter was Tommy's father. I was seventeen years old. I thought it was true love. I thought he would leave Kendall and marry me." Tears gathered in her eyes. "Instead, when I told him I was pregnant, he threw some money at me and told me to get an abortion."

"My God." George clenched his hands and turned away from her. He paced to the window and stared at the gathering dusk for a long moment.

"I thought you were going to tell me it was some guy who went to high school with you," he said at last. "My God, Amy! You slept with Carter? When he was married to Kendall?"

"You don't know how much I've regretted that over the years. Believe me, you can't say anything to me that I haven't already said to myself."

He turned to face her. "I thought I knew you as well as one person can know another. And now you tell me about this other side of you—a side you've been hiding."

"It was nine years ago, George," Amy said, her own temper stirring. "I've changed. Are you still the same person you were when you were seventeen?"

"He was my sister's husband," George replied. He stared at Amy, pain in his eyes. "Tommy is Shelby and Jenna's half brother. Every time I look at Tommy, I'm going to think about how you betrayed my sister."

Amy paled. "Yes, but it's not Tommy's fault. He's just a child." Tears burned her eyes, and she willed them not to fall. "Be as angry at me as you like. But don't take it out on Tommy."

"Kendall adored Carter. And you tried to steal him from her."

"Are you sure she adored him?" Amy shot back. "I'm not."

"And that's supposed to make it okay? That's supposed to justify what you did?"

"I'm not trying to justify it," she said, brushing tears from her cheeks. "I know there's no excuse."

George kicked at the throw rug in front of the door. "What am I supposed to say to her?"

"The truth. I'm not asking you to keep this a secret." Her mouth quivered. "I'd rather not share the news with everyone in Sturgeon Falls, but if that's what it takes, so be it."

"You think I'm going to tell anyone else? Don't worry, your secret's safe with me."

George took another lap around the living room, then stopped abruptly. "So that's why Townsend hangs around." His mouth twisted in derision. "He's still cleaning up after Carter."

"Don't talk like that about Gabe. He's been wonderful to Tommy," she said, jumping to her feet. "He's been a father figure, someone to do 'guy' things with when we're in Milwaukee. And he's been good to me, too. Gabe has done nothing wrong."

"If Townsend is such a damn saint, why don't you

marry him?" George shoved his hands into his pockets and turned away from her.

"You think I never thought of that? It's hard being a single mother. When Gabe came to me after Carter died and said he knew about Tommy, I thought about marrying him. I was terrified and alone and didn't know what to do."

She touched George's back, flinching when he stepped away from her. "But Gabe was never interested in me that way. And as much as it would have solved my problems, I wasn't attracted to him, either. So he became Tommy's uncle and my friend."

"I suppose Townsend told you to keep your mouth shut. Not tell me about Tommy," George said with a sneer.

"As a matter of fact, he pushed me to tell you. But I was afraid." She felt her mouth quiver and bit her lip.

"Yeah, you waited until you thought I was hooked, didn't you?" Pain and anger warred in his eyes.

"No. I'm trying to do the right thing." She took a step closer. "I could have waited until after we were married. I didn't have to tell you at all."

"And now I have to choose between you and my sister."

She felt as if he'd punched her in the gut. "No! Why would you have to choose?"

"What am I supposed to say to her? 'Hey, Kendall, I'm going to marry Amy. And by the way, she slept with Carter while he was married to you, and Tommy is Carter's son.'"

Amy could see him doing the mental calculations.

"My God! You got pregnant with Tommy while Kendall was pregnant with Jenna. Do you think Kendall is going to forgive and forget something like that?"

"I hoped she would. It was a long time ago."

"Not long enough. Kendall is all the family I have, and we spend a lot of time together. How can I ask her to welcome you into the family?

"People have a huge capacity to forgive," Amy said quietly. "I hope you can forgive me. And I hope Kendall can. I'll go over there tomorrow and tell her the truth."

"No. Don't go near my sister. I'll tell her myself."

"All right." She looked at George, standing by the window, so far away from her. "And what about you and me? What happens now?"

"I don't know." He turned and looked out the window. "I need to think." He turned away from the window, refusing to look Amy in the eye.

"I love you, George," she cried. "And I thought you loved me, too. That's why I told you—I didn't want this secret between us anymore." She wiped the back of her hand across her eyes.

"I thought Carter could do no wrong," he said, his voice full of pain. "He was the golden boy, the athlete the rest of us wanted to be. And now I find out he cheated on my sister. With the woman I thought I loved."

"I know you're hurt, George. But like I said, all of this happened a long time ago."

"So you figured I'd shrug and say, 'So what'?"

"I hoped you'd say that we could work it out. That

we could talk about it. I thought that's what people who love each other do—talk out their problems and figure out how to solve them." A sob formed in her throat, and she choked it back. "It sounds as if you're not interested in working anything out. Did you ever really love me—or was it just sex for you all along?"

"Now you're putting this on me?" he asked, disbelief apparent on his face. "That it's my fault?" He grabbed his keys from the table where he'd tossed them. "I have to leave."

The door slammed, and moments later George's car peeled out of the driveway, tires squealing. Amy stood by the window for a long time, hoping he'd come back once his temper had cooled.

Finally she threw herself onto the couch, tears rolling down her cheeks. Damn Gabe. She should have listened to her own instincts. She should never have told George.

She shifted as something hard jabbed her hip. Sliding over, she reached behind and pulled out the tiny ring box.

The diamonds glittered brilliantly through her tears. She stared at the ring for a moment, then snapped the box shut. Some dreams were as insubstantial as the bright flashes of light that glinted off a diamond ring. Look at them the wrong way, and they disappeared completely.

CHAPTER ELEVEN

Sunday morning

GABE PUSHED OPEN the door of the kitchen and paused, watching Kendall work. She pulled a pan of muffins from the oven, set them on the counter, then turned back to omelets cooking on the stove. The fragrance of apples and cinnamon filled the air as heat rose from the pastries.

The room looked different than it had last night. After midnight, the dim artificial light, the quiet, the sleeping house had been an intimate cocoon. Gabe's blood thickened as he remembered how Kendall had felt pressed against the counter, remembered how she'd tasted. The soft sounds she'd made when he touched her.

Now the kitchen was brightly illuminated. The counter was covered with mixing bowls, muffin pans and plates. And Kendall was avoiding his gaze.

"Gabe," she said, concentrating on the stove. Her face was flushed and her hair tousled. "Have a seat in the dining room and I'll get your breakfast."

"I'm in no hurry," he said. "You don't have to treat me like a guest."

"You *are* a guest," she said, flipping the omelets. Bacon and sausage sizzled in a separate pan and she turned them before reaching for the muffins. With a quick snap of her wrist, she dumped the muffins into a napkin-lined basket, setting four aside before carefully arranging the rest and tucking them in with the corners of the napkin.

Next, she plated the omelets, adding bacon to one and sausage to the other, with three strawberries arranged on each plate. In the dining room voices rose in admiration.

After serving her guests, Kendall returned to the kitchen and picked up the mug of coffee that was sitting on the counter. She took a sip and grimaced. "Cold," she said, pouring it into the sink. As she reached for the coffeepot, she turned to Gabe. "Do I even have to ask if you want a cup?"

"You know me too well," he said. "You always have."

Her hand stilled, then she reached for a clean mug and filled it. Nodding toward the kitchen table, she said, "Cream's over there."

Kendall resumed her work, spooning batter into another muffin pan. After sliding the pan into the oven, she stepped back to the stove. "What can I get you?"

"Nothing right now," he said, sipping the coffee and watching her brisk movements. "I'll wait until the rush is over."

Filling the sink with water, she washed out the mixing bowl. With her hands immersed in suds, she said, "Why don't you go into the other room. There's not a lot of space in the kitchen."

"I won't get in your way. I prefer the view in here."

"There's a better view from the dining room. You can see the beach from the window."

"I don't care about the beach."

Her shoulders stiffened. "Guests aren't allowed in the kitchen."

"I was in the kitchen last night," he said in a low voice. "You didn't seem to mind it then."

The bowl she was washing slipped out of her hands and splashed into the sink. "I wasn't cooking last night."

"No? You felt pretty hot to me."

Her hands stopped moving. "Please, Gabe. We agreed last night was a mistake."

"I didn't say it was a mistake." Water sprayed the wall as Kendall rinsed the bowl a second time. "Is that why you're so nervous? Thinking about last night?"

"I'm not nervous," she replied. The bowl clanged against the sink one final time as she set it in the dish drainer. "I'm just busy."

"I can see that." Gabe leaned against the counter, wondering how long it would take Kendall to look at him. "How did you sleep?"

Her gaze locked on his and she didn't look away for a moment. Then her face heated and she turned away. "I slept just fine."

"I bet you had trouble falling asleep, though."

Her eyes flashed and she opened her mouth, but before she could speak he cut her off smoothly. "Because of Elena. I was afraid you'd be worrying about her."

As she stared at him, a reluctant smile flickered on

her mouth. "Very good, Gabe. I'm impressed. And yes, I am concerned about Elena. But it didn't keep me awake."

"Good." He finished his coffee and poured another cup.

"How much coffee do you drink in a day?" she asked.

"Too much. It's a bad habit I got into when I was working fifteen-hour days, getting my company off the ground." He added cream and took a drink, savoring the flavor. "Why do you ask? Worried about me?"

"Your bad habits are your own business. I just want to be sure I have enough on hand," she retorted.

It was Gabe's turn to smile. "You're pretty quick yourself, Kenny."

Before she could answer, the door swung open and Dylan staggered into the kitchen, his eyes bloodshot and his face pasty. "For the love of God, coffee," he said with a groan.

As Kendall poured him a cup, Gabe saw her mouth twitching. "Into the dining room, Dylan." She herded him toward the door. "I'll make your breakfast. The usual?"

The reporter shuddered. "No breakfast. I may never eat again."

"Then how about a side order of my father's guaranteed hangover recipe?" she asked.

"You're a saint in heaven," he replied, his tone fervent as he steadied himself on the door frame. "I'll kiss your feet if it gets rid of this headache."

She opened the refrigerator and reached for tomato

juice. When she handed him her concoction a few minutes later, she said, "You should stay away from that cheap swill they serve at the Blue Door."

"Believe me, I've learned my lesson," he muttered. He downed the hangover cure. "Thanks. Do you mind if I curl up here and die in peace?"

"No guests in the kitchen," she reminded him with a smile. "You'll have to die in the living room."

He looked at Gabe, and Gabe saw his curiosity stir despite the massive hangover. "What's he doing in here, then?"

"I'm a friend of the family," Gabe said smoothly.

Suddenly, the girls burst into the kitchen and Smith winced and shuffled out. "Where's Uncle George?" Shelby asked.

Kendall glanced at the clock and frowned. "He's late. Uncle George was going out last night," she said. "But I don't think he would have forgotten you."

"You going somewhere with your uncle?" Gabe asked.

"He takes us to church. 'Cause Mom can't usually go," Jenna explained. She picked up a muffin and took a delicate bite.

"Yeah, and we have ice-cream cones afterward," Shelby added, shoving a piece of muffin into her mouth. "Even in the winter."

The back door banged open and George stormed into the room. "You guys ready to go?" he growled. Then he spotted Gabe and his mouth thinned to a hard, angry slash. "What are you doing here, Townsend?"

Gabe held up his mug. "Having a cup of coffee."

George glared at his sister. "I thought you didn't allow guests in your kitchen."

Kendall slid between George and Gabe. "What's wrong?" she asked her brother quietly.

"Nothing." He tried to move away from her, but she blocked his way.

"There most certainly is something wrong."

George shot Gabe a look filled with venom, then slammed the door open. "Ask your buddy Townsend. I'll be in the car when the girls are ready."

Jenna's eyes were huge as her uncle ran down the steps. "Is Uncle George mad at us?"

"Of course not, honey." She watched her brother disappear and her attempt at a smile wobbled. "He probably stayed up too late."

Gabe shoved away from the table and stood up. *Oh, God. What had happened with Amy?* "Thanks for the coffee, Kendall. I've got to go."

"Oh no, you don't." She grabbed his sleeve before he could get away. "What did George mean? What am I supposed to ask you about?"

He detached her hand and set his coffee cup on the counter. "You'll have to ask your brother."

She moved to block his exit from the kitchen. "Tell me what's going on, Gabe."

He let his gaze touch on Shelby, then Jenna, who watched the two adults with avid interest. "It's between Amy and George," he said in a low voice. He moved her aside. "Have a good time at church," he said to the girls.

As he pushed through the swinging door, he heard

Jenna ask, "What's wrong with Uncle Gabe? Why is everyone crabby this morning?"

"I don't know, honey," Kendall answered, sounding troubled.

Gabe pulled out his cell phone to dial Amy and found a text message from her. "Call me," it read.

"It's Gabe," he said when she answered the phone.

"It was awful," Amy said between sobs.

"I'll be right there."

As Gabe turned onto County B, he saw a flash of sunlight glinting off the windshield of another car in Kendall's driveway. Ignoring it, he pushed the speed limit and drove south toward Sturgeon Falls. The prospect of dealing with Amy's tears terrified him, but it was no less than he deserved. He'd been the one to talk her into her confession, after all.

Minutes later he was there. When he pounded on the door, it took Amy a long time to open it.

Her eyes were puffy and swollen and her nose was red. "Gabe," she said, her voice hoarse, and began crying again.

"Let me come in," he said. Drawing her into his arms, he held her while she cried, deep wrenching sobs that shook her entire body. "I didn't make coffee," she apologized, her words indistinct.

"Don't worry about coffee." He drew her down onto the couch and eased her away from his chest. "What happened?"

"Exactly what I was afraid would happen," she answered bitterly. "He called me a slut and walked away."

"George called you a slut?" His fists clenched for a moment, then he wrapped her in his arms again.

"Not in so many words. But it's what he meant."

"Bastard."

Amy's steady, silent tears seeped through his shirt. "He's not a bastard. It's my fault. I knew I shouldn't have told him." She sniffled against his chest. "I knew it was a mistake."

"He'll be back. George was shocked and angry. Once he cools down, once he thinks about it, he'll be back."

"Why couldn't I have just lied?" She eased away from Gabe and wiped her nose with a crumpled tissue. "Just told him it was some guy from high school?"

"Because you're an honorable person. You don't want to build the rest of your life on a lie," Gabe said.

"He wouldn't have left," Amy said. She twisted around and grabbed something from the table. "Before I told him, he asked me to marry him." She opened the box and looked at the ring, then began to sob again. "He said I was making him choose between me and Kendall."

"I'm sure he said a lot of things he regrets now," Gabe replied. "Go have a shower, and I'll make breakfast."

"Didn't you eat at Kendall's?" she asked. "I'm sure it was perfect. Everything about Kendall is perfect."

"Stop it, Amy," Gabe said. "None of this is Kendall's fault." Kendall was going to be devastated, too. Would she be crying, as well?

God, he hoped not. It would break his heart to watch her cry over her faithless husband.

Amy closed her eyes and took a deep, shuddering breath. "I know. I'm being a bitch. But it hurts so much, Gabe. I was upset after Carter dumped me, and scared. So scared. But it didn't hurt like this. Like there's a big hole in my chest where my heart used to be. It even hurts to breathe."

"I know." He wished he could reassure Amy, tell her it would hurt less after a while. But he couldn't.

She stood up to leave the room, then looked over her shoulder. "He thought you were Tommy's father."

"I imagine he's not the only one."

"Doesn't that bother you?"

"Why should it?"

"I don't want anyone to think you abandoned your own child," she said fiercely. "I don't want anyone believing that of you."

"They're going to think what they think," Gabe said with a shrug. "I can't stop them." He looked around Amy's small living room, saw the pictures on the wall that Tommy had drawn, the macaroni necklace he'd made for his mother, the pencil holder he'd fashioned out of an orange-juice can and some colored paper. Similar artwork decorated Gabe's condo back in Milwaukee. "You and Tommy are part of my life. You've both given me so much. If it's caused gossip, it was worth it."

"Why did you come back for the dedication?" Amy asked, her tears drying on her face. "There's nothing in Sturgeon Falls for you except grief."

"You guys are here, aren't you?" he said. He managed a grin. "I think that outweighs any grief I get from guys like Jim Donaldson."

"Really, Gabe." Amy turned to face him. "Is coming back here worth it? Is it worth the pain?"

He thought of Shelby, grinning at him after she'd executed a scissors move in her soccer game. He thought of Jenna, swinging her new tennis racquet wildly at a ball. He thought of Kendall in the kitchen the night before, the way she'd tasted, the way she'd felt when he held her. The way she'd made him feel.

"Yeah, it's worth it." He turned Amy around and gave her a gentle push toward the bathroom. "Getting to boss you around for a change is worth it, too. Now go have that shower while I start breakfast."

AN HOUR LATER, the breakfast dishes done, Amy led Gabe toward the door. "Leave," she said, trying to smile. "You've seen enough tears for one day. You've gone way beyond the call of duty."

"Do you want me to get Tommy?"

"That's okay. I'll go in a little while."

"Are you sure?" He touched her cheek, wiping away the white tracks of tears. "I know you don't want him to see you upset like this."

"No, thanks." Her smile wobbled and her eyes filled again. "I'll be fine for Tommy. I would never let him know that he was the reason George left."

"You did the right thing," Gabe said, putting his hands on her shoulders. "Remember that. And if George can't deal with it, it's a reflection on him. Not you."

She looked away. "Is that supposed to make me feel better?"

"Not today. Not tomorrow. Eventually."

"Are you speaking from personal experience?" She looked him in the eye. "Did you do the right thing when you left here seven years ago? And does that give you a lot of comfort when you're alone at night?"

He dropped a kiss on her head, then looked away from her. "It's not the same thing at all."

"That's what I figured you'd say." Amy curled her arms around herself. "I know this is the price I'm paying for the wrong I did," she said quietly. "I may understand, but I don't have to like it."

"Krippner is a fool," Gabe said.

"Yeah, but he was my fool. I'm fine now. Get out of here."

"Okay, but I'll see you tomorrow," he promised.

"I'm not sure why you'd want to subject yourself to more of this, but thanks." She stepped onto the porch with him and gave him a fierce hug. "You're a good man, Gabe."

"That's what all the women say when they cry all over me." He brushed her hair away from her face. "Take care of yourself. And Tommy."

Out of the corner of his eye he saw a car cruising slowly down Amy's street, stopping in front of her house. He turned to see Dylan Smith sitting in a battered economy car, scribbling on a piece of paper.

"Dammit." He opened the door and pushed Amy inside. "Stay in here until that guy is gone," he said to her. "Don't go for Tommy until you're sure he isn't around."

"Who is it?"

"A goddamn reporter."

Amy shrank back from the door. "What does he want?"

"I'm going to find out."

Gabe strode down the sidewalk and leaned in Smith's car window. "What the hell are you doing?"

Smith closed his eyes and flinched. "For God's sake, Townsend, you don't need to yell. I'm doing my job."

"And what exactly is that supposed to mean?"

"It means I'm following leads for my story."

"The only thing you followed is me."

Smith's smile was a pale imitation of his usual cocky grin. "Last time I checked, there wasn't any rule against driving on public roads."

"What do you want? What are you looking for?"

Smith shoved his piece of paper into the back pocket of his jeans. "Just looking for a story," he said. "People love this human-interest stuff."

Before Gabe could answer, the reporter gunned the engine and took off, making Gabe jump back.

He watched Smith disappear around the corner, then ran to his own car and jumped in. He didn't slow down until he pulled into Kendall's driveway.

Kendall came out of the kitchen just as Gabe walked in the front door. Ignoring her, he stormed up the stairs and tried to open the reporter's door. When he realized the door was locked, he ran into his own room, grabbed a tool from his kit bag and returned to Smith's door.

Shoving his pick into the old-fashioned lock, he had the door open in less than thirty seconds.

"What do you think you're doing?" Kendall's shocked voice came from the top of the stairs.

"Trying to find out what Smith is up to," he answered as he stepped into the room. His gaze swept from one side to the other, noting a mound of clothes on the floor, a laptop computer—turned off—on the desk and toiletries scattered on the dresser. A pile of papers was partially covered by the computer, and Gabe walked over to look at them.

"Gabe, stop." Kendall grabbed his arm and tried to pull him back into the hall. "You can't do this. You can't break into another guest's room."

"Watch me," he said as he shook her off. "He followed me this morning. He was waiting when I came out of…"

"When you came out of where?"

"That's not important. I want to know why he followed me." He grabbed the papers from under the laptop and rifled through them, staring unbelievingly. A cold, hard anger grew inside him.

"Any of this stuff look familiar?" He shoved the papers at her.

"I'm not going to look through Dylan's belongings," she said, putting her hands behind her back.

"No?" He selected one sheet and read from it. "'Mrs. Van Allen, my bookkeeper has brought your account to my attention. You're two months overdue on your bill for the brake repair we did in April. Please contact me so we can set up a payment schedule.'" He looked at her. "That sound like it belongs to Smith?"

She'd gone white. "What?" She snatched the paper out of his hand. "What's he doing with this?"

"Did you throw it away?"

Her hand was shaking as she lowered the paper. "Yes."

"You don't have a shredder?"

"I've been meaning to get one." She looked back at the paper in her hand. "I guess it's a priority now."

Gabe shuffled through the rest of the papers, seeing other documents with Kendall's name on them. And some of his own. "This is a draft of my speech that I threw away yesterday." He looked up at her, his eyes grim. "Get rid of him, Kendall. Get him out of your house. Today."

She looked at the note in her hand, then back up at Gabe. "I can't. He's the only guest, besides you, this week. I can't afford to throw him out."

"Would you rather have him going through your garbage?"

"I'll get a shredder today." Her hand tightened on the note. The humiliation that showed on her face made Gabe want to punch Smith senseless. "Besides, it's better to have him here, where we can keep an eye on him."

Gabe wanted to tell her that he'd pay for Smith's room, just to get rid of him. But that would humiliate Kendall even more. "You're probably right," he said grudgingly. "Better to know what he's doing."

She looked down again at the paper in her hand. "What do we do with these?" she whispered.

"Take them."

Her hand tightened and she crumpled the paper in her fist. "I'll take them when I clean the room."

Gabe took the piece of paper out of her hand, smoothed it and put it back into the stack of papers. Then he replaced them beneath the computer. "That will work."

"I'll get my cleaning stuff right now."

A car's tires crunched on the driveway and Gabe grabbed her arm. "There's a car coming."

She looked out the window. "It's my brother and the girls." Frustration filled her eyes. "I'll get in here as soon as I can."

"Go downstairs," he said. "I'll lock the room."

She nodded at him and headed toward the kitchen. Gabe replaced the papers and locked the room, then followed Kendall. It looked as if it was going to be a day full of ugly revelations.

CHAPTER TWELVE

Sunday afternoon

GABE FOLLOWED KENDALL down the stairs and then veered into the dining room. Maybe George would have enough sense not to tell his sister what he'd learned from Amy. At least not until he cooled down.

"Girls, why don't you take these muffins over to Elena's house and see how she's doing. Tell her mother I'll stop by later to see them." Kendall's voice was muffled by the kitchen door, but still audible.

"Okay," Shelby said, and then the back door banged shut.

In the dining room, Gabe poured himself another cup of coffee. He should head back to his room. He didn't want to eavesdrop on Kendall and George. This would be a private, personal conversation.

But George had been angry and upset this morning. Would he take it out on Kendall?

Gabe had no idea. He didn't really know George. Since none of the men in Kendall's life had put a priority on her well-being, however, Gabe was prepared for the worst.

Kendall's father had encouraged her to marry Carter, seeing only the dollar signs attached to the Van Allen name. And Carter had changed after he married Kendall. He'd gone from being a spoiled but essentially well-meaning kid to a man more concerned with the pursuit of his own pleasure than with his wife and two young daughters. He'd acted as if Kendall and the girls had been burdens.

And Gabe himself had walked away, just when Kendall had needed him the most.

It didn't matter that she'd refused to have anything to do with him. He could have stayed, toughed it out, been here when she needed help.

Instead, guilt had made it easier for Gabe to walk away.

Now he headed back to his room, prepared to give George Krippner the benefit of the doubt. And stopped when he heard George's voice, raised in anger.

"I liked Carter. I wanted to be like him. Hell, all my friends wanted to be like him, too. And it turns out he was a complete asshole. He was screwing Amy while you were pregnant with Jenna."

"I had no idea." Kendall's voice was shocked, barely audible.

"Your buddy Townsend knew. He's known all along."

"I don't believe that," she replied.

George snorted. "Amy said he did. He knew from the beginning."

"Tommy Mitchell is my girls' half brother." Gabe heard the astonishment and disbelief in her voice.

"Yup." It sounded as if a chair had just skidded across the floor. "And won't that make for fun family parties?"

"It's in the past, George. I thought you loved Amy. Can't you let it go?"

Gabe's hand tightened on his coffee mug. In spite of her own pain, Kendall was trying to comfort her brother.

"He slept with Amy! He's Tommy's father! How can I let that go?" The back door rattled in its frame, as if George had given it a kick. "I thought you two had a happy marriage. I wanted the two of us to be like you and Carter." Gabe heard the sound of glass shattering. "Pretty funny, huh?"

Gabe stormed through the kitchen door. "Stop it, Krippner. I know you're angry as hell, but that's enough." He looked at Kendall's colorless face. "You're upsetting your sister. Maybe you should leave."

Fury glittered in George's eyes. "You'd like that, wouldn't you? So you can pretend to be her friend, pretend to care about her kids. Where were you when that son of a bitch she was married to was cheating on her? Covering up for him. That's where you were."

"Your sister was right. This is ancient history. What difference does it make now?"

"I don't know Amy at all. Just like I don't know Carter. Or you," he said to Kendall.

Kendall grabbed her brother's arm and shook him. "No, I didn't tell you Carter and I had problems. Why would I have? The intimate details of my marriage were

An Important Message from the Editors

Dear Reader,

If you'd enjoy reading romance novels with larger print that's easier on your eyes, let us send you TWO FREE HARLEQUIN SUPERROMANCE® NOVELS in our NEW LARGER PRINT EDITION. These books are complete and unabridged, but the type is set about 20% bigger to make it easier to read. Look inside for an actual-size sample.

By the way, you'll also get a surprise gift with your two free books!

Pam Powers

Peel off Seal and Place Inside...

she'd thought she was fine. It took Daniel's words and Brooke's question to make her realize she was far from a full recovery.

She'd made a start with her sister's help and she intended to go forward now. Sarah felt as if she'd been living in a darkened room and some-one had suddenly opened a door, letting in the fresh air and sunshine. She could feel its warmth slowly seeping into the coldest part of her. The feeling was liberating. She realized it was only a small step and she had a long way to go, but she was ready to face life again with Serena and her family behind her.

All too soon, they were saying goodbye and Sarah experienced a moment of sadness for all the years she and Serena had missed. But they ad each other now and that's what

She held

See the
larger print
difference!

Like what you see?
Then send for TWO FREE
larger print books!

YOURS FREE!
You'll get a great mystery gift with your two free larger print books!

none of your business. You were nineteen when Carter died. You thought the sun rose and set in him." She shook him again. "Go home and settle down, George. Think about Amy. And Tommy. Are you willing to give them up for something that happened so long ago?"

George pulled away from her. "Every time I look at Tommy, I'll see Carter. I'll know that Amy slept with him. I don't know if I can live with that."

The sight of Kendall with her arms wrapped around herself, eyes aching with pain, made Gabe furious. He stepped in front of her and gave George a shove, making him stagger backward. "For God's sake, Krippner. What the hell is wrong with you? You just told Kendall that her husband cheated on her. And *she's* trying to comfort *you*. Can you think of anyone besides yourself?"

"You'd know about that, wouldn't you?"

"Get out."

"Why? So you can comfort Kendall? You were real good at that seven years ago, weren't you? You took off and never looked back." He glared at Gabe. "She doesn't need anything from you. Or are you just hanging around to drop another little bomb? What other secrets of Carter's are you hiding?"

George slammed out the door and pounded down the stairs.

"I'm sorry you had to find out this way."

Kendall watched her brother's car disappear, taking the last of her illusions with it. Gabe's voice barely registered. Kendall felt as if she were floating above her own body, detached. She was amazed that Carter still held the power to hurt her. And once again, Gabe had witnessed her humiliation.

Would Carter and Gabe always be linked together? Would she ever be able to think about Gabe without Carter's shadow hanging over the two of them?

"Is it true?" Kendall asked. Her tongue wouldn't work properly, making the words slur together. It was numb, just like the rest of her. Numb, except for the humiliation and shame that slid along her skin like a writhing snake.

"That Tommy is Carter's son?"

She nodded.

"Yes, it's true," he said.

She reached blindly for a chair, dropping into it like a dead weight.

"Shelby and Jenna have a half brother."

"Yes."

"Carter cheated on me." She could barely form the words. "He had a child with another woman."

Gabe crouched low beside her chair. "That's not a reflection on you, Kendall."

He tried to take her hand, but she pulled away. "Don't touch me." Every nerve in her body was raw and exposed. The slightest touch would cause unbearable pain.

"Carter was wild those last few years," Gabe said, his voice grim. "He was like a spoiled kid who did whatever he could to get attention. He wasn't the Carter I grew up with."

Guilt stabbed Kendall, the guilt she felt because of her own role in making him that way. "Are you saying it's my fault he cheated on me?" Maybe she had pushed him into Amy's arms. Her voice rose. "Do you think it was my fault that he was so wild?"

"Of course not, Kenny."

"Don't call me that!" She shoved at Gabe and he fell backward onto the floor. "Don't ever call me that again."

"What Carter did doesn't change who you are," he retorted. "You're the same person you were this morning."

"Am I?" She looked around her kitchen, a room she'd remodeled with her own hands. A room as much a part of her as her breathing. Now it was as if Carter's ghost leaned against the granite counter, watching her with a mocking smile. The past seven years of independence, of accomplishment fell away, knocking her back with a vicious punch.

She jumped to her feet and stared out the window. The sky above the orchard was bright blue and cloudless, a perfect early-summer day. Not the kind of day when the ground would suddenly shake beneath your feet.

Her throat swelled tight and she bit her knuckles to keep the tears from bursting free. Gabe wrapped his arms around her and pulled her to him. "Cry, Kendall. It's okay to cry." He smoothed his hand down her back, tucked her head against his shoulder.

She shoved him away. "Don't. It's not okay." She wouldn't take the comfort he offered. Any sympathy, any softness was going to make her completely fall apart.

She refused to fall apart in front of Gabe.

That weakness would open a chasm beneath her, an abyss she was not prepared to face.

"You don't have to deal with this alone. Let me share some of the burden," he said quietly.

"Is that what you call it?" She flung herself away, letting anger fill the cold places inside. "I thought sharing went two ways. You never told me about Amy. About Amy and Carter."

"When was I supposed to tell you? When you came to visit me in the hospital after the crash?"

Kendall looked away. She'd wanted to visit Gabe, wanted to know he would be all right. But she hadn't been able to do it. When she realized her first thought had been for Gabe instead of her dead husband, shame had overwhelmed her. She couldn't face Gabe. Couldn't face her own feelings.

"You could have told me before. When you first knew about it."

"When do you think I knew?"

She gripped the edge of the counter, picked up the coffee she'd been drinking earlier. "Carter told you everything. You were closer to him than…" *Than I was.*

"So you think I knew about Amy all along?"

"Carter would have bragged to you," she said, her voice bitter. "Especially after Tommy was born. He always wanted a son." She'd never forget the flicker of regret that she'd seen in his eyes when he'd found out that each of his children was a girl. He'd tried to hide it, but she'd known.

"You're wrong about that," he said quietly. "He loved his girls."

"He had a funny way of showing it." Remembering his inattention, his casual indifference toward them, her eyes filled with tears again.

Gabe turned her around, gently held her arms to keep her from pulling away. "He was ashamed of what happened with Amy," he said quietly. "He didn't tell me until the night he died. And then, it was only because we were—" He clamped his mouth shut.

"You were what?"

"It's not important. He regretted what had happened. Regretted that he'd harmed his marriage."

He hadn't been alone in harming their marriage. She'd played a part, too. "I don't believe that. Carter never regretted anything he did."

"He knew he'd screwed up."

Gabe's words beat against her heart, and she pushed them away. She didn't want to think that Carter had changed. Didn't want to think he was capable of changing.

If she did, it would mean she hadn't tried hard enough. That they could have salvaged their marriage.

If she'd wanted to.

She pushed that thought away, too. "Does everyone in Sturgeon Falls know the truth?" She bit her lip to keep it from trembling. "Everyone but me?"

"Stop it." He tightened his grip on her arms and gave her a gentle shake. "No one else knows. Just you, me and George. Sturgeon Falls is a small town. Do you honestly think you wouldn't have heard about this before now if everyone knew?"

She pulled back and put some space between them. "All right. Even if you didn't know earlier, why didn't you tell me after Carter died?"

"When should I have told you?" he repeated. He shoved his hands into his pockets. "When we stood at Carter's grave? In front of his two daughters? Or maybe later, when you were trying to rebuild your life? When you made it clear you wanted nothing to do with me?"

She flinched and looked away. He was right. She'd rejected every overture Gabe had made. She refused to talk to him when he called, sent his letters back unopened.

"Carter was dead," he said. "You were angry at me." He lifted his shoulders slightly. "You didn't want to listen to me. And to be honest, I didn't want to tell you. I didn't want to cause you any more pain."

"Did you know Amy was planning to tell George? Is that why you came back now?" she asked, feeling as if her heart was splintering inside her. "So you could be here for the big revelation? Was this your revenge for the way I shut you out of our lives?"

"Is that what you think?"

The pain that filled his eyes cut into Kendall. Shamed her. "I'm sorry, Gabe. That was unfair."

"I came back because of the stadium dedication," he said. "Because I owe it to Carter. He was my friend. He made a place for me in his family when I was growing up, and I'll never forget that. And I encouraged Amy to tell George while I was in town. So I could be here if she needed me. If you needed me."

"Why, Gabe?" she asked. "I wouldn't even speak to you. Why would you come back for me?"

"I wasn't there for you when you needed me after Carter died. I wanted to be here now."

"I didn't want anything to do with you," she said, her voice unsteady.

"That doesn't matter. Friends stick by you, no matter what."

"Is that what we were, Gabe? Friends?"

"Yes. We were friends. Weren't we?"

What she saw in his eyes made her heart ache and her throat tighten. "Don't," she whispered. "Don't look at me like that."

"Like how?"

"Like this is important. Like I matter to you."

"You *do* matter," he said. "This *is* important."

"You feel obligated to me. Because of how Carter died. I'm not going to be an obligation," she said, her voice fierce now. "I swore I would never be another person's burden for as long as I lived."

"You're not a burden." He touched her cheek. "You don't let anyone help you, do you?"

"I don't need any help."

"You don't need to talk about the past, either?"

"No." Her throat grew tight and she looked away from Gabe. "It won't change a thing."

"Maybe it would."

"It doesn't matter if we talk about it or not. We could

discuss it to death, but Carter's ghost will still be there. It's always going to be there."

"Not if we don't let it." He reached for her hands. "If you won't talk about the past, how about the present—and the future." He squeezed her hands tight, pulled her closer. "I regret not seeing the girls all these years. I think of how much fun I had with Shelby. How much I loved watching Jenna when she was a baby. I want to spend time with them now, get to know them now. If you'll let me."

The scene in the kitchen last night played again in her memory, stirred need inside her. Need she had to deny. "You killed their father. How do you think they're going to feel when they figure that out?"

He dropped Kendall's hands and turned away from her. "You don't pull any punches, do you?"

"I'm realistic. I don't want you to build up any false expectations."

"Me? Or Shelby and Jenna?"

"I don't want them hurt, either," she said, and the need to protect them strengthened her resolve. "I don't want them becoming attached to you. It will only devastate them when they learn the truth."

"Are you going to tell them what happened?" he asked, his voice quiet.

"I won't have to. They'll hear it, sooner or later. Sooner, if they're spending time with you. You know how people love to spread gossip."

"So I should go. To protect Shelby and Jenna. To protect you."

"I don't need protecting."

"I think you want to be protected, Kendall. From yourself. From what you felt when I kissed you last night." He turned around to face her. "I wasn't alone in this kitchen. You were right here with me. All the way."

"That was a mistake. I was tired, stressed. That's all."

"Stress?" He skimmed a finger over her cheek, and let it trail down her neck to her collarbone. Heat flashed through her. "It certainly was stressful for me," he murmured, skimming his finger along the ridge. "I'm glad it was for you, too."

She knocked his hand away. "That's not what I meant and you know it."

Before he could answer, she heard Shelby and Jenna in the yard. Relief swept over her. "The girls are back," she said, opening the door.

"Hi, Mom," Jenna chirped, stopping as she looked from Kendall to Gabe. "What's wrong?"

"Nothing's wrong, sweetheart." Kendall forced herself to smile. "How's Elena?"

"She's okay." Jenna continued to study her mother. "Where's Uncle George? Is he still crabby?"

"Uncle George had to leave." She turned to Shelby with relief. "Hi, Shel."

Shelby rummaged in the cookie jar for a chocolate-chip cookie. "We saw Elena," she announced with her mouthful.

"How is she doing?"

"Her forehead is all black-and-blue," Shelby said with relish.

"It's really gross," Jenna added, wrinkling her nose.

"And she has a headache," Shelby finished up.

"I'll go down and see her later. Maybe there's something they need. But first we have chores. We need to clean the guest rooms," she reminded her daughters.

"Okay." Both girls pounded up the stairs.

Gabe frowned. "I forgot about Smith," he said in a low voice. "About those papers in his room. What are we going to do about him?"

"*We're* not going to do anything." Her voice was firm. "I'm going to clean his room. And remove those papers."

"And what happens when he finds those papers missing?"

"What's he going to say to me? 'Where are the papers I took from your garbage?'" She gave him a level look. "He's smarter than that."

Gabe's jaw worked and she could tell he was unhappy. "Dammit, Kendall. You didn't sign up for this."

"I signed up for everything related to this business. And I can handle it." She turned to leave the room. "If you want to do something, you can go get me a shredder. I'll give you my credit card."

"I don't need your damn credit card," he growled as he stalked out the back door. He paused before letting it close behind him. "Keep your cell phone with you. In case you need to call for help."

"You're being a little melodramatic, aren't you?"

"I hope so." He held her gaze a long moment. "I really hope so."

CHAPTER THIRTEEN

Sunday afternoon

"GIVE ME THE BOX," Jenna demanded, her voice rising. "It's my turn to arrange the shampoo and soap. You're supposed to hang up the towels."

"Make me." Shelby's voice held an "older sister" superiority, and Kendall sighed as she cleaned Dylan's room.

"That's not fair," Jenna wailed. "Give it to me!" The sound of plastic bottles and bars of soap hitting the bathroom floor across the hall had Kendall throwing down her dust rag.

"What's going on?" she yelled.

Silence. Then the sound of scrabbling, and tiny bottles of shampoo and conditioner plunking back into the plastic shoe box where they were stored.

"We finished our chores, Mom." Shelby's voice was subdued. "What should we do next?"

Normally, she gave them each another job, something different every week. Today, she glanced out the window, watching for Dylan's car, and decided she didn't want her daughters around if there was going to be a confrontation.

"Have you put the dirty sheets and towels next to the washing machine?" she asked.

They nodded.

"Then you can go outside and play. Just stay away from the orchard and the lake until I'm finished up here."

"Really? We don't have to do any more chores?" The girls exchanged an astonished look. "Okay."

They raced down the stairs, as if fearing their mother might realize she'd made a mistake. Kendall grinned and turned on the vacuum cleaner.

When she switched it off, she found Dylan leaning against the door, watching her.

"Dylan." She glanced at the garbage bag sitting open against the wall, then jerkily rewound the vacuum cord. "How's the headache?"

"Better," he said, straightening as he walked into the room. "Your concoction is magic."

"My father swore by it." She eased past him to set the vacuum in the hall, casually twisting the top of the garbage bag together as she grabbed it. "Give me another couple of minutes here and I'll be out of your way."

"No hurry," he said.

She saw his gaze travel around the room and stop at the desk. The papers were gone.

"You did a very thorough job of cleaning my room," he said, his voice dry. "I left a mess today."

"No problem," she said with a bright smile. "My job

is to make sure you have everything you need." She held his gaze. "Within reason, of course."

"Of course." He grinned, acknowledging defeat. "You do a good job of it, too."

"Thanks." She replaced the blanket and quilt on the bed, ran her dust rag along the top of the dresser one last time and stepped out into the hall. "It's all yours," she said lightly.

"Then I guess I'd better get back to work," he said equally lightly.

His door closed. Kendall took a deep breath and picked up the garbage bag, gripping it tightly in shaking hands, and headed down the stairs. Ducking into her office, she pulled out the papers she'd taken from his desk, shoved them into the file cabinet and locked it securely.

She'd finished her cleaning and was tossing the rest of the trash in garbage containers outside the back door when she heard a car pull to a stop out front.

Gabe.

She took a deep breath. Of course it was Gabe. He was her only other guest.

Ignoring her erratically beating heart, she snapped the lids on the garbage cans and scanned the yard for the girls. Shelby was playing in the sand on the beach, and Jenna was sprawled on her stomach nearby, reading.

"Don't get any closer to the water," she called.

Even from this distance she could see Shelby roll her eyes. Grinning, she gave them a cheery wave.

When she walked through the door, Gabe was waiting in the kitchen. "I put the shredder in your office," he said in a low voice.

"Thanks." She tried to walk past him without meeting his eyes, but he stopped her by putting a hand on her arm. "Are you going to tell me what happened? I know Smith is here—I saw his car."

"Let me finish and we'll go outside," she murmured.

She moved more slowly than usual as she dealt with her remaining chores. She was in no hurry to face Gabe again. The rawness of their most recent encounter throbbed like an open wound, and she was reluctant to poke at it. When she could delay no more, she found Gabe sitting on the back porch. His black hair was unruly, as if it had been blown by the wind. He rested his head against the railing, his eyes closed, but as soon as she joined him, he looked up at her.

"I need to see how Elena is doing," she said. "We can talk when I get back."

"I'll come with you."

He stood close as she descended the steps. She edged away, walking toward the girls. "We're going to Elena's," she called to them.

"I want to come," Shelby yelled. Both girls scrambled to their feet and ran toward the orchard, ahead of Kendall and Gabe. Jenna hugged Harry Potter to her chest. The book looked almost bigger than she was.

Gabe gave her a knowing half smile. "Chaperones?"

"I don't need chaperones," she said with a level look. "I can take care of myself. But I don't like them on the beach by themselves."

"Right. I'll stick to business. Did Smith come back while you were in his room?"

"He did," she answered. She told him what had happened. "He knew I had the papers. He acted like it was a big game. Like I'd won this round, but it wasn't over."

"For damn sure it isn't over." Gabe's voice was grim. "Not until I find out what he's up to."

"It wasn't illegal to go through my garbage," she reminded him. "He'd say he was just doing what was necessary to get the story."

"Yeah, but what story is that?"

"Stay away from him, Gabe. Don't make a big deal out of this. If you do, he'll keep digging." She pushed at one of the low-hanging branches, making the leaves quiver. "I don't want him to find out about Amy and Tommy."

"He won't hear it from Amy or from me. You better warn George not to say anything."

"I'll try. But George is angry enough to do something stupid."

"Then you'd better try to keep him away from the house." He stopped her again with a hand on the arm. "I don't want to get into a fight with your brother. And if he says anything to Smith, there'll be a fight."

"I'll do my best," she said and stepped away from him. Away from his touch.

They emerged from the shadows of the orchard and approached a tract of neat, single-story houses where migrant workers lived during the cherry-picking season. Shelby and Jenna waited impatiently in front of one of them.

As Kendall lifted her hand to ring the bell, she heard a familiar voice inside. Dylan. Speaking Spanish.

Gabe reached out and stopped her from ringing the bell. "What the hell is he doing here?"

They stared at each other for a moment, then Kendall said, "Let's find out."

Elena's mother opened the door. "Hello," she said.

"I came to see how Elena is feeling," Kendall explained in Spanish.

"Please come in," the woman said, smoothing the front of her dress with her hands.

They stepped into the tidy living room. Dylan sat on the couch next to an older woman, and Elena was sprawled on the floor, reading a magazine. She jumped up when she saw the girls. "Hi, Shelby. Jenna," she said, her eyes brightening. "You came back."

"Dylan. What are you doing here?" Kendall said.

"Talking to Señora Guttierez," he said smoothly.

"Señor Smith has been very kind," Elena's mother said. She glanced at him and smiled. "Very respectful." Her expression softened as she looked at the older woman. "My mother doesn't get much company. And the children have heard all her stories many times already."

"What are you and Señora Guttierez finding to talk about?" Kendall asked Dylan.

"This and that," he said, standing up. He turned to the older woman and said in Spanish, "I enjoyed our visit. I'll come back later, when you don't have other visitors."

As he headed toward the door, Kendall stepped in front of him. "We need to talk."

"Any time," he said, brushing past her.

There was a moment of awkward silence as the door closed behind him, then Kendall smiled at Elena's mother. "I didn't realize you knew Señor Smith."

"My husband met him on Saturday night. When he heard that my mother was with us, he asked if he could talk to her. He is interested in the old days at the orchard."

"The old days?"

"When she came here to pick the cherries as a young woman. When old Mr. Van Allen was in charge of the orchard."

"That was a long time ago," she said. Gabe moved closer to her.

Elena's mother smiled. "My family has been coming here for many years."

"He's staying at my house. I apologize if he was bothering you."

"Bothering us?" The woman looked bewildered. "Of course not. It's good for my mother to have company."

"Yes, of course." She swallowed and looked at the girls on the floor. Elena was thumbing through Jenna's Harry Potter. "How is Elena doing?"

"She is doing well. Thank you for taking her to the doctor. We are grateful for your help."

"I'm sorry about the accident."

"The roots of the trees are hard to see in the dark, but she shouldn't have been running in the orchard at night. Her head hurts," Mrs. Montoya said, glancing at her daughter. "But she'll be fine in a day or two."

She hurried into the kitchen, returning with the pan that had held the muffins. "And thank you for the pastries."

"You're welcome."

They chatted for a few more minutes, then Kendall said, "We'll leave you to enjoy your Sunday. Let me know if Elena needs anything."

"Thank you."

"Elena needs to rest, girls," she said to Shelby and Jenna. They stood up reluctantly, and Jenna took her book back from Elena. The girl's gaze followed them to the door. After promising to come back the next day, they headed back through the orchard to the house.

"What is that bastard up to?" Gabe whisper grimly.

"You understand Spanish?" she asked.

"Enough to know that Smith was trying to dig information out of an old woman."

She glanced at him as they threaded their way through the cherry trees. "Dylan's a charming guy. I want to know what he's trying to charm out of my neighbors and employees."

"We'll find out."

But Dylan wasn't there when they reached Van Allen House. Gabe's eyes were cold and hard as he looked at the spot where the reporter usually parked. "I'll be waiting for him when he gets back."

"Gabe, I'll talk to him," she said. "He's staying in my house, talking to my employees. I'll handle it."

"You do what you want," he said, his eyes implacable. Ruthless. He looked like a stranger, and it made her uneasy. "I'll do what I have to do."

"I want you to leave him alone," she said. "I don't want you harassing him."

"Harassing him?" He smiled coldly. "I don't harass people. I'm just going to ask him a few questions."

"You're going to intimidate him."

"You say that like it's a bad thing."

"It *is* a bad thing. He might…"

Leave. She clamped her mouth shut. She couldn't say that to Gabe. That was exactly what he wanted— to get Dylan out of her house.

She couldn't afford that. The money Dylan paid for his room would cover some bills. Like the one for her brake job that Dylan had found in the garbage. "If you try to frighten him, he'll be convinced that we're trying to hide something. And he'll just look harder."

"He's questioning an old woman who can barely speak English," Gabe retorted. "I think he's already looking pretty damn hard."

"Just stay away from him. Let me handle it."

He stared at her for a long moment. Then his eyes thawed and he gave her a wry smile. "I'm trying to protect you and you're stomping all over my male ego. Can't you throw it a bone and let me handle the reporter for you?"

She reached for him instinctively. "Thank you, Gabe," she said. "I know you're trying to help. And I appreciate it. I really do. But this is my business. Dylan is my guest and it's my job to deal with this problem."

He looked down at the hand on his arm. "All right. I'll back off. I'll let you handle Smith." He brought her hand to his mouth, brushed his lips over her knuckles. "But if he gives you a hard time, all bets are off."

She left her hand in Gabe's for a heartbeat too long, then drew it away. "He's not going to give me a hard time. Dylan gets his information by charming people, not by threatening them. I'm immune to charm."

He smiled wryly. "Good to know, Kenny."

"You wouldn't try to charm me, Gabe. You're too honest for that."

Gabe watched her as she walked away, her words echoing in his ears. *If only you knew, Kenny.*

His lack of honesty was what had drawn him back to Sturgeon Falls. He had to make things right before he could move on with his life. But he worried that the same lack of honesty would drive a final wedge between the two of them, rather than resolving things. He hadn't been able to resist kissing her last night. And if he had a chance to kiss her again, he would take it. Because it would probably have to last him a lifetime.

He'd returned to his room to work on his speech when he heard the front door slam some time later. He knew it wasn't the girls—from his window he could see them in the yard. Maybe it was Smith.

He walked downstairs and headed into the kitchen. When Kendall raised her eyebrows at him, he nodded toward the coffeepot. "I need my fix," he said.

"You're going to have to learn to lie better than that," she said. "He's not here." She nodded toward a tall woman with short, wavy blond hair who leaned against the counter drinking iced tea. "This is Carter's cousin, Charlotte Burns. Charlotte, do you remember Gabe Townsend?"

"Of course." Charlotte leaned forward and shook his hand firmly. "You were Carter's friend, weren't you?"

"Guilty as charged," Gabe answered. He studied the striking woman in her faded jeans, work boots and flannel shirt. "I'm sorry, but I don't remember you."

"Of course you don't." She grinned at him. "I was younger than you and Carter. I worshipped from afar."

"Charlotte's mother and Carter's mother were sisters," Kendall explained. "She spent time with Carter's family when she was growing up."

The blonde continued to smile, but shadows filled her bright blue eyes. "One big happy family," she said lightly. She took another drink of tea, then set the glass on the counter with a snap. "I have to get going, Ken. I'll see you later."

"You're not going to stay and have dinner with us?" Kendall gestured toward a newspaper-wrapped package on the kitchen table.

"Not tonight. I have a fish for Kat, too, and then I have to go back to the boat. My engine's been giving me grief. I need to whack it a few times with my wrench."

Kendall hugged Charlotte and walked her to the door. When she returned, she picked up the package and slid it into the refrigerator.

"Salmon," she explained to Gabe.

"Your cousin brings you fish? And her cat?"

Kendall grinned. "Charlotte runs a charter fishing boat out of Sturgeon Falls. You'd be surprised how many people want to fish but won't eat what they catch." She grinned again. "And Kat is Katriona Macauley, her best friend. She's a doctor with a practice in town."

The kitchen door swung open and Dylan walked in. "Townsend." He nodded to Gabe. "Hey, Kendall, who was that gorgeous blonde in the pickup truck?"

"That was Carter's cousin, Charlotte," she said.

"Darn," he said lightly, but his eyes sharpened. "I was hoping she was a new guest."

"Nope." She slid in front of Gabe. "Dylan, what were you doing at the Montoyas' house? Why were you questioning Elena's grandmother?"

"You make it sound as if I had her on the rack," he said, flashing his dimple. "I was talking to an old woman who enjoyed having company."

"Spending some time with an elderly woman out of the goodness of your heart?" Kendall narrowed her eyes. "I doubt it. I don't know what you're after, but I don't want you harassing my employees, especially on a Sunday. It's their only day off. You have no business disturbing them."

"I wasn't harassing her. We were just talking." He shrugged. "Older people like to reminisce."

"Then go and reminisce with your own grandmother. I won't have you taking advantage of vulnerable old people."

Smith flinched, and the smile faded from his face.

"I don't have any grandparents," he said quietly. "I enjoyed talking to Señora Guttierez, and I think she enjoyed talking to me. Her family works for you, but that doesn't mean you own them. I'll talk to her whenever I choose."

Kendall watched in stunned silence as Dylan shoved himself away from the counter and left the kitchen.

CHAPTER FOURTEEN

Sunday evening

GABE PUSHED AWAY from his desk and stretched. The
figures on the laptop screen blurred and wavered, reminding him he'd spent too long staring at them. The
squeak of his desk chair on the wooden floor echoed
loudly in the silence, a silence broken only by the soft,
distant murmur of waves lapping at the beach.

The moon glinted above the black water of Green
Bay and barely illuminated the shadows in Kendall's
yard. She really needed better lighting at the back of her
house, Gabe thought as he stared down at the shadowy
yard. There were too many places to hide out there.

Closing his laptop, Gabe opened the door to his
room and heard shrieks of laughter drifting up the stairs.
Loneliness swept over him as he looked back at his tidy,
neat, empty room, then he shut the door and headed
toward the laughter.

Kendall, Shelby and Jenna sat at the dining-room table,
playing a board game. Shelby raised her arms in menace,
then stuck her upper teeth over her lower lip. Jenna
watched for a moment, then shouted out, "Vampire!"

Grinning, Shelby dropped back into her chair. "You got it, Jen."

Jenna happily reached for her game piece and moved it.

When Kendall looked up and saw Gabe leaning against the door frame, she stilled for a moment, then gave him a bright smile. "We're playing Cranium," she said. "Would you like to join us?"

"You're in the middle of a game," he said. "I don't want to disrupt it."

He got himself a glass of water, and by the time he returned it was Shelby's turn again. She pulled another card and grinned. "I got another Cameo."

"Shelby always gets the Cameo cards," Jenna complained. "It's not fair."

Gabe slid into the seat next to Jenna. "What are Cameo cards?"

"Those are cards you have to act out," she explained. "They're Shelby's favorite. She always gets them, and she's really good at it."

"What are your favorites?"

"The Doublemeanies and the Code Crackers," Jenna said. "You have to figure out words."

"I bet you're good at those because you like to read so much," Gabe said.

He leaned back and watched Shelby raise her arms, spin in a circle and weave from side to side as she acted out a whirling tornado. She *was* pretty good at it.

"Nice tornado, Shel," he said. "That was pretty good acting."

"I'm going to be an actress when I grow up," she informed him.

"Is that right?"

She nodded. "Starting when I'm in high school. They have school plays."

"You don't have to wait until you go to high school," he said. He glanced at Kendall, remembering their earlier conversation about Shelby and acting. "There's a group in Tin Harbor that has classes on acting and puts on plays in the summer. I know T—" No, he shouldn't mention Tommy Mitchell. "You should check it out."

"Really?" Her eyes lit up. "Can I, Mom?"

"I'll look into it, okay?" Kendall said with a forced smile. She shot Gabe a look that held resignation and a hint of resentment.

"Okay." Shelby grinned as she flopped back into her chair. "Your turn, Mom."

Gabe lingered in the dining room, enjoying the girls' attempts to one-up each other and Kendall's teasing refereeing. Finally, when the game was over and Jenna had triumphed, Kendall stood up.

"I'll get a bedtime snack while you put the game away," she said as she disappeared into the kitchen.

Gabe followed her. "Can I help?"

"There's nothing to do," Kendall answered, lining up bowls on the counter and grabbing a carton of ice cream from the freezer.

"What's wrong?" he asked.

"Nothing." She closed the freezer door with a little too much force, then dug an ice-cream scoop into the carton.

Gabe put his hand over hers, took the scoop and began to serve the ice cream. "Tell me what's wrong, Kendall."

She sighed. "I wish you hadn't told Shelby about those theater classes."

"Why not?" He frowned. "She wants to be an actress, there are classes close by. What's the problem?"

Kendall slid a dish towel over the handle of the oven door. "I've heard about that group," she said quietly. "They do a great job, but classes are expensive and the kids have to provide their own costumes and makeup." She rearranged a stack of plates. "You saw that note from my mechanic. I can't even pay for my car repairs. Still, I should have figured out a way for Shelby to get involved in acting. And I will."

Before he could respond, Kendall had picked up two bowls of ice cream and pushed through the door into the dining room. He took the other two and followed her.

"Can we look at the pictures while we eat our ice cream, Mom?" Shelby asked. "You promised we could pick out the ones we want for the ceremony."

"Sure. I'll go get them."

"No! Let's look at them in your room. That's where we always look at them," Shelby said.

"All right," she sighed. "But you have to be careful not to spill ice cream on my bed."

Gabe dropped his spoon into the bowl as they headed for the stairs. He was pushing away from the table when Shelby stuck her head around the corner.

"Aren't you coming, Uncle Gabe?"

"I think this is a family activity, Shel."

"You *are* part of the family." She grinned at him. "So come on."

"I meant just you and your sister and your mom."

"Mom!" Shelby yelled. "Can Uncle Gabe come and look at the pictures, too?"

The pause was too long. Then Kendall said, "Sure."

"Maybe another time, Shel. Okay?"

"No." She stamped her foot. "You're part of the family and you need to help pick out the pictures."

Oh, God. What was he supposed to say to that? "All right. But just for a minute."

He followed Shelby up the stairs to the third floor, hesitating at the door to Kendall's room. It was painted a buttery yellow, with white furniture and scarred but polished hardwood floors. The rugs scattered around the room were slightly threadbare and old, just like the ones downstairs, and the quilt and curtains were patterned with yellow and blue flowers.

Like the rest of the house, this room was peaceful and welcoming.

Unlike Kendall, whose shoulders stiffened when Gabe appeared. She didn't look at him as she knelt on the floor in front of a bookcase. "Come on in, Gabe."

"This wasn't my idea," he said in a low voice."

She rocked back on her heels, clutching a photo album. "I know," she sighed. "I should have asked you myself. You're in a lot of these pictures."

Kendall looked at her daughters, bouncing on the

bed, then glanced at Gabe. Her cheeks reddened slightly. "Girls, let's sit on the floor. We won't all fit on the bed." She settled herself on the floor without looking at him. Gabe sat next to Jenna.

One memory after another leaped out at him as they turned the pages of the album. Carter on the beach, holding a fish he'd caught. Carter and Kendall, arms looped around each other's waists, gazing into each other's eyes.

"That one," Jenna said, pointing to the picture. "That's my mommy and my daddy."

"That's a good choice," Kendall said, slipping it out of its pocket. "That was right after I met your daddy."

"That's you, Uncle Gabe," Shelby said, pointing to another picture. He and Carter stood in the orchard, leaning against a tree.

"Your dad and I worked at the orchard every summer," Gabe replied.

Kendall turned a few more pages and found pictures of Shelby as a baby. In most of them, Kendall was holding her, looking radiant. Finally they found one where Carter was holding Shelby. He looked uncertain and ill at ease.

"Is that me?" Shelby asked.

"It is." Kendall slipped that picture out of its slot. "Let's find one of Jenna with Daddy, then one with both of you and your father."

"You skipped some pages, Mom," Shelby said after they'd found more pictures of Carter and the girls.

"Those were before you were born," Kendall said. "You wouldn't be in them."

"I know, but I want to look at them."

Kendall's hand tightened on the photo album, then she turned to the pictures she'd skipped over. She was flipping through them when Shelby stopped her. "There's you and Uncle Gabe," she said, glancing at them and then back to the picture. "You guys were *young*."

Gabe laughed. "That makes me feel really old."

His smile faded as he looked at Kendall. She sat frozen, staring at the picture.

She tried to flip the page quickly, but he stopped her. His heart jolted when he saw the photo.

"That's our beach, isn't it?" Jenna asked.

"Yes," he managed to say. "That was taken at a big Fourth of July party your mom and dad had."

"Where's Daddy?" Shelby asked, studying the picture.

"He was probably taking the picture." Kendall clapped the album shut. "Time for bed, girls."

The girls protested, but Kendall shoved the photo album back on the shelf. Gabe stacked the empty bowls and headed downstairs.

He'd loaded the dishes in the dishwasher and was looking around for something else to do when Kendall pushed through the kitchen door.

"Thank you," she said without meeting his eyes. "For cleaning up."

"It was nothing." He watched as she fiddled with a bowl of fruit, rearranging the apples and pears. "The girls didn't notice anything unusual about that picture from the Fourth of July party," he said quietly. "Don't worry about it."

"I'm not worried," she answered.

"It upset you to see it."

"I wasn't upset." She moved the fruit bowl, and an apple fell out and rolled across the green granite counter.

They reached for it at the same moment. Sparks jumped from her hand to his. Pulling away, Kendall put the apple back, then shoved her hands into her pockets. "I was surprised—that's all. I wasn't expecting to see it."

"Those pictures brought back a lot of memories."

She struggled to smile. "The girls always like to look at them." Taking a deep breath, she reached for the light switch. "It's late. I'm going up to bed. Good night, Gabe."

"Wait, Kendall. Before you go, there was something I wanted to ask you."

"What?" She looked at him warily.

"About Shelby," he added.

"Oh. Okay." She relaxed a little. "What?"

"I'd like to pay for her to take those acting classes in Tin Harbor."

"No," said too quickly. "Thank you, but no."

"You let me buy Jenna a tennis racquet."

"Those classes cost a heck of a lot more than a tennis racquet." She narrowed her eyes. "Unless you spent a lot more than you should have on the racquet."

"Don't worry," he said. "It was an appropriate racquet for a beginner."

"Fine. But you're not going to pay for the acting."

"You can't swallow your pride for your daughter?"

She flinched. "Pride has nothing to do with it."

"No?"

She looked out the window, even though there was nothing to see but darkness, and she sighed. "Maybe it does," she said quietly. "I should have realized that she'd want to be part of that group. I should have arranged it myself. I shouldn't have needed you to point it out to me." She crossed her arms. "You see them, Gabe. And right away you understand who they are. Maybe I'm a little jealous."

"So I can give Shelby the acting classes? And tennis lessons for Jenna?"

"I'll think about it." She looked over her shoulder at Gabe. "I don't want the girls thinking of you as the source of expensive gifts. That's not the way to build a relationship with them."

"Am I going to have a relationship with them?"

"It looks like you already do. Whether or not you pursue it is up to you."

"I'm welcome to come back? To spend time with the girls?"

"I already told you, if that's what you want, I won't keep them away from you." She leaned back against the counter. "You were right. You can tell them about Carter. He was their father. They want to know about him, and you can give them that."

"What brought on this change of heart?" he asked, moving closer. "I thought you couldn't wait to get rid of me."

She slipped past Gabe and pushed through the door into the dining room. "Looking at those pictures tonight. Thinking about our conversation this afternoon. About Carter, about the kind of person he became. That's not the side of him I want the girls to know."

She stepped to the buffet, fiddled with the basket of silverware. He wondered if she even realized she'd put the dining table between them. "You were a good friend to Carter. I saw it in those pictures. And I see that you care about Shelby and Jenna. You can give them their father."

"I'm not sure I deserve your trust," he murmured, guilt stirring inside him again. "But I promise I won't abuse it."

"I know you won't." She struggled to smile. "You're going to have to work to come up with G-rated stories about him, though."

"I'm sure I can find one or two," he replied.

"Good night again, Gabe," she said. "It's been a long day."

"I'll walk you upstairs."

He waited while she turned off the lights and locked the doors, then followed her up the stairs. When she got to her room on the third floor, she reached for the doorknob without looking at him. "I'll see you in the morning," she murmured.

"Wait," he said, touching her arm.

She turned around—reluctantly, he thought. "What?"

"Thank you, Kendall." He saw wariness in her eyes. "For allowing me to be part of their lives."

"I'm doing it for them," she whispered.

"I know." He drew her closer. "There's nothing between us, right?"

"There can't be. You know that." She trembled, but she didn't move away. "I can't need you."

He didn't want to need her, either. It was too painful. It brought back too much guilt, too many memories. But it didn't seem to matter. One look at her, one touch swept everything away. He brushed his mouth over hers. One taste, and he was lost.

He bent his mouth to hers again, closed his eyes as he drank her in. Her sweetness filled his mouth, made his blood pound. She tasted faintly of the chocolate she'd had on her ice cream, the tea she'd been drinking. Of the taste that was Kendall. The taste he'd never forget.

Trapped between his body and the wall, she softened against him until her body wrapped around his. Her nipples were hard where her breasts pressed into his chest, moving with every flutter of breath, every sigh.

When he cupped her face in his hands, pressed a kiss to her neck, she opened her eyes. "Gabe." She put her hands on his wrists. "Stop."

"Are you sure you want me to stop?" He swiped his mouth over hers, tugged at her lower lip.

She shivered. "No. Yes." She eased away from him and stepped into her bedroom. "Good night," she said as she closed the door softly.

He put his hand on the cool wood of the door, imagined he could feel her moving around inside the room. "Good night, Kenny."

AN HOUR LATER, Gabe threw back his quilt and swung his legs off the bed. Kendall's room was directly above his. Instead of sleeping, he'd been listening to her move around. Wondering if her restlessness had anything to do with him.

Even if it had, he reminded himself, she wouldn't admit it. Kendall was the most stubborn person he'd ever known.

It sounded as if she'd finally gone to bed. Maybe now he could get some sleep himself.

The moon, already setting, glittered over Green Bay, illuminating the swell of waves. It outlined the sea grass along Kendall's beach, and Gabe looked away.

That beach held too many memories.

As he eased back into bed, he heard a door rattle downstairs. Where had Smith been this evening? Had he been at Elena's house, pretending to listen to her grandmother while scrounging information about Carter? Or had he been to the Blue Door, looking for other sources?

He listened for footsteps on the stairs, but instead he heard the door rattle again. Had the idiot forgotten his key?

Good. Let the bastard sleep in his car tonight.

But Smith wouldn't sleep in his car. He'd call Kendall, wake her up to come down and let him in.

Gabe slipped on his boxers and stepped into the

hall. A night-light glowed along the baseboards, illuminating the stairs. He hurried downstairs, afraid the reporter would call Kendall before he could get the door open.

There was no one on the front porch.

The door rattled again. It was the back door. Sprinting into the kitchen, he fumbled with the unfamiliar locks and finally got it open. No one was there.

Hurrying down the steps, he scanned the dark yard and the even darker orchard. Nothing.

The grass was cool beneath his bare feet, and the breeze carried the fresh scent of the lake. Was someone hiding in the shadows, watching him?

It was impossible to tell. The darkness was too complete. As Gabe began to walk around the house, he heard the front door open.

He ran back through the kitchen, getting to the stairs at the same time as Smith. The reporter looked at him without his usual smile. Or his usual charm. "Why are you wandering around the house in the dark?"

"Were you just trying to get in the back door?" Gabe asked in a low voice.

"Why would I try the back door? The key is for the front door."

"Just checking."

"How come?"

"Does it matter?"

Dylan studied him, let his gaze linger on Gabe's bare chest and his boxers, and a knowing smile passed over his face. "Sorry, old man. For interrupting."

"What's that supposed to mean?" Seeing the smirk, Gabe clenched his fists and moved closer.

"You and Kendall. Sorry I disturbed you."

"There is no me and Kendall," Gabe said, his voice cold. "So you didn't interrupt anything."

"No?" Smith gave him a cocky smile. "That's not what it looks like from the cheap seats."

"You're wrong, Smith. Or don't you care about that? Anything to make the story a little spicier, right? Whether it's true or not?"

Dylan snorted. "Give me a break, Townsend. I have eyes. I know how to add. Two and two have always made four." He smiled again. "Or, in this case, should I say one and one always makes two?"

"I'm a guest here. That's all."

The reporter rolled his eyes. "If you say so."

"I suppose your version of the truth will end up in your story. Whether or not it's true. A little sex always sells more newspapers, doesn't it?"

The humor disappeared from Smith's eyes. "I don't need sex to sell my story, Townsend. I've got plenty of other information to use." He headed toward his room, then turned to look back at Gabe. His face was in the shadows. "But you're right about the sex. People are always interested in other people's sex lives. Especially when those other people are pillars of the community." He continued up the stairs and said over his shoulder, "You *would* call the Van Allens pillars of the community, wouldn't you?"

"What the hell is that supposed to mean?" Gabe

stormed after the reporter and stepped in front of him, blocking his way. "What are you writing about?" he asked, struggling to keep his voice low. "It sure as hell isn't about a football-field dedication."

Dylan reached around Gabe and opened his door. "I don't talk about my stories before they're published." He gave Gabe a smile completely devoid of humor. "I don't want any of my secrets to come out prematurely." He shouldered past Gabe and went into his room. "I'm sure you know what I mean."

The door snicked shut.

KENDALL STUMBLED down to the kitchen in the dark the next morning, her eyes raw from lack of sleep. Another restless night. She'd had a few of them since Gabe showed up at her front door.

As she mixed the batter for a batch of muffins, she heard the front door close. Moments later, she heard a car start.

Looking through the dining-room window, she saw Gabe heading down the driveway and talking on his cell phone. Driving way too fast.

She watched until he turned onto County B. Then, feeling a little hurt because he hadn't told her where he was going and knowing she was a fool to feel that way, she went back to the kitchen and her breakfast preparations.

Gabe was an adult. He didn't owe Kendall a thing.

He especially didn't have to tell her where he was going or what he was doing.

They didn't have that kind of relationship.

They never would.

When his car turned into the driveway again, later, while she was cleaning his room, she yanked the sheets from his bed, tossed them into the hall and hurried to replace them.

Kendall heard Gabe walk into the dining room, and then the kitchen. A moment later, he came pounding up the stairs looking for her.

Her fingers gripped his quilt, then she fluttered it over his bed and smoothed it into place. By the time he reached the bedroom hallway, she was closing his door.

"Good morning, Gabe," she said with a bright, neutral smile.

When she tried to move, he put a hand firmly on her arm and jerked his head toward Dylan's room. "Is he in there?" he asked in a low voice.

"As far as I know. He hasn't come downstairs yet this morning."

Gabe took his dirty sheets from her arms and headed down the stairs. "We need to talk."

CHAPTER FIFTEEN

Monday morning

"OUTSIDE," GABE SAID, clutching Kendall's arm again and steering her toward the back door. "I don't want him to hear us."

"Let's go down to the beach," Kendall said, gently slipping her arm from his grasp. "We'll have more privacy there."

She slid into an Adirondack chair, the wood smooth against her bare legs. Gabe perched on the edge of another, facing her. "What's the big secret?" she said. "Why did you sneak out of here this morning in the dark?"

"I didn't sneak," he said, studying her as he spoke. "I was trying not to wake anyone." He gave her a slow smile. "I'm glad you noticed I was gone."

She shrugged and stared out over the water. "I heard you leave." *I wondered where you were going.* She wouldn't say it. Couldn't say it.

"I drove into Green Bay."

She sat up in the chair. "To check on Dylan?"

"I talked to his editor at the *Green Bay News-*

Gazette." Gabe's mouth thinned to a grim line. "Dylan Smith is on a leave of absence right now."

"What?" She bounced out of the chair.

"He's their investigative reporter, but he's taken an unpaid leave of absence to do some personal research. He turned in his last assignment a few weeks ago." Gabe stood, paced down the strip of sand. "The editor asked him what the research was about, told him it didn't have to be unpaid if it could turn into an article for the paper. Smith said he'd let him know. That he wasn't sure if anything he found would make a story."

"So what's he doing?" Kendall crouched down on the beach and picked up a flat rock. She skimmed it over the waves on the lake, watching it bounce four times before it disappeared into the water. "Why did he lie about his story?"

"He might be coming after you," Gabe said.

She swiveled to face him. The wind had lifted Gabe's hair from his forehead, highlighting his bleak gaze. "Why would you think that?"

"I heard someone at the door last night. I thought it was Smith, and that he'd forgotten his key, so I went downstairs to let him in." He glanced at her, then away. "I didn't want him to wake you up."

"Thank you," she said. She wanted to smooth away the lock of hair that had fallen over his forehead. Instead, she tucked her hands in her pockets.

He explained what had happened, how he'd confronted Smith on the steps and what Dylan had said.

She dug her toes into the damp, cool sand. "I'm hardly a pillar of the community."

"You're a Van Allen. And he's staying in your house. Connect the dots, Kendall."

"It's more likely he's after Carter," she retorted. "Trying to dig up dirt on him. And he'll find it, won't he? Because there's plenty of dirt to find."

"He can't hurt Carter."

"But he can hurt Carter's daughters. He can destroy their illusions. He can sabotage that damn football stadium dedication. I Googled him, but I only found his other stories. There wasn't a hint of what he's doing here." She wrapped her arms around herself and looked out at the blue-gray water of Green Bay. In spite of the bright unclouded sky, the water was choppy and rough. Like the day.

"The editor said this was personal research," Gabe reminded her. "Does Smith have some connection to Carter?"

"I have no idea." She kicked a stone into the water. "But there was a lot I didn't know about Carter, wasn't there?"

"He went through your garbage can," Gabe said. "The papers he had were about you. And he was pretty damn interested in our supposed relationship."

"Then I don't have to worry about anything, do I? Since we don't have a relationship."

"Stop it, Kendall. We need to figure this out."

His voice was gentle, and she wanted to scream at him. Wanted to tell him to stay away from her, not to tempt her. Not to be a man she thought she could rely on.

"Who have you had relationships with since Carter died?"

"Who have I slept with, do you mean?"

"Kendall." He put his hands on her shoulders, and she stiffened. "I'm not trying to pry. I'm trying to figure out what Smith is after."

She shook off his hands. "You're not trying to pry? Really? I think asking me who I've had sex with is a damned prying question."

"Okay. Let me rephrase that. Who have you been involved with that Smith would be interested in?"

"If he's looking for a sex scandal involving me, he's going to be disappointed. Okay? Is that what you want to know?"

"No secrets in your past?" he asked, his voice light.

"You know all my secrets," she said, turning to face him. "Are you going to tell him?"

"You know I wouldn't talk to Smith about you. Hell, I wouldn't tell him his hair was on fire," he answered, taking a step closer. "And you're wrong about those secrets of yours." He touched her cheek, let his hand linger. "I don't know all of them. But I'd like to."

For a moment, she allowed herself to lean into his touch. Then she drew away. "So what do we do now?"

"Tell me your secrets?"

The pause was heavy with unspoken things. Finally she turned away.

"What do we do about Smith?" She picked up a new smooth stone, tossing it from hand to hand as she walked along the beach. The rocks and pebbles bruised the bottoms of her bare feet, but she kept walking. She needed to distance herself from the tenderness in Gabe's eyes, the softness. It tempted her to do things she shouldn't do. To feel things she shouldn't feel.

She could sense Gabe close behind her, but she didn't turn around. Finally he said, "I'm going to follow Smith. See where he's going, figure out who he's talking to."

"He won't like that."

Gabe shrugged. "So what? As he said himself, there isn't any rule about driving on public roads."

"All right." She gripped the stone more tightly to keep from touching Gabe. "Just don't take any stupid chances."

"Hey, I'm a guy," he protested. "There's no such thing as a stupid chance. There are only smart chances."

She smiled, allowing herself to relax. "Okay, you… guy. At least be careful."

"I like knowing you're worried about me."

As they made their way back to the house, Smith stepped onto the porch with a mug in his hand. When he saw them, he waved, then leaned against the door to watch as they approached. Kendall edged a bit farther from Gabe.

"I'm going in the front door," Gabe muttered. "I don't want to talk to him this morning."

He disappeared around the side of the house, and Kendall painted a smile on her face. "Good morning, Dylan. What would you like for breakfast?"

THE SUN WAS BLAZING in the early afternoon, but the still-cold water of Green Bay numbed her feet. Kendall ignored the pain. Wading farther out, she carried the string of floating plastic buoys she used to mark the edge of the swimming area. As the water climbed higher against the wet suit she wore, she felt the chill through the thick neoprene. Still, the suit kept her insulated and dry.

Dragging the heavy anchors behind her, feeling them bump over the sandy bottom of the lake, she finally reached the place where they belonged. It took a few minutes to position the string of buoys, and by the time she was finished, her hands were as cold as her feet.

As she headed back toward shore, she saw her brother standing on the rocks, watching her. Her step faltered, and she wondered if George was still angry. She wasn't in the mood for another ugly scene.

"You shouldn't be in the water alone," he chided her, grasping her arm as she stumbled onto the sand. "Even with a wet suit."

"It only takes a minute to set out the buoys," she said, allowing her feet to absorb the heat of the sand. "Then it's done for the summer."

He shifted from foot to foot, avoiding her eyes. "You should have let me do it."

"I will next time," she answered easily. "I just wanted to check it off my list." She turned her back to the sun, letting it warm her. "What are you doing here? I thought you'd be wearing your tool belt and pounding nails today." She studied him. "You *are* working with the construction crew again this summer, aren't you?"

"Yeah, I'm working with them. I just took a couple

of days off." He kicked at the sand, sending a spray of fine grit into the air. "I had planned for Amy and Tommy to go away with me for a few days."

"I'm sorry, George," she said, enfolding him in a fierce hug. "I'm so sorry."

He clung to her for a moment, then eased her away. "You have nothing to be sorry about," he muttered. "I came over to apologize. For losing my temper yesterday and taking it out on you. Townsend was right. I wasn't thinking of you at all."

"It's okay. I understand."

"Don't let me off so easily, Kenny." He gave her a little shake. "Yell at me. Tell me what a loser I am. I shouldn't have told you about Tommy and Carter."

"Okay, jerkface," she said with a smile, using her favorite childhood taunt. "You're a loser. Does that make you feel better?"

He slung an arm around her shoulders. "Much."

She leaned against him. "What are you going to do?" she asked quietly. "You love Amy. You wanted to marry her. Did that change so quickly?"

"I don't know." His voice was tortured. "When I think about Amy, all I can see is her and Carter."

"It was a long time ago," Kendall said. "She was so young, and people make mistakes."

"What about you? If I married Amy, she'd be over here a lot, just like I am. You and the girls would be at our house. Could you be able to be friends with her? What about Tommy? How would you handle that?"

She should lie to George, tell him it would all be fine.

Tell him she wouldn't have a problem with Amy and Tommy. But she couldn't say the words just yet.

"I don't know," she finally answered with a sigh. "I don't know how I'd be with Amy and Tommy. It's not Tommy's fault that Carter cheated on me. I can't blame him." She closed her eyes as the pain sank in. "But I won't pretend it's not hard to know Carter did that while I was pregnant with Jenna. While he was supposed to be spending time with me, building a family with me, he was having sex with another woman."

"What about Amy?" he said quietly. "If we work this out, will you be able to forget what she did? Will you find a way to be her friend?"

"I know I should say yes, that I can forget it and put it behind me. But I just don't know, George. It's too soon. It's too raw."

"I guess it's a good thing Amy's not in the picture, then." His voice was bitter—and lost.

"What do you want me to say? Do you want me to pretend? To tell you everything is peachy keen?" She kicked at a tuft of beach grass, watched it bend and then bounce back. "That would insult your intelligence. And it wouldn't be fair to Amy and Tommy.

"I'm trying to be honest with you. I'm not saying I'll feel like this forever. But this is how I feel right now."

They walked a few more feet, and George sighed. "I know, Kenny. I'm sorry—I'm just not thinking straight."

Kendall took his arms and held him in front of her. "You do what you have to do, George. This isn't about me. This is about you and Amy. And Tommy."

"It's not that simple," he retorted. "You're my family. I'll have to give you up if I marry Amy. I'm not sure I can do that."

"You're being awfully damn dramatic, George, and I want it to stop. You're not going to have to give us up. Quit worrying about me, and get your own head straight about how you feel. Can you look at that child and simply see Tommy? See the person he is? Or will you always see Carter staring back at you?

"And the same with Amy. Can you put what she did in the past and leave it there? Because if you marry her, you can't ever bring Carter up again."

"I don't know what I want. Except for you, Kenny. You're my sister. You'll always be my sister. My family."

She gave him another fierce hug. "Same goes, George. You know that." She grinned up at him. "Even if you are a jerkface."

The pain in her brother's eyes eased. "Nice talk, Ken. What if the girls heard you?"

"They're not here. Shelby is at soccer practice and Gabe is giving Jenna a tennis lesson."

"What's going on with Townsend?" he asked casually.

"Nothing. He's here for the stadium dedication. He'll give his speech on Wednesday, talk about what a great guy Carter was, then go back to Milwaukee. End of story."

He slanted her a glance. "I always thought the two of you would get together after Carter died."

"Nope," she said, even as the pain splintered her heart. "He's just a ghost from the past."

"I didn't like him," George admitted, "because I thought he was Tommy's father, that he'd taken off and left Amy behind. But he was good yesterday, standing up for you. Maybe he's not so bad after all."

"Wow," she managed to say. "The George Krippner seal of approval. But there's nothing between me and Gabe."

They'd reached the kitchen door. "Do you want to stay for dinner?" she asked.

"Nah," he said. "I'll give the girls a little more time to forget what a bear I was yesterday." He leaned down and kissed her cheek. "I'll see you later, Ken."

She wandered into the house. With both girls gone, the quiet echoed off the walls and filled her head. Maybe she could relax. She headed toward the stairs for the Lindsay Longford book she'd been reading, then stopped when she saw, through the windows beside the front door, a package sitting outside.

It was addressed to Gabe. From Milwaukee. Gabe hadn't told her he was expecting a package, she thought as she wrestled the box into the house. What did he need that was so heavy? He'd only be here a few more days.

Leaving it sitting in the hall, Kendall ran upstairs and retrieved her book.

The box wasn't any of her business. It belonged to a guest.

But she couldn't help glancing at it from time to time. What was in it?

CHAPTER SIXTEEN

Monday afternoon

GABE DUCKED and laughed as the tennis racquet whistled past his ear. "Hey, Jenna, does my head look like a tennis ball?" Keeping one hand on the steering wheel, he took hold of the racquet and pushed it gently to the floor.

"Wait until we get home, okay? We'll practice hitting balls against the garage wall."

"Okay," Jenna said, bouncing on the seat. "I had fun today, Uncle Gabe."

"I did, too." Jenna's excitement was contagious. Gabe had smiled so much that now his jaw hurt.

"Can we practice again tomorrow?" she asked, her eyes shining. Please?"

"Sure. As long as it's okay with your mom." Uncomplicated joy was an emotion he'd lost touch with a long time ago. He'd grab every opportunity to share in Jenna's.

The driveway was empty when they got home, so Smith had to be out snooping around somewhere. Gabe should have been following him today, but he'd promised Jenna a tennis lesson. Smith would have to wait.

After Gabe showed Jenna how to practice her returns against the garage wall, he headed toward the house. The box sat next to the door, with a plain label, just as he'd asked of his secretary. He smiled with satisfaction. His early-morning phone call had paid off.

Lifting the heavy package, he carried it up the stairs and deposited it in his room. It could wait until later.

The house was quiet and peaceful, with sun pouring golden light through the windows. Where was everybody?

Heading downstairs, he spotted Kendall in the living room asleep on the couch. Her hair was tousled and her light brown eyelashes lay against her cheeks like feathers. A book rested against her chest, and one hand dangled off the edge of the couch.

He'd never seen Kendall sleeping. She looked innocent and young. Vulnerable.

He wasn't used to seeing her this way, with her defenses down.

His heart rolled over in a wave of tenderness. He couldn't look away and he longed to gather her close, press his mouth against hers and revel in her taste.

Her eyes fluttered open. When she saw him, her lips curved into a soft smile. "Gabe."

"Hey, sleepyhead," he murmured, crouching next to the couch. He tucked a lock of hair behind her ear, let his hand linger on her cheek. "I didn't mean to wake you. Go back to sleep."

She put her hand over his, held it to her cheek. "I'm not sleeping," she said, her thick, raspy voice giving the lie to her words. She pressed his hand more snugly to her face and her eyes fluttered closed again.

"Kenny." Beneath her hand, he smoothed his fingers over the petal-soft skin of her cheek, felt her quiver in response. "You shouldn't have let me catch you sleeping," he whispered, his mouth hovering over hers. "It makes me want all kinds of things I can't have."

"Mmm. Me, too." She turned her face to press her lips into his palm, left them there. The slow in and out of her breathing filled his hand, rippled across his skin like fire.

She was asleep. She had no idea what she was saying, what she was doing. If he were an honorable man, he'd ease away from her and forget her words. Forget the feel of her mouth against his hand.

But he'd never been an honorable man where Kendall was concerned. He'd never been able to put her out of his mind, not even when she married his best friend. He'd savored every opportunity to touch her back then. Most of those moments had been accidental and innocent—bumping her arm while playing some game, helping her out of a car, passing her the salt at dinner.

But two of those moments hadn't been so innocent. They might have started out accidentally, but they'd quickly become carnal and greedy, drenched in heat and desire.

And Kendall had been an equal participant.

Gabe had waited far too long to see her sleep. To watch the rise and fall of her breath, to feel her melt into him. Telling himself to leave, he lingered all the same, savoring every breath of Kendall's against his skin.

When he slid his hand from beneath hers and pulled an afghan over her, Kendall's eyes fluttered open. "Gabe?" she said, her voice uncertain.

"It's okay, Kendall. You were taking a nap."

She shoved both hands through her hair, dark blond tendrils curling around her fingers. "I never have naps." Her eyes were heavy-lidded and bewildered as she blinked and studied the sunny room. "Where's Jenna? You were supposed to be playing tennis with her."

"She's hitting a tennis ball against the garage wall."

The muffled thump of the ball hitting brick could be heard, and Kendall stood up and walked to the window.

As she watched her daughter, she stretched, her movements slow and languid. Her shorts rose higher on her legs and her back bowed. From the side, Gabe saw her T-shirt stretch across her chest, saw the hard points of her nipples pressing into it.

Painfully aroused, he turned away. "I'll see you later, Kendall."

"Wait." She turned to face him, and he tried to avoid looking at her chest. "You have a package. In the hall."

"I saw it, thanks."

"What…?" He could see her curiosity—and also her determination not to ask questions. "Thank you for taking Jenna to play tennis."

"It was my pleasure."

He hurried to his room, anxious to get away from her. If he didn't, he'd wind up begging.

A half hour later, Gabe was stretching outside the front door, getting ready to go for a run, when a silver minivan pulled up. Shelby jumped out, tears pouring down her face.

"Shelby?" He put his hands on her shoulders, took in her red eyes and nose, the tracks of tears on her dusty face. "What's wrong? Are you hurt?"

Her lip quivered. "Where's Mom?"

A woman got out on the driver's side, looking flustered. "Where's Kendall?"

"She's in the yard, I think." He wrapped his arm around Shelby's shoulders, and she leaned into him. "What happened?"

A baby began to cry inside the car and the woman turned back. "Shelby can tell her. I have to go."

As the van pulled out of the driveway, Gabe called, "Kendall? Are you out here?"

Kneeling next to one of her flower beds, Kendall heard Gabe call, then realized that Shelby was crying. Dropping her trowel, she peeled off her gloves and ran toward the front of the house.

Gabe had his arm around Shelby's shoulders and was looking baffled and alarmed. When Kendall got close, Shelby flung herself into her mother's arms, sobbing.

"What is it, sweetheart?" she murmured, gently rocking her daughter. "What's wrong?" She forced herself to concentrate on Shelby and not look at Gabe.

"Sheila hurt her leg at practice," Shelby wailed. "She couldn't walk. They had to carry her off the field. They called her mom to take her to the hospital." She burst into tears again. "I'm afraid she's going to die."

Kendall's arms tightened. "People don't usually die

when they hurt their leg," she said. "Didn't Coach Ted tell you that she'd be okay?"

"No! He just said she wouldn't be able to play in our tournament next weekend. And that our team won't be able to be in the tournament now."

Kendall saw Gabe's shoulders relax, the panic fading from his face. She tried not to smile. Clearly, he'd never dealt with a ten-year-old girl in the midst of a meltdown. She brushed Shelby's tangled hair away from her face. "Are you upset about Sheila or upset about the tournament?"

"Both," she said, hiccupping a sob. "We practiced so hard for that tournament. And I don't want Sheila to die."

"Sheila's not going to die, Shel," Kendall said calmly. "I'll call her mother in a little while and find out what's wrong with her leg. Okay?"

"But we still can't play in the tournament."

"Why not? Why can't you just play with one less person?"

"Because Madison and Ashley are going to be gone, so they can't sub. And now we don't have enough players."

Gabe edged closer. "I have an idea, Shelby."

"What?" Her face was suddenly full of hope.

Gabe glanced at Kendall, seeking permission to talk. She nodded.

"Elena's a pretty good soccer player. Maybe you could ask her to play in the tournament with your team."

"Yeah! Elena could play." The tears disappeared, replaced by excitement. "Let's go ask her." She pulled away from Kendall and hopped up and down. "Right now."

"Not right now," Kendall said firmly. "You go inside and get cleaned up, then we'll think about it."

"Okay." She raced into the house.

"I shouldn't have said that, should I?" Gabe said ruefully.

"It's not a bad idea," she answered, gazing toward the orchard. "But it may not work."

"Why?"

"Elena would have to have a uniform and shoes and all the rest of the equipment. And I doubt her parents could afford that."

"Could she borrow a uniform from one of the girls who isn't playing?"

"Probably. But she couldn't really borrow shoes or socks or shin guards."

"Don't take this the wrong way. I'm not trying to interfere. But I'd be happy to pay for her equipment."

Kendall forced herself to look away from Gabe's hands. She remembered waking from her uncharacteristic nap and finding his hand on her face. Remembered her own hand covering his, pressing it closer to her skin. Remembered the heat that had flowed through her, thick and intoxicating.

"It's a good idea," she said, not meeting his eyes. "But I'm not sure Elena's parents will agree."

"What about Shelby's coach? Do you need to talk to him?"

"Probably. I'd better go do that now."

Gabe followed her inside. "Weren't you going for a run?" she asked.

"I needed a diversion," he replied. "The drama of Shelby's soccer tournament is much more interesting."

She smiled and shook her head, just relieved he hadn't brought up those moments on the couch. "She's so competitive. She's been talking about this tournament in Green Bay for weeks."

"Then I hope we can find a way to make it work." He brushed her face, his fingers barely touching her skin.

She stilled and the electricity crackled.

He gave her a half smile. "Dirt," he explained.

"Oh." She rubbed at her face, but her skin still tingled where Gabe had made contact. And then Shelby pounded down the stairs and Gabe and Kendall jumped apart. "Let's go to Elena's," Shelby shouted.

"I need to call Coach Ted first," Kendall said. "To make sure it's okay if we ask her."

"He'll say yes," Shelby said. "Why wouldn't he?"

"Shelby, let's go outside and wait for your mom," Gabe suggested, steering her toward the door. "We'll watch Jenna practice her tennis."

Kendall watched them disappear. Gabe seemed so in tune with the girls. So aware of their moods. How had he managed that in just a few days?

Watching him with her daughters was a bittersweet experience.

But it wasn't fair to compare Gabe to Carter. Her husband had been much younger than Gabe was now when the girls were born. Carter hadn't had a chance to grow into fatherhood.

Whereas Gabe seemed to be a natural. As Kendall waited for the coach to answer his phone, she leaned through the doorway of her office to look out the front door. Gabe and Shelby stood next to the garage while Jenna hit the ball. She was showing off, Kendall realized, her heart melting. And Gabe was encouraging her.

He understood Jenna's insecurity in regard to sports. And he knew that she needed to be better than Shelby at something. Kendall's heart melted a little more.

"Hello?"

The voice of Shelby's coach in her ear drew her attention from the scene outside. "Hi, Ted, this is Kendall Van Allen. I have an idea."

TWENTY MINUTES LATER, Kendall and Gabe stood in the orchard with Elena's mother. The girls had run off to find Elena, and now Mrs. Montoya looked from one of the adults to the other, puzzled and wary. "You want Elena to be on your daughter's soccer team?"

Kendall touched Gabe's arm, signaling him to let her speak. "They're supposed to be in a tournament next weekend and several of her teammates can't play. They need another player, and Shelby thought of Elena." Kendall smiled. "She said Elena is a good soccer player."

Elena's mother gave her an answering smile, her pride evident. "She plays with my husband and sons."

"Would she be able to play with Shelby's team?"

The woman's smile faded and she glanced away. "I don't think that would be a good idea."

Gabe squeezed Kendall's arm, then stepped forward. "Mrs. Montoya, she could borrow a uniform from one of the other girls. And since she would be doing the team a favor, they would provide any other equipment she needed. Mrs. Van Allen will make sure she gets to the games and back. Will you talk to your husband and think about it?"

Mrs. Montoya studied them for a moment, then nodded. "Yes, we will talk about this." She hesitated. "Elena likes soccer very much."

"And we'd like to have her play with Shelby's team," Kendall said.

She turned when she heard the girls behind her, running through the orchard. They were dribbling a soccer ball through the trees, laughing and calling to each other. Even Jenna was trying to participate. "Let's go practice," Shelby yelled, and they took off toward the house.

Elena's mother watched them over Gabe's shoulder and her eyes softened. "We'll let you know."

"Thank you," Kendall said to Elena's mother. "We'll wait to hear from you."

She and Gabe headed home, following the girls. "Thank you," she said to Gabe.

"For what?"

"For saying the team would provide the equipment. For protecting Mrs. Montoya's pride."

"I understand about pride," he said quietly.

"No one wants to take charity," Kendall said. She

kicked at a clod of dirt beneath one of the trees. She felt Gabe watching her, but she didn't look up.

"This conversation isn't about the Montoyas, is it?" he finally said.

When Kendall didn't answer, he continued. "When I asked if I could pay for Shelby to take the acting classes, did you think that was charity?"

She looked at the ground, concentrating on not tripping over a root. "I don't like charity any more than the Montoyas."

He pulled her around to face him. "You think I offered to pay because I felt sorry for you?"

She shrugged. "Didn't you?"

He stared down at her but she still couldn't meet his eyes. "You know I didn't, Kendall."

She snapped her head up. "Okay, smart guy, then why didn't I jump at your offer?"

"You're afraid I'm getting too close. To both you and the girls."

"I already said you could have a relationship with the girls."

"What about you?"

"What about me?"

"Do we have a relationship?"

She pulled her arm away from him. "I don't know what we have." Oh, she knew. The heat and the need were consuming her.

And so was the guilt.

"You don't? I thought you were a lot smarter than that, Kenny."

She heard a hint of laughter in his voice and looked up at him. Big mistake. Beneath the smile in his eyes she saw longing and desire. And something else, something that scared her. Something she'd stopped dreaming about a long time ago.

Her heart pounded and her nerves jumped. "I must not be very smart," she whispered. "Because if I were, I would have closed the door the moment I saw you standing there. I wouldn't have ever let you into my house."

"Why, Kenny? What are you afraid of?"

"You know. You know exactly what I'm afraid of."

"I do." His mouth hovered a breath away from hers. "Because I'm afraid of the same thing."

When he kissed her, she closed her eyes and let desire carry her away. She pressed into him, legs to legs, chest to chest, and forgot everything but Gabe.

The sounds of the girls, shouting and laughing, slowly penetrated the fog of desire that filled her head. She opened her eyes to find him watching her. He licked at her mouth, sucked on her lower lip, then eased away. "I know," he said, brushing his mouth over her ear. "Not the right time or place." He nipped at her neck, made her whimper. "I've been patient for a long time, Kendall. I can be patient for a little longer."

He kissed her again, a deep, searing kiss. "How about you?"

"No. Yes," she managed to reply.

He brushed her hair away from her face, smoothed her shirt. "Soon," he murmured.

CHAPTER SEVENTEEN

Monday evening

GEORGE KRIPPNER slouched on the couch and stared moodily at the television as he clicked the remote control, flipping from a news show to a stand-up comic to a baseball game to an old, romantic movie. When Cary Grant and Grace Kelly kissed and fireworks exploded outside their window, he pressed the off button and threw the remote on the coffee table. It slid off and clattered to the floor.

Nudging his running shoes out of the way, he stood up and went into the kitchen. He'd intended to go for a run, had even dressed for it, but the hell with that. He pulled a bottle of beer from the refrigerator and took a long drink.

Someone knocked at his door and he paused in midsip, then he set the bottle on the counter and went to see who was there. It was probably one of the kids in the building, selling candy for their baseball or soccer team. They all knew he was an easy touch.

Pasting a smile on his face, he opened the door. The smile faded as he saw Amy standing there.

He fought to control the instinctive burst of joy he felt at seeing her. "Amy," he finally said.

He glanced around his messy living room and cringed. An empty tortilla chips bag lay on the floor, and a bowl on the table held the crusty, dried-up remains of salsa. Three pairs of dirty socks festooned the couch and sticky rings from beer and coffee dotted the coffee table. Magazines and books were scattered across the floor.

This looked like the home of an utterly pathetic loser.

Red crept into her face as the moment lengthened and grew more awkward. "Hello, George," she said, straightening her shoulders. "I know you don't want to see me, but may I come in for a moment anyway?"

"Yeah," he said, stepping back from the door, scrambling for something to say. "Sorry. I was expecting someone else."

Surprise and shock passed over Amy's face, followed by a look of deep pain. She thought he'd been expecting a woman.

Before he could say anything, Amy thrust out her hand. "You left this at my house. I figured you'd want it back."

She uncurled her hand to reveal the black velvet ring box. His heart pulled tight when he saw it, remembering how happy he'd been when he bought it, how excited he'd been to give it to her.

He stared, unable to take it back. Unable to make that final gesture, to confirm that all his dreams were in ruins.

Amy's fingers tightened around the small box, then she placed it carefully on top of his television. "I'm sorry I came over," she said quietly. "Sorry I interrupted. But I didn't want you to think I'd keep the ring."

She turned away, fumbling with the doorknob. "Amy, wait," George said. He wasn't sure why he'd stopped her, just that he didn't want her to leave. Not yet.

She stood there, her back to him, her hand on the knob. Waiting. He had no idea what to say.

"I didn't think you'd keep the ring," he finally said. "You're not that kind of person."

"Thank you for that, I guess." She pulled open the door. "Goodbye, George."

"Hold on, Amy. How's Tommy?"

"Tommy is fine," she said, and he thought he heard her sniffle as she slipped out of his apartment.

Don't let her leave. The words pounded at him and he took a step toward the door, then another. But he couldn't make himself open it, couldn't bring himself to call her back. Yet again, his pride reminded him that Tommy was Carter Van Allen's son. And by the time he'd shoved that pride away and opened the door, Amy was driving away.

GABE WALKED INTO Van Allen House just as the sun was dropping into the bay. He'd been following Dylan Smith since shortly before dinner, but he hadn't learned a thing.

The reporter had driven to the marina in Sturgeon Falls, then wandered around the docks. Was he looking for Carter's cousin, Charlotte? He'd been awfully interested in her the other day.

There was no sign of Charlotte, or whoever it was that Smith was looking for. The reporter drove to the public library and Gabe trailed behind, feeling faintly foolish. Despite being in the security business, he didn't enjoy this cloak-and-dagger stuff.

By the time Smith returned a batch of microfiches and left the library at closing time, Gabe was sick of the game. When the reporter pulled into the parking lot at the Blue Door, Gabe kept going.

Lights were on, but the house was silent. He didn't see the girls or Kendall. He headed toward his room but then stopped. He was too edgy, had too much restless energy to make himself sit at his computer and work.

He wanted to see Kendall. He needed to see her. But when he went back downstairs and into the kitchen she wasn't there. Frowning, Gabe stepped into the shadows beyond the door, wondering where she could be.

The sun was a thin slice of orange, suspended over the water of the bay. It gave off just enough light to let Gabe see Kendall sitting in one of the beach chairs.

As he approached her, he saw she'd been reading a book, which now lay on her lap. She rested her head against the back of the chair. "Hello, Gabe," she said as he got closer.

"What are you doing down here?" he asked, easing onto another chair.

"Just being." She glanced at him, then closed her eyes again. "The girls are in bed, and I didn't feel like sitting in the house."

"Want some company?"

She lifted one shoulder. "Suit yourself."

"Did you hear from Elena's mother?"

Kendall smiled. "She said yes. Shelby and Elena and Jenna played soccer until all three of them were exhausted. That's why the girls are in bed and asleep already."

"I'm glad it worked out," he said, pleased to think he'd put the smile on her face.

She looked over at him. "You're so good with the girls," she said, her voice soft. "Do you spend a lot of time with someone who has kids in Milwaukee?"

"Are you asking me if I'm dating anyone?"

Even in the dimming light Gabe saw her face redden as she turned away. "That's none of my business."

"You don't think so?"

"Of course not."

"I'd like it to be your business."

Her hand tightened on the arm of the chair, then she leaned back again.

He studied her in the fading light. Tall pine trees swayed in the gentle breeze, setting their fresh scent adrift on the air. Kendall looked mysterious, her face in shadow and her pale legs gleaming in the dim light.

"You look like some exotic creature of the night," he said in a low voice.

Her mouth curved. "I don't think exotic creatures of the night are usually in bed by ten o'clock."

His blood heated as he took her in, sprawled in the chair, completely relaxed. "It's almost ten o'clock now. Are you going to disappear?"

She regarded him intently. "Why did you come down to the beach, Gabe?"

"Because you were here." He watched her quietly, until his heart steadied. "I dream about this beach sometimes."

"You and Carter spent a lot of time here."

"I'm not with Carter in my dreams," he said.

"Who are you with?" she whispered.

"Don't you know, Kenny?"

She held his gaze and swallowed hard, her throat rippling in the fading light. "Tell me."

"You. I'm with you. And we're not sitting peacefully in chairs."

"What are we doing?"

Gabe looked at her as heat rushed through him. "Everything. We're doing everything I've dreamed about for too many years to count."

Instead of looking away, as he'd half expected, she continued to watch him. Her lips opened and her eyes grew slumberous. "Why, Gabe?" she asked. "I haven't seen you for seven years. Why would you dream about me?"

"I've always wanted you." As she continued to hold his gaze, it felt as if she were touching him. "I wanted you before you married Carter. I wanted you after you married him, and I wanted you after he died. I knew I couldn't have you, but I wanted you just the same. You're part of me, and you always will be."

"I wanted you, too," she said, her voice so low that he could barely hear her. "Not at first. I was too infatuated with Carter. But the more time you spent with us, the more I thought about you. Especially after…"

"After that Fourth of July." He closed his eyes. "You have no idea how hard it was to pretend that kiss didn't matter. To pretend everything was normal."

"Why did you?" she asked. "Why did you back off?"

"What should I have done? Ask you to break your engagement with Carter? My best friend? Ask you to run away with me?"

When she didn't answer, he rolled out of his chair and knelt next to hers. It was too dark now to read the expression in her eyes. "You acted the same, Kenny. As if nothing had happened. Like you had forgotten all about it. I thought that was what you wanted."

She turned to face him. "I never forgot," she whispered. "You made me feel things I'd never felt with Carter. Before or after."

He stared at her, not sure he'd heard her correctly. "My God, Kenny," he breathed. "What am I supposed to say to that?"

She closed her eyes and he felt heat rise in her face. "Nothing. Forget I said it. I don't know why I did."

"Too late," he answered. "You think I could forget that?" He leaned over the arm of the chair, pressed his mouth to her neck. "Not a chance."

She shuddered beneath his lips, reached out to draw him closer. "What are we going to do, Gabe? I don't want to feel this way. I don't think you do, either."

He trailed his mouth over her throat, nipped at her collarbone. Let the need wash over him in an endless wave. He felt himself drowning and welcomed the sensation. "I didn't plan on this happening. I knew it wouldn't be smart, and I thought you wanted nothing to do with me. But I'm tired of pretending. And knowing that you want me, too..." He moved up to her mouth, desperate to taste her. "Tell me to stop, Kendall. Because I don't know if I can stop myself."

Kendall closed her eyes, lost herself in Gabe's touch, in his mouth. She'd avoided him for so long, tried so hard to stay away from him. Why, just this once, couldn't she have what she'd craved for so many years? Why couldn't she be selfish and think only of herself? And Gabe.

He kissed her slowly. As if he was storing the memory inside him. When he drew her lower lip into his mouth, sucking it gently, she moaned and his tongue swept inside.

She tried to press closer to him, but the arm of her chair was in the way. With a frustrated growl, she leaned over the wood, needing to feel Gabe against her. She wanted his solidity, his strength.

"Hold on," he murmured, sliding into the chair next to her. It was too small for both of them to fit into, so he eased her on top. Pushing her hair out of her face, he held her steady as he studied her.

"You're so beautiful," he whispered. "I always thought you were the most beautiful woman I'd ever seen."

She slid her fingers into his hair. The only other time she'd touched his hair, it had been cold and wet with lake water. Now it slipped through her fingers like a soft summer night, caressing her skin and smelling like

Gabe. Like the scent she'd kept in her heart for all these years.

"Kenny." He struggled to sit up, and she let him go. "I want to see you," he said. He ran his hands down her arms, smoothed his fingers over the tiny band of skin exposed between her shirt and shorts. "I want to touch you. I want to know you in the moonlight."

He cupped her through her shirt, leaning forward to brush his mouth lightly over one nipple. When she sucked in a breath, he brushed his mouth over the other. "Can I take that as a yes?"

"Yes," she said, her voice shaking. "Please, Gabe."

He picked up her hand, then slowly pressed her hand to his heart. Let her feel it racing beneath her fingers.

"I'm shaking just as much as you are," he murmured. "I've wanted you for so long."

He grasped the bottom of her shirt and eased it over her head, letting it fall to the ground. Then he simply stared at her lacy black bra.

"Holy Mother of God," he breathed. "Is this what you've been wearing beneath those T-shirts?"

She smiled, intoxicated by her effect on him. "I like sexy underwear."

"So I see." He cupped his hands over her breasts, slid his thumbs over her nipples. An involuntary cry escaped her, and Gabe's eyes darkened.

"Is there more where this came from?" he asked as he reached around to unclasp the undergarment.

"I have a whole drawerful," she answered. Sexy underwear was her secret vice, her one indulgence. Up until now, no one else had known.

The lace fell into his hands, and her breasts were bared to him. "We'll have a fashion show," he said, his voice thick. "Some other time."

For a long moment he just stared at her. Then he reached out, brushed his finger gently against one nipple. She felt the shock of it all the way through her body. When he touched her again, it tightened into a hard little nub.

"Kenny," he said with a sigh before drawing her gently into his mouth.

She shifted on his lap, feeling his erection press into her, and he groaned against her. "Hold still," he said. "Or I'll embarrass myself."

She fumbled with the buttons on his shirt, needing to feel his skin against hers. But her fingers were clumsy and she couldn't get them to work. Finally, frustrated, she yanked the shirt over his head and tossed it aside. She spread her hands over his chest, which was solidly muscled and covered in dark hair. When he tried to turn her over, they both got stuck in the chair.

"Hold on," Gabe said, lifting her up and off. He grabbed the blanket that had been covering the chair, took her hand and led her into the grove of pines. He smoothed the blanket over a bed of needles on the ground and drew her down next to him.

"Better than the beach," he said. "Less sand." He brushed the hair from her face.

"Hmm." She reached for the waistband of his slacks,

unbuttoning them and drawing them down his legs. "Now it's my turn to look at you."

She brushed her hand over him and felt his response. But when she bent to take him in her mouth, he stopped her.

"Not this time," he said. "I've waited too long for this for it to be over in a moment." He peeled her shorts down her legs, stopping when he saw the scrap of lace that matched her bra. "Oh, yeah," he said, sliding his finger beneath elastic. "Who would have thought you'd be so naughty?"

"Up until now, it's been to remind myself what being naughty was like," she said.

His hand tightened on her hips. "Let's find out."

He swept the lace down her legs, then kissed her, a joining of mouths that had her pulling him close. After he fumbled in the pocket of his jeans, Kendall opened the foil packet and slid a condom onto him. And when he eased into her, she felt as if she was where she was meant to be.

Gabe moved slowly at first and she savored every thrust, every sensation that spiraled tighter inside. But as the fire ignited and spread, she wrapped her legs around him and pulled him closer.

"Gabe," she gasped, clutching at him as sensation swept through her. Teetering on the edge, she rose to meet his thrusts. With a guttural groan he poured himself into her and she shattered in his arms.

CHAPTER EIGHTEEN

Monday evening

THEY LAY TANGLED together for a long time, their sweat-slicked skin cooling in the night air. Finally Gabe pulled the edges of the blanket over Kendall. "You must be cold."

"Mmm," she said, curling more tightly into him. "You're keeping me warm."

He pressed a kiss into her hair and tightened his arms around her. "I know better ways to keep you warm."

His erection stirred against her belly and she smiled. "Want to tell me about them?"

"I'd rather demonstrate." He nuzzled her neck, then kissed her deeply. Desire spread through her again and she wrapped her arms around Gabe and drew him close.

She swung her leg over his, and he rolled her onto her back. Something sharp poked.

"Yowch." She sat up and reached beneath the blanket, pulling out a pinecone.

He tossed it away and bent to kiss the bruised spot. "I guess we could have picked a better location."

"This is perfect," she said, staring at the moon over the lake. "It's magic."

"It's not the lake or the night or the moon. It's you. You're the magic. You always have been."

The guilt she'd managed to suppress for the past hour came roaring back. "Don't say that, Gabe. I don't want to talk about the past. Not tonight."

"How about the future?" he said, brushing his face along her neck. The rasp of his beard stubble made her shiver. "Can we talk about that?"

What *was* the future? Would Gabe be part of it? She had no idea. She didn't know what she wanted, other than this stolen moment. "Not the future, either."

"No past, no future? Just now?" he said, his words rumbling against her neck.

"Yes. Just now. In fact, I don't want to talk at all." Before he could answer, she fastened her mouth to his and pushed him onto the ground.

Later, when she opened her eyes again, the moon had slipped below the lake. Stars splashed across the sky in the darkness, a billion twinkling dots of light above them. She was cold, and Gabe wrapped them both in the blanket.

"This probably wasn't the best place to get naked," he said. "This is still the North Woods and it's still early June." He stood up, walked to the chairs and retrieved their clothing. His skin gleamed, the faint light reflecting off his broad shoulders and strong legs. After he handed Kendall her shorts, blouse and underwear, he pulled on his own slacks and shirt.

Tucking her bra in the pocket of her shorts, she

pulled on the rest of her clothes. Then she picked up the blanket and gave it a shake.

Gabe helped her fold it, then tucked it under his arm and slid his hand into hers. She clung to him as they made their way back to the house.

She busied herself locking up, feeling awkward and unsettled. What did they do now? Say good-night and go to their own bedrooms? Share a bed and worry that one of the girls might come looking for her?

Before she could say anything, Gabe drew her into the living room. "You're uncomfortable. That's the last thing I wanted."

"I'm not sure how to act. I've known you for so long—" *wanted you for so long* "—and everything is different now." She leaned into him, needing to feel his strength. "Do I take you to my room? Do I go to your room with you?"

"Do you pretend this never happened?" he murmured into her ear.

She pushed away from him. "I don't want to talk about that right now."

This time, instead of letting it go, he took her hands. "You didn't want to talk about it earlier, but we have to talk about it sometime." He smoothed one hand over her face, lingering there. "*I'm* not going to pretend this never happened."

His words pounded at her heart, made her want to weep. "No," she said quietly. "I won't pretend this never happened. I'm glad it did. I wanted it to happen. I've wanted you for so long, Gabe."

She twisted away from him and stared out the window into the dark, seeing nothing. But she couldn't think clearly when she was so close to him. When she could see his eyes, see what he felt. For her.

"I was consumed by guilt the entire time I was married to Carter," she said in a low voice. "Because he wasn't enough. The whole time we were married, you were there, too."

She leaned her forehead against the cool glass. "I couldn't give myself completely to Carter because a piece of me belonged to you. Do you know how that made me feel?"

He wrapped his arms around her from behind and kissed her again. "Yes. I know exactly how you felt." He drew her against him, solid and strong. He felt like a man she could rely on. A man who would be there for her, no matter what.

"I carried just as much guilt as you did," he acknowledged. "You were my best friend's wife. And still I dreamed about you." His arms tightened around her. "You were there in all my fantasies."

She wanted to stay like this forever, safe in Gabe's arms. Protected. His heart beating against her.

Even so, she forced herself to move away. "I need time to figure this out, Gabe. I don't know how to get past the guilt. How not to feel like a bad person for wanting you."

"You're not bad." He swung her around so they were face-to-face. "You were stuck in an impossible situation, and you behaved honorably."

"I didn't behave so honorably on that last night," she whispered. "At the holiday party. When I kissed you."

"We had no choice, Kendall. You know that. When Phil, Carter's friend, held mistletoe over our heads and insisted we kiss, we had to do it. We had to play along and act like it was a big joke. You know what would have happened if we'd refused. That drunken idiot Phil would have teased Carter mercilessly. It would have been awkward for everyone."

"But it wasn't just a party kiss, was it? It wasn't an innocent, play-along-with-the-joke peck on the cheek. You kissed me. And I kissed you back. I meant it. And so did you."

"We didn't seek each other out," he reminded her. "We didn't betray Carter."

"Not physically, no. But I betrayed him in my mind. So many times. And that's just as bad." She wanted to look away, wanted to bury the guilt deep inside her, but she forced herself to face him. "I don't feel guilty because I kissed you. I feel guilty because while I was kissing you, I wished you were my husband. And my husband left the party after I kissed you, and then he died."

"And the man you were kissing killed your husband."

"I didn't say that."

"But you were thinking it." He gave her a strained smile.

"It was an accident. I know that. I've known it all along—even when I was blaming you. You didn't intend to crash the car. The weather was bad and you lost control. You didn't intend for Carter to die. But I can't forget that the last time I saw him, I was betraying him."

"Punishing yourself for the rest of your life won't bring him back." Gabe slid his hands down her arms and took her hands. "Haven't you done this long enough?"

"I can't get past the guilt." She squeezed his hands, then let him go. "I don't know how."

"Okay, Kenny." He drew her back into his arms, and she held him tightly. "Let's not talk about it anymore tonight. I'd rather just hold you. I'd rather kiss you." He brushed his mouth over hers, and she opened to him. One touch, one kiss and she was trembling in his arms.

"Let's wait and talk about this when we're both less emotional." He kissed her again, and he was hard against her once more. "I want to hold you tonight while you sleep, to wake up with you in the morning. I'll always want that. But I'm not going to push you."

She wanted him to push her. One more kiss, one more slow sweep of his hand down her back, and she'd be dragging him to her room. She didn't know what to do about the future with Gabe, but she knew what she wanted tonight. She wanted to spend the night with him, to hold him while he slept. To make love with him again.

Before she could say anything, the stairs creaked, then a door above them closed. Gabe's mouth flattened. "Smith." He ran up the stairs, two at a time, and Kendall ran after him.

By the time she reached the top of the stairs, he'd flung open the door to Dylan's room. "What the hell were you doing, Smith, spying on me and Kendall?"

Dylan crossed his arms and leaned against the dresser. "I wasn't spying on you. I started down the stairs to get something to drink, and when I heard you talking, I went back up to my room. I didn't want to intrude."

"Oh, that's a good one. You rummage through Kendall's garbage and pull out her personal papers, and you expect us to believe you didn't want to intrude?"

The reporter's face turned a dull red. "That was a mistake," he said quietly. "I was looking for connections with Carter's family and I went too far. Kendall took the papers, and I was glad she did. I shouldn't have taken that stuff."

"Easy to say now."

Dylan turned his palms up. "Think what you want. I'm obviously not going to change your mind."

Kendall grabbed Gabe's arm and yanked him out of the room. "Come on, Gabe. That's enough. Good night, Dylan."

He shook off her arm. "I'm not finished with him."

"Yes, you are." She opened the door to his room and pulled him inside, then shut the door. "You're going to make it worse," she said in a harsh whisper. "Now he's going to wonder what we were talking about."

Gabe stared at her, his eyes hot, his jaw working. Finally he sighed. "You're right. He either heard us or he didn't. And we can't change that now."

"You're not going to go after him again, are you?"

"No," he said. "As much as I'd like to punch him, I can control myself."

"Good." She grabbed onto the front of his shirt and gave it a shake. "No fighting. I don't want you to get hurt."

"I can take care of myself. You should be worried about Smith."

"He doesn't matter." Kendall took a deep breath. "It's you, Gabe. I care about you."

He held her gaze. "So tonight wasn't a mistake?"

"No," she said, knowing it was the truth. She stepped into his arms, holding him tightly. "Whatever else happens, it wasn't a mistake."

"What happens next, Kenny?"

"I don't know." She leaned against him, needing his strength. "I have a lot of thinking to do."

"And you're going to do that thinking alone."

She smiled and touched his face. "Yes. I can't think when I'm with you."

His smile looked forced. "I guess I'll just have to stick close and not give you a chance to overthink this."

"Good night, Gabe." She pressed against him for one last kiss, soaking in the memory of him and the feel of him against her. "I'll see you in the morning."

CHAPTER NINETEEN

Tuesday morning

GABE HESITATED outside the kitchen the next morning. He could hear Kendall working by the stove. One of the girls giggled, and then a pan clattered against the countertop.

As if this encounter with Kendall wasn't already awkward enough, he had to deal with the morning after in front of her daughters. But he wouldn't back away now. Plastering a smile on his face, he pushed open the door.

"Uncle Gabe!" Shelby called. She hopped off a stool and grabbed his hand. "Come see what I'm doing."

Kendall smiled at him, her eyes softening. "Good morning, Gabe."

There was no self-consciousness in her eyes, just a welcome. He ached to kiss her. Instead, he opened the refrigerator and reached for a carton of orange juice.

"Good morning, Kendall. Did you sleep well last night?" he asked.

Kendall's eyes twinkled. "I was a little…restless. How about you?"

"Me, too." He bit his lip to hide his grin. "Must have been the moon keeping you awake."

"Must have been." She nodded at the carton in his hand. "No coffee this morning?"

"I need some instant energy. I'm feeling a little worn out. And drained."

A smile quivered and pink tinged her cheeks. Before she could respond, Shelby tugged at Gabe's arm.

"Uncle Gabe!" Impatient, she drew him away. "Look what I'm doing."

He turned away reluctantly. "What's that?" he asked, peering into a bowl of dark brown batter that Shelby held out. "Aren't you too old to be making mud pies?"

"It's chocolate-cherry muffins," she exclaimed. "My favorite. That's what we're having for breakfast. And I'm making them."

"You're making them?" He raised his eyebrows. "I thought your mom was the baker in the family. Have you been secretly making all those breakfast muffins?"

"No, silly," she said. "I'm just helping Mom today."

"That's good, Shel," he said. "It sounds as if your mom is a little tired today. Probably she can use the help."

Kendall turned away, but he saw the grin on her face. "Let's put the cherries in the batter and get them in the oven," she said. "I'm sure Gabe is hungry."

"Okay." Shelby dumped in a cup of dried cherries, spilling some of them on the counter. "Oops." She scooped up the runaways and added them to the bowl. After Shelby had helped spoon batter into the muffin pan, she slid off the stool. "Can I set the timer?" she asked.

"Fifteen minutes," Kendall said as she wiped off the drips.

Shelby punched the buttons to set the timer, then skipped out the back door. "I'm going to practice soccer while the muffins cook."

Gabe watched her run down the steps, kick her soccer ball and start dribbling across the lawn. Then he reached for Kendall. "Good morning," he murmured against her lips.

"You already said that." She smiled as she looped her arms around his neck.

"I know, but my good morning just got better." He kissed her, meaning to keep it light, but heat exploded instantly. Kendall pressed closer, her arms tightening.

Gabe leaned back, framing Kendall's face in his hands. "Could I have done that in front of Shelby?" he murmured.

Kendall eased away from him, no longer smiling. "I don't know, Gabe. You said you'd give me time."

"I was hoping you'd had a revelation during your restless night."

"I did. I was sorry I made you leave," she whispered. "But that's not the kind of revelation you want."

"It's a beginning." He smoothed his hand down her cheek. "What do you want me to do, Kenny? The dedication ceremony is tomorrow. I have business to take care of afterward, but do I come back? Do I think about moving my business here?"

"I'm trying," she said, wiping her hands on her jeans. "I'm going to go through some things I should have gotten rid of a long time ago. Okay? I have to start there."

"All right, sweetheart. I'll let you do this your way." He kissed her again, more deeply. "But I really don't want to sleep alone tonight. Do you?"

"No," she whispered against his lips. "I don't. I missed you too much last night."

His body tightened in anticipation. "That's a start."

He heard footsteps clattering down the stairs and pulled away. By the time Jenna burst into the kitchen, he was two feet from Kendall.

"Mom! Is it time to go?" Her gaze darted to a single red rose sitting in a bud vase on the counter. "That's pretty. Where did it come from?"

"Mr. Smith gave me that," Kendall said, and Gabe felt an unpleasant flash of jealousy.

"Oh. So is it time to go?" Jenna repeated.

"After breakfast, Jen," Kendall replied. She glanced at Gabe. "The girls and I are going into town to decorate the stadium for tomorrow. Would you like to help?"

He thought of the box upstairs. This would be a perfect time to set up its contents. "Thanks, but I have some work to do," he said. "And don't worry about breakfast. Just leave a couple of Shelby's muffins on the counter." He ruffled Jenna's hair. "Have fun. I can't wait to see what you guys do."

After leaving the kitchen he headed upstairs and locked the door to his room. Then he opened the box and took out the equipment and tools he'd asked his assistant to send.

LATER THAT AFTERNOON, Kendall sat on the beach with her book, watching Gabe build a sand castle with Shelby, Jenna and Elena. It was a warm day for early June and the girls had begged to play in the sand.

"It has to be a Harry Potter castle," Jenna said. "It has to be magic."

"Okay, Jen, how do we make it magic?" Gabe asked.

"It has to have lots of towers. And a dragon."

"You can't make a dragon out of sand," Shelby said scornfully. "Right, Elena?"

"Maybe we should look in the book to see if there are dragons," Elena answered. She glanced around. "Is the book here?"

"It's in the house," Jenna said. "Okay, no dragons. But we need lots of towers."

"We need more water to make the towers," Shelby said, thrusting a bucket at Gabe.

"This isn't fair," Gabe protested, hiding a smile. "Why do I have to do all the hard work?"

"Because you're our slave," Jenna said, bouncing up and down. "Remember? You said you'd be our slave if we took the garbage cans out to the road for Mom."

"Did I really say that?" he asked, walking to the edge of the water and filling his bucket. "I don't remember saying that."

"You did say it," Jenna cried, turning to Kendall. "Mom! You remember, don't you?"

"Oh, yeah. I remember," Kendall said, every one of the stolen moments with Gabe vivid in her memory.

"Gee, how could I have forgotten that conversation?" Gabe asked Kendall in an innocent voice. "Am I just getting old? Or is it lack of blood to the brain?"

Fighting a grin, Kendall opened her book and pretended to read as Gabe brought back the water and the girls worked on the castle.

A few minutes later, George called out, "Hey, you guys. Are you having fun without me?"

Kendall twisted in her chair and smiled at her brother. "Hey, yourself. What are you doing here in the middle of a workday?"

He bent and kissed her cheek. "Just came by to see my favorite sister and my favorite nieces."

"We're your only nieces," Jenna said with a giggle. "And Mom is your only sister."

"Then I guess it's a good thing you're my favorites," George said with a grin. He squatted next to the misshapen turrets made of crumbling sand. "Good castle, guys."

"It's Harry Potter's castle," Elena said.

"Yeah?"

"This is our friend Elena." Shelby remembered her manners and introduced her friend.

"Hey, Elena," George said.

"Uncle Gabe is helping us," Jenna informed him. "He has to, 'cause he's our slave."

"Is that right?" George gave Gabe a tiny smile. "I'd make him work harder if he was my slave."

As the girls slopped more sand onto the pile, George wandered over to the chair next to Kendall's and sat down. She closed her book and looked at him.

"What's going on?" she asked in a low voice.

"Why do you think something is going on? I stop by all the time."

"Yeah, you do. But you usually don't look so sad."

George looked away, staring at Gabe and the girls. "Amy came over last night. To give me back the ring. I'd left it at her house on Saturday."

Kendall sat up. "Did you take it?"

"No." He closed his eyes. "I didn't take it, but she just put it down. And walked away."

"You didn't try to talk to her?"

He pressed his hands to his face. "I wanted to. But by the time I realized it, she'd already left."

Kendall reached over and took his hand. "What are you going to do?"

"I don't know." He looked at her with weary eyes. "I thought everything was perfect," he said. "Then she told me about Carter."

"Now things aren't perfect anymore," she said. "And that's what's bothering you?"

George shrugged his shoulders. "I don't know what's bothering me," he muttered.

She reached down and scooped up two handfuls of sand, then closed her fists. "This is what you want, right?" she said, holding them up. "Perfection."

"Doesn't everyone?"

"There's no such thing." She opened her fingers a little and let the sand sift through them. "This is real life." She closed one fist again, but let the sand continue to flow out of the other. "Nothing is perfect. Do you want this?"

She opened the closed fist to show him the sand that was left. "Not perfect, but still good. Or this." She opened the other fist to show her empty hand. "Nothing at all."

She dusted the sand from her hands and took his. "If you love Amy, it doesn't matter what happened in the past, does it? And if you love Tommy, it doesn't matter who his father is. All that matters is what you want."

George looked at Gabe and the girls, watching them laugh as they threw wet sand at their misshapen creation. "That's what I want," he said. "A family. I want to build sand castles with Tommy and Amy." He looked over at her. "Do you think it's too late for us?"

Kendall glanced over at Gabe. "I don't think it's ever too late. But I'm not the person you should be asking. You need to ask Amy."

George nodded. "I screwed up, big-time, didn't I?"

"Yeah, you did. And now you have to fix it."

He leaned down and kissed her. "Thanks for the kick in the rear, Kenny."

"Any time."

She watched him walk across the lawn, head down. Then she looked again at Gabe, her daughters and Elena. What did she want? Did she want perfection? Or did she want what Gabe had offered?

Did she want Gabe in her life? In her daughters' lives?

Yes, she whispered. She wanted Gabe.

She had been honest with Gabe about her feelings. And he had been honest with her. Maybe they could build something strong, something good, from the truth.

Maybe the truth was strong enough to overcome old feelings of guilt.

It would have to be strong. The failure of her marriage had been as much her fault as Carter's. She had known almost immediately that it had been a mistake, but she hadn't done anything. Instead of leaving him, she'd stayed with Carter, trapping them both. He'd known she didn't love him, but he'd never said a thing. Instead, he'd just become wild and reckless.

Would she ever be able to go to Gabe without shame muscling its way between them? She didn't know. But she could get rid of the things she'd kept simply to remind her of her guilt.

Shelby looked up. "Where's Uncle George?" she asked. "Why didn't he stay to see our castle?"

"Uncle George has a lot to do," Kendall said, trying to keep her voice light. "He just stopped by to say hello."

"Uncle George can be your slave next time," Gabe said.

"No, we want you, Uncle Gabe. You're better at building castles than Uncle George." Suddenly serious, Jenna said, "Me and Shelby don't want you to leave."

"I'd like to stay, too, Jen," he said, ruffling her hair. "But we can't always get what we want."

Kendall stood up. "I have some things to do," she said. "Baggage I need to get rid of, and I've put it off for too long. Gabe, will you stay here with the girls?"

"Sure. We haven't finished our castle, have we, guys?"

AT TILDA'S GARDEN Amy looked up from the plants she was watering and saw George. He walked toward her with a serious expression on his face. Her heart jumped and her stomach dropped. Then she carefully turned off the water and set the hose out of the way.

"I need to talk to you," he said as he stopped in front of her.

"I can't talk now, George," she said, trying to keep her voice steady. "I'm working."

"Tilda isn't going to mind if you take a break." He took her arm. "Could we go into the potting shed?"

She freed her arm. They'd snuck into the potting shed when George stopped by to see her after school. He'd crowd her against the counter and say he couldn't live another minute without kissing her.

"No. Not the potting shed."

"Then behind the greenhouse. Please, Amy," he said quietly. "You have every right to tell me to get lost. But I hope you'll listen to what I have to say."

"All right." Amy glanced around and saw there were only a couple of customers. "But only for a minute."

She led the way through the greenhouse to an area where landscaping rock was stored. Pushing aside some broken pieces with her foot, she turned to face George.

He stood looking at her for a moment, then he took her hand. "Amy, I've been an ass. I'm so sorry. Can you ever forgive me?"

Her heart began to pound and she drew her hand away. "What do you want?" she whispered.

"I want you back," he said. "I'd like to pretend I

didn't act like the world's biggest idiot, but that's not possible. Will you give me another chance?"

"Nothing has changed," Amy answered. "I'm still the same person I was on Saturday. My son is still Carter's son."

"That's the point, Amy. You're the same person you were on Saturday, the same person I fell in love with. What you told me hasn't changed the way I feel about you."

"No? That's not what you said the other night. Which version am I supposed to believe?"

"You're not going to make this easy, are you?"

"How can I, George?" she asked. "You broke my heart. You said you loved me, and then you called me a slut. Can you blame me for being skeptical?"

"You're not a slut. I didn't say that," he blurted, horrified.

"Maybe not in those words. But that was certainly the message."

"Okay." He wrung his hands together. "I screwed up. I already knew that. How can I fix it?"

"I'm not sure." Amy wrapped her arms around herself and tried to hold back her tears. "What's going to happen the next time we have a fight? Which George is going to show up?"

"Not the one from Saturday night," he said. "That guy was too ugly to live, so I killed him off."

A tentative smile fluttered at the edges of her mouth. "What made you change your mind?" she asked.

"I talked to Kendall and she reminded me that people

change, that you were just a kid when all this happened."

"That's generous of her."

"She's not Saint Kendall," he said. "She said she didn't know if she could forgive you."

Gulp. "That's honest. What else?"

"I saw Townsend playing on the beach with Jenna and Shelby this afternoon," he said. "And Kendall. They looked like a family, Amy. The girls are nuts about the guy, and he looks like he's nuts about them. And I realized that I felt that way about Tommy. It didn't matter who his father was. It's Tommy I love."

He reached out to touch her, and then let his hand drop. "I love you, too, Amy. And I'll turn into a miserable man if you don't marry me. Think of all the poor kids who'll have an ogre for a teacher. Can't I get you to sacrifice yourself for the greater good?"

She smiled again and swallowed hard. "What about Tommy? I won't allow you to hurt him, ever," she said fiercely. "If you're going to resent him because of who his father was, I can't marry you. Unless you can love him like your own son, this isn't going to work."

"I do love Tommy," he said quietly. "I already consider him my son. I was shocked and hurt when you told me about Carter, and I reacted without thinking."

"Tommy isn't Carter. Tommy is Tommy. His own person. *My kid.*"

"It doesn't matter who his father is. I want to be his dad—the guy who takes him to Packers games. The guy who teaches him how to drive. The guy who teaches him how to be a man."

George shoved his hands into his pockets. "After what I did on Saturday, maybe I don't deserve to teach him anything. But I hope you'll give me a chance to earn back your trust."

"I want to believe you, George." Amy's throat grew tight and tears threatened to fall. "More than I want to take my next breath."

He dug into his pocket and pulled out the ring box. "I knew as soon as you left the other day that I'd made a huge mistake. Will you please take this back? Put it on your finger and never take it off? I love you, Amy. I'll always love you. Please marry me."

She stared at the ring, then looked at George. "I've made plenty of my own mistakes," she said. "The one with Carter was only the biggest one. How can I not forgive you?"

Moisture swam in his eyes. He reached for her, pulling her tightly against him. "I love you, Amy. Forever." He reached for her left hand and slipped the ring on her finger. "Okay, now for the big question. How soon will you marry me?"

She sniffled into his shirt. "It's going to take at least a year to plan a wedding."

"A year? I have to wait a year?"

She looked up and saw shock on his face, then grinned through her tears. "I'm not worth the wait?"

"You're worth anything. But I'm not a patient guy." He studied her face. "You're joking, right?"

"Yes, I'm joking. How about a couple of months?"

"That's still too long, but it's better than a year."

"Aren't you forgetting something, George?"

"What? What am I forgetting?"

"When you ask a woman to marry you, it's customary to kiss her when she says yes."

"Oh, I haven't forgotten. I'm just saving the best for last." He bent his head and took her mouth. Her heart fluttered and the lump in her throat dissolved.

"I love you, George," she murmured.

A long time later, as she and George walked to his car, Tilda came around the corner. Her curly gray hair blew around her face, and she shoved it back with one gloved hand as she studied them.

"Have you two been in the potting shed again?" Her voice held a laugh. "Give those counters a break. They've been taking a real beating lately."

George held up Amy's hand and the ring sparkled in the sun. "We won't need your counters anymore, Tilda. Amy's making an honest man of me."

"It's about time," she said, hugging Amy. "You're a smart man, George Krippner."

"No, I'm a lucky man."

"Remember that the first time you have a fight," Tilda said.

"I will, Tilda." George brought Amy's hand to his mouth and kissed the ring. "Believe me, I will."

CHAPTER TWENTY

Tuesday afternoon

KENDALL LIFTED the flat white box down from the shelf in her bedroom closet and set it on the bed. She ran her finger over the label Memory Box, then let her hand drop away. She'd painted those hopeful words on the lid when she was young and naive.

When she'd assumed that all the memories she and Carter made would be happy ones.

The girls' voices drifted up the stairs, blending with the sound of a Disney movie they were watching, and she smiled. She couldn't completely regret her marriage. It had given her Shelby and Jenna.

Taking a deep breath, she opened the box. Her wedding photos were on top, and she set those aside. The girls would want to look at them some day.

She moved her wastebasket next to the bed and sat down. The cards Carter had given her for her birthday and their anniversary were tucked beneath the wedding album, and she tossed those into the trash. There were only a few of each. Once they'd gotten

married, Carter hadn't bothered much with senti-
ment.

She looked through matchbooks from restaurants
where they'd eaten, postcards from the one vacation trip
they'd taken and ticket stubs from movies they'd seen
while they were dating. There were a few letters that
Carter had written to her before they married, and she
set those aside with the wedding photos.

After sorting through the rest of the mementos de-
tailing the story of her marriage, she reached the bottom
of the box. A dried red rose lay on top of some papers,
and she picked it up. It crumbled into dust in her hand,
and she let the remnants dribble into the wastebasket.

It was one of the many roses Carter had given her.
Most of them had been pleas for forgiveness.

The wastebasket was overflowing, and there were
only a few things set aside for Shelby and Jenna.
Memories of their father would have to come from their
photos and from the stories they were told.

From Gabe.

They didn't need the sad trinkets in this box to learn
about their father. Gabe could bring Carter alive for
them in a way no one else could.

She shouldn't have kept him away for so long.

The last things in the box were the documents related
to the accident. A photo of the aftermath, which she
tossed away without a look. The police report. And a
list of items found in the car, which she assumed had
been returned to Gabe.

She unfolded the sheet of paper and read the short

list. A Green Bay Packers hat, found on the back seat. A handful of CDs, also on the back seat. Empty soda cans on the floor of the passenger side. Three dollars and fifty-six cents in change on the floor.

And a wristwatch caught on the handle of the driver's-side door.

She stared at the list for a long time, sickness gathering inside. Finally, she stood up and ran down the stairs to Gabe's room. When she knocked on the door, her hand was shaking.

"Come in," he called.

She slipped inside and closed the door behind her. Gabe's eyes heated when he saw her. "Kendall." He jumped up from his desk and gathered her into his arms.

She clung to him for a moment, the stepped away. "I need to ask you something," she said.

"Anything." His smile faded. "What's wrong?"

"I was going through some old papers and photos," she said. She looked down at the sheet in her hand and blinked hard. "I found this. I guess I never looked at it before."

Gabe took the paper from her and glanced at it. "Yeah, I got one of these, too. What's the problem?"

"The last thing on the list."

He looked down again and stilled. "What about it?" he finally said.

She closed her eyes and took a deep breath, then looked at him. "You weren't driving the car, were you? Carter was driving that night."

"Why would Carter be driving? It was my car."

"I know it was your car. And Carter was driving it."

He stared at the sheet of paper for a long time, then crumpled it into a ball and tossed it in the wastebasket. "That damn watch."

"You never wore a watch, Gabe. Not in all the years I knew you. Carter teased you about it constantly. The watch that was caught on the driver's-side door wasn't yours—it was Carter's. It means he was driving."

"I wish you hadn't see this," he said. "I never intended for you to know."

"Why?" she whispered. "Why did you take the blame?"

"I didn't start out intending to." He took her hand. "It just sort of happened."

"How?"

He stared down at her hand, brushed his fingers across her palm. "By the time the police got there, Carter was in the passenger seat. I was trying to drag him clear because I could smell gasoline and I was afraid the car was going to explode. The driver's door was too smashed to open. I guess the watch got caught on the handle when I was pulling him out."

She gripped his hand. "How could you have dragged him into the passenger seat? You had a broken arm. And a broken jaw."

"I don't know." He shrugged. "Adrenaline, I guess."

"Why did you let him drive your car? You knew his license had been revoked three months before the accident."

He kissed each of her palms. He held on tightly, as if he wouldn't ever let her go. "I followed him outside when he left the party, and we had a fight. An ugly, mean fight that escalated into a shoving match. He took a few swings at me but he couldn't connect." He looked away. "He'd had too much to drink.

"I told him I'd drive him home, then come back and get you." He sighed. "Under the circumstances, that was exactly the wrong thing to say, but I wasn't thinking clearly. I just wanted to give him time to cool down.

"He grabbed my car keys and said he'd drive himself home. I tried to get them back, but he jumped in the car and took off. I barely managed to get into the passenger seat.

"I blame myself for what happened. I tried to get him to stop, but the more I told him to pull over, the angrier he got and the faster he went. I've always wondered if he would have made it home if I hadn't jumped in the car with him. If I hadn't tried to stop him."

"You were trying to help him." She squeezed his hands. "How can you blame yourself?"

"Maybe I should have just let him go."

"That's why you took the blame, isn't it? Because you thought it was your fault."

"I wasn't thinking right about anything afterward. When the police came to talk to me in the hospital, they assumed I'd been driving. It was my car. Carter was in the passenger seat. And with my jaw wired shut, it was hard to talk. It was easier to go along. It didn't matter. Carter was dead."

"Didn't they ask you about the watch?"

"Nope. Not once."

"Why didn't you say something later?"

"After that visit from the police, I did some thinking. My auto insurance wouldn't have paid any claims if they'd known Carter was driving. Not with his license revoked. You wouldn't have gotten a settlement from them for his death."

"That's why you took the blame?" she asked, her head whirling. "You allowed everyone to think you'd been driving, so I would get the insurance money?"

"It was the only thing I could do for you," he said. "I couldn't help you or the girls any other way. I knew Carter had gone through most of his inheritance and that he didn't have much life insurance. Money wouldn't bring him back, but it would make your life a little easier."

"Gabe." She dropped onto the bed. "I don't know what to say. I'm overwhelmed. Stunned. Confused."

"You don't have to say anything. If you hadn't found that damn list, you never would have known. I never intended for you to know."

"But I do know," she said. "I'll pay the money back to the insurance company."

"I already did that. They got their money, and I wasn't prosecuted for fraud. It's over. Can't we leave the accident and everything related to it in the past?"

"How can I forget about it? That was a lot of money, Gabe—enough to turn this house into a bed-and-breakfast. Now I'll have to pay *you* back."

"You don't have to pay me back. My company is successful. I have more money than I need," he said, his voice rough. "Dammit, Kenny. You're struggling to make it here, and you want to give me money? No way."

"Gabe, I can't—"

"Stop." He cupped her face with his hands, pressed a kiss to her mouth. "This isn't about your pride. This is about making a living, about supporting Shelby and Jenna and yourself. You can't pay me back right now. You can't afford to. And I won't take the money."

"You're making this harder for me," she objected. "I'm trying to figure out what to do about us. This makes it more complicated."

"It doesn't. What's between you and me isn't about the money or Carter or the girls. It's about us. Only us." He drew her close and kissed her again.

She wanted to lose herself in the kiss, but instead she eased away. "What did you and Carter fight about at the party?" she asked, afraid of what he would say and knowing she'd have to face it if she wanted a future with Gabe.

"What do you think we fought about, Kendall? We fought about you."

"Because he'd seen us kissing."

"Yeah, because of that kiss. I told him it was nothing, that it didn't mean a thing. It was just a holiday kiss because someone had dangled mistletoe over our heads and insisted."

He tightened his grip on her hands. "I could barely bring myself to say the words," he said in a low voice. "I didn't want to deny what I felt for you. But I couldn't tell my best friend that I was in love with his wife."

"You didn't have to tell him. He knew," she said, remembering the look on Carter's face when he'd watched them. "He knew how I felt, too."

"I think he'd always known." He dropped her hands and paced the room. "I hated him sometimes," he said in a low voice. "Not just because he had you, although that was bad enough. But he liked to rub it in. Liked to make little remarks about you, about stuff you'd done for him. Bragging, like he'd won the prize he knew I wanted."

He clenched his hands and stared out the window. "I think he asked you out that first time because he knew I wanted to. Carter was always competitive. About everything."

"That's why you took the blame. Because you felt guilty. Because you'd fought about me."

"There's more than enough blame to go around," Gabe said, "but beating ourselves up isn't going to bring him back. We have the right to be happy."

"I am happy."

"Are you, Kendall? Is that why you haven't dated anyone since he died?"

"I have too dated."

He didn't say anything and she turned away. "I be-trayed him, Gabe." Her voice caught and she fought back tears. "Not just that night, but the whole time we were married. I didn't love him. And because I betrayed him, Shelby and Jenna lost their father."

"You've already served your sentence, Kenny. People convicted of manslaughter get out of prison in less time. Can't you forgive yourself?"

"Can you?"

"Yes," he said softly. "I've paid enough for what happened. And so have you."

"I want to believe you. I do. I'm just not sure if I can."

"It's all right, Kendall. Take as much time as you need to think this through. I've been in love with you forever. I'll wait as long as I have to."

IT WAS ALMOST MIDNIGHT, but Gabe couldn't sleep. He thought of Kendall in the room above him and he wondered if she was sleeping. Or was she restless, too? Wishing she wasn't alone?

It had been so hard to step back today, to tell her the next move was hers. But he wasn't hoping for just one night. He wanted forever. And Kendall needed time. Especially after her discovery earlier today.

He jumped out of bed and paced across the room. The moon had already set and the lake looked dark and mysterious. A gentle breeze lifted the curtains hanging next to the window, and the faint rustling sound was some night creature on the prowl.

He stilled. Or maybe not. The noise drifted in again. It sounded like a foot scraping on wood.

Someone was behind the house. Gabe crouched

beneath the window and peered out. Was there a deeper shadow near the cellar door?

"Closer," he whispered. "Get closer, dammit. Trigger the damn lights."

As if the prowler had heard him, the shadow moved until it seemed to become part of the door. Suddenly the yard was filled with light. And crouched by the cellar door, frozen in place, was the prowler.

Elena.

She stood up and bolted for the orchard. Gabe leaned out the window and yelled, "Elena! Wait. Don't run. I'll be right down."

She glanced over her shoulder and stumbled to a halt. Even from this distance, Gabe could see her terror.

"It's okay," he said softly. "Just stay there."

He threw on a pair of shorts and a T-shirt, then tore out of his room. He heard someone moving around on the floor above him. Kendall. He couldn't wait for her. Elena was ready to bolt.

By the time he got out the back door, Elena was edging toward the orchard. Gabe stopped several feet away and crouched in front of her. "It's okay, Elena."

"Are you going to call the police?" she asked, her lower lip trembling.

"Of course not," he said, trying to keep his voice soothing. "But we need to talk. Is something wrong? Are your parents sick, or one of your brothers?"

She shook her head slowly, tears running down her face as she looked at the ground.

The kitchen door banged, and he heard Kendall's

footsteps behind him. "What's going on?" she said. Then she stopped. "Elena?"

Gabe stood up and took her hand, drawing her into a crouch next to him. Elena was already scared. She didn't need two adults towering over her.

Kendall shivered, and he saw she wore only a thin shirt and boxers. Her pajamas. He looked away, but wrapped an arm around her shoulders, trying to keep her warm.

"You need to tell Mrs. Van Allen why you came to the house so late," he said softly. "Do you need something? Did your parents send you?"

The girl shook her head again, and Gabe looked at Kendall helplessly. He had no idea how to handle a terrified ten-year-old.

Kendall reached for his hand and squeezed it, then leaned forward. "What were you doing here, sweetheart?"

Tears flowed down her face. "I just wanted the book," she sobbed. "I wanted to read it. I thought I could borrow it at night when Jenna was asleep."

"What book?" Kendall scooted forward and took Elena's hand. "What book did you want to read?"

"The Harry Potter book." Her mouth quivered. "I started to read it when Shelby left it in the orchard, and I wanted to finish it." She dug her bare foot into the grass. "I read the other ones, but I haven't read that one yet."

"Why didn't you ask Jenna to let you borrow the book?" Kendall asked. "I know she would have lent it to you."

"My mother wouldn't let me." Her voice was barely audible. "She said she didn't want me bothering you."

"Oh, Elena, you're not a bother. You *couldn't* be. The girls like you and so do I," Kendall said.

"She said I couldn't ask."

And Mrs. Montoya wouldn't let him buy the book for her, either, Gabe thought. He knew the soccer equipment had been hard for Elena's mother to accept. It was only because she thought the team was buying it that she agreed.

"Could your parents take you to the library to get it?" Kendall asked her.

"We can't have library cards here because we don't live here all the time."

"Who told you that?" Kendall asked. Her voice was soft, but there was steel beneath her words.

"The lady at the library."

"I'll talk to the library lady tomorrow. You'll get a library card," Kendall promised.

"Really?" Elena looked up, her eyes full of hope.

"Really." Kendall stood up and held out her hand. "In the meantime, Gabe and I will walk you home. You shouldn't be out so late."

"I had to wait until everyone was asleep to leave. Sometimes Papa stays up late and falls asleep on the couch," she confided.

"You tried to get the book before tonight, didn't you?" Kendall asked. Her voice was soft with understanding.

Elena nodded. "But I couldn't get in. The windows were too high to climb through. That's how I get out of my house when my father is sleeping on the couch."

Kendall glanced at Gabe over Elena's head and grinned. "You're pretty adventurous, aren't you?"

"I like to read," Elena said, and Gabe's heart broke.

"You'll get all the books you want from the library," Kendall promised.

They held Elena's hands as they made their way cautiously through the orchard, walking slowly to avoid the uneven roots at the base of the trees and the ruts in the dirt between the rows. When they reached her house, it was completely dark.

"Over here," she whispered. She crept around to the side and pointed to a window without a screen. "That's my room. My *abuela's*, too. But she never wakes up."

Gabe heard gentle snoring coming from the room. Kendall crouched down in front of Elena. "We'll talk about this tomorrow," she murmured. "You can't sneak out of your house at night and wander around. It's too dangerous."

"Are you going to tell my mama and papa?" Her mouth trembled, but she held Kendall's gaze. Gabe squeezed the child's shoulder.

"I think you need to tell them, Elena. So I don't have to. Okay?"

The girl nodded, and Gabe thought he saw tears sparkling in her eyes. Then she gripped the windowsill and began to hoist herself up.

He grabbed her around the waist and lifted her to the window, and she scrambled inside. Then she replaced the screen and pulled down the blinds.

He reached for Kendall's hand, holding it tightly as

they navigated their way back through the orchard. When they were on the lawn behind the house, he said, "Can you really get the library to give your workers library cards?"

"I'm going to make sure that all the workers from all the cherry farms in the area get library cards if they want them. And that's just a start." He heard the determination in her voice and had no doubt she'd succeed. "I'm going to check on the schools, too. I suspect some of them discourage the workers from enrolling their kids because they get here late in the school year. That's going to change."

"That sounds great, Kendall, but how are you going to do it? All those things cost money. And they're going to say the workers don't pay any taxes."

"But I do. Do you have any idea how much I pay in taxes every year for the orchard and my bed-and-breakfast?"

"A lot?"

"Yes, a lot." She smiled grimly. "Sturgeon Falls stretched their city limits to include me because they wanted my tax money. If the library won't give the workers library cards and the schools don't make more of an effort to get their kids enrolled, I'll secede from the city.

"I agreed to be annexed because I wanted the city services. But I can live without them. They can't live without the tax money from the orchards. I can convince the other orchard owners to do the same thing. I don't think it's going to be hard to get the city to see things my way."

"Good for you," he said, kissing her. "I'll come with you tomorrow when you take Elena and her family to the library. In case you need someone to watch your back."

"There isn't going to be a fight," she said, leaning into him. He could feel her smile against his mouth. "I'll be polite and charming, but they'll have library cards before we leave."

"I'm crazy about you," he murmured against her lips. "Have I told you that?"

"No," she said, looping her arms around his neck. "But I kind of guessed."

Her shirt was so thin he could feel her skin through it. As he caressed her back, she shuddered and rose to fit her body against his. But when he cupped her hips and pulled her more tightly against him, she drew away.

"This isn't right," she said, touching his face and letting her hand drop away. "It's not fair to touch you and kiss you, then tell you to stop."

"Then don't tell me to stop." He kissed her and felt her melt against him. "Come to my bed, Kendall. Spend the night with me."

"You said you'd give me time."

"And I will. But I reserve the right to lobby." He skimmed his hand down her back, lingered on her hips.

"Gabe." Her tiny moan vibrated in his mouth, and he took the kiss deeper. "I'm weak enough to buy what you're selling," she murmured.

As she clung to him, kissing him back, he moved her

toward the stairs. The lights he'd installed came on in a brilliant flash of white.

She pulled away from him. "Where did those come from?" she asked. "I almost forgot about this."

"I installed them this morning while you and the girls were decorating the stadium, and I'm not going to apologize. I had no idea your prowler was a ten-year-old girl. I want you protected."

"You should have asked me before you did this." She opened the door and he followed her into the kitchen.

"Yeah, I should have asked you," he said. "But it wouldn't have made any difference. If you'd said no, I would have done it anyway."

She sighed. "I should be angry," she said. "But how can I be?" She moved into his arms, hugged him fiercely. "Thank you, Gabe."

"That's it?" he asked, holding her tightly. "That's the big fight?"

"That's it." She tilted her head up to grin at him. "Disappointed?"

"Nah. I'm sure we can find better uses for the time we would have spent fighting. And better uses for the energy."

"I'm sure we can." She looped her arms around his neck, then grew quiet. He turned around to see what had caught her attention.

The rose that Smith had given her sat on the counter. The same kind of red rose that Carter used to give her when he'd screwed up.

She kissed him once more, then eased away. "I'll see you in the morning, Gabe."

CHAPTER TWENTY-ONE

Wednesday afternoon

THE DISMISSAL BELL clanged as Kendall walked into the stadium the next afternoon with Shelby and Jenna. A makeshift stage stood at one end of the field, decorated with red-and-white pom-poms they'd glued in place yesterday. Pots of red, white and blue flowers lined the front and sides of the stage, and red-and-white streamers decorated the chain-link fence that surrounded the stadium.

Gabe was talking to the high school principal. Kendall hadn't seen Gabe in a suit for ages. The dark-gray material made his shoulders look wider, made his black hair look blacker. An air of authority emanated from him.

He looked every inch the successful businessman, someone who had started a company and made it flourish. Then he saw her and smiled, and her heart leaped. Even in the unfamiliar suit, he was still Gabe. Still the man who made her heart race and her palms sweat.

The foam boards bearing pictures sat on easels next to the stage. One board held the photographs of Carter that she and the girls had set up the day before. The other held pictures of Carter's days at Sturgeon Falls High School—pictures of him playing football, basketball, baseball. Pictures of his team holding the trophy after they won the state football championship.

"Where are we supposed to sit, Mom?" Shelby asked.

"On the stage, Shel." She smiled down at her daughter. "Let's go check it out, okay?"

As they headed toward the stage, she heard her brother's voice behind her. "Hey, Kenny."

George grinned at her. He held Tommy's hand and had his arm wrapped around Amy's shoulders.

"Uncle George," Jenna cried, running to him. "I didn't know you were going to be here."

"And miss your big day?" He swung her into the air and kissed her. "No way."

Kendall's face felt as if it would crack as she smiled. "Thank you for coming, George," she said. "You too, Amy."

"I didn't want to intrude," Amy said. "But George wanted us to be here."

Kendall looked down at Tommy, who was looking around the stadium as he stood next to Jenna and Shelby. "I'm glad you came," she said, realizing that she meant it. "Glad Tommy can be here."

"He doesn't know," Amy said quickly. "I haven't told—"

Kendall reached out and touched her arm. "It's okay," she said softly. "You'll tell him someday. And he'll remember this. He'll be glad he was here."

"Thank you," Amy whispered. She tried to smile, but her eyes filled with tears. "That's pretty generous."

"No, it's the right thing." Kendall smiled again, and it was easier this time. "None of this is Tommy's doing."

Amy glanced at George, and he nodded. "Hey, guys, let's go find Shelby's and Jenna's seats," he said to the three children. "They're big shots today."

Amy turned to Kendall. "I want to apologize to you. It probably doesn't make any difference, but I *am* sorry. What I did was wrong, and the way you found out was wrong, too. I should have told you myself, a long time ago, but I was a coward."

Kendall took a step closer to her. "You're not a coward, Amy," she said quietly. "It took a lot of courage to tell George about Carter. You could have married him and never said a word."

Amy watched her steadily. "I know it's going to be hard for you, me being married to George. I can't change what happened in the past, but I wanted you to know I'm sorry that I hurt you."

As Kendall registered the remorse in Amy's eyes, a weight fell away from her heart. "You know what, Amy?" she said. "I don't think it's going to be hard at all. You make George happy. He loves you and Tommy. And that's good enough for me."

"Thank you, Kendall," Amy said, tearing up again. "That means a lot to me. And it will mean everything to George. I don't know if I could be as forgiving, if our positions were reversed."

Kendall took her hand. "How old were you when you got pregnant?"

Amy flushed. "Seventeen."

"And Carter was twenty-two. He took advantage of you."

"It wasn't all on Carter," Amy said. "I might have been only seventeen, but I was old enough to know better."

Kendall squeezed her hand. "So was Carter, and let's leave it at that. George is a lucky guy. I'm glad you're going to be part of our family."

"Me, too," Amy whispered.

"Mom, we're supposed to be on the stage." Shelby tugged at her arm. "Come on."

"Hold on, Shel." She turned to Amy. "You and George and Tommy are coming to the house after the ceremony, aren't you?"

"I wasn't planning on it," Amy said cautiously.

"You tell George we're expecting you." She smiled. "I want my family there."

Kendall hurried to the stage as groups of high-school kids streamed into the stadium. As she stepped onto the stage, Gabe took her arm and helped her up.

"Are you okay? I saw you talking to Amy."

"I'm fine." She glanced at the bleachers, where George was settling himself between Amy and Tommy. "In fact, I'm more than fine."

The principal interrupted before Gabe could say anything else. "Mrs. Van Allen, thank you so much for coming today."

"We wouldn't have missed it," Kendall said.

He gestured toward the other end of the field, where the scoreboard was covered with a white cloth. "I think you'll like what we've done."

"I'm sure I will."

"We'll get started as soon as everyone's seated." He peered at the filling bleacher seats. "All the teams that use the stadium will be here. We're very excited."

"It's an honor we wouldn't miss," Kendall answered.

"It's well deserved," he said. "After all, Carter was the best athlete we've ever had at Sturgeon Falls High. It seemed only right to name the stadium after him." He gave her a sidelong glance. "And the Van Allen family has always been generous in their support for our school. I'm sure that support will continue." He beamed at her. "I'll give you a call next week to discuss our plans for the stadium."

Gabe cut in smoothly. "Dr. Barnard, where would you like Shelby and Jenna?"

As the principal guided the girls to their seats, Gabe drew her aside. "Don't let the old windbag corner you," he murmured. "He's already hit me up for a donation for 'stadium renovation.'"

Kendall grimaced. "Thanks for the warning."

He gazed down at her. "Hang in there for forty-five minutes, and then this will be over."

"It's going to be fine, Gabe." She nodded at Shelby and Jenna. "Look how excited they are."

The girls wriggled in their seats, staring at the crowd with awe. Gabe went over and put a hand on each of their shoulders. "Everyone is here because of your dad," he said. "They didn't know him, but they know what he did when he went to school here. They're all proud that the school is naming the stadium after your father."

"Yeah?" Shelby looked at him. "Will it still be named after my dad when I go to school here?"

"Yep," Gabe said.

"Then my school will have a stadium with the same name as me. How cool is that?"

"Pretty cool," Gabe said with a smile.

The marching band, which was lined up outside the stadium, played the first notes of the school's fight song and marched into the stadium. Kendall sat down and Gabe sat next to her. His leg bumped hers once, then again, and she looked down to hide her smile. He was telling her he was there. Watching her back, as he'd said yesterday.

She liked the feeling.

The fight song swelled to a crescendo, then ended as the principal strode to the microphone. Gabe reached for her hand and squeezed it reassuringly. She squeezed back, then let go.

She'd been dreading this ceremony, dreading the memories it would stir. Worrying that she wouldn't be able to hide her complicated feelings about Carter. But glancing at the girls, she knew it would be fine. This day wasn't about her. It wasn't even about Gabe. It was about her daughters and a memory they'd cherish of their father.

Shelby and Jenna stared at the principal, spellbound, as he began to talk about the Van Allen family and Carter. Kendall smiled and relaxed.

THIRTY-FIVE MINUTES LATER, Gabe finished an anecdote about Carter and paused as he waited for the laughter to subside. He wanted to turn around and see how Kendall was doing. Hell, he wanted to be sitting next to her, holding her hand. He'd been trying all week to erase Carter from her memory, and here he was, standing on a stage bringing him back to life.

"You're all going to be playing in Van Allen Stadium from now on," he said. "Play your games the way Carter lived his life—full out, no holds barred, embracing both the good and the bad. Because if you do, you'll be successful, whether you win or lose your game."

He glanced at the crowd, then looked back at Kendall, Shelby and Jenna. The girls were enthralled. Kendall had taken the girls' hands. When he caught her eye, she smiled at him. It was shaky, but it was still a smile.

He turned back to the podium. "Carter died too young, before he had a chance to fulfill all his dreams. By naming your stadium after him, you'll be remembering his athletic feats, the excitement he brought to football, baseball and basketball games. And you'll be aspiring to his competitiveness and his love of sport. That's the legacy Carter Van Allen leaves to Sturgeon Falls High.

"The people who loved Carter, his friends and his

family, will cherish those memories, but we have more personal ones, as well—his charm, his infectious wit, his larger-than-life personality. That's Carter's gift to us. And his greatest legacy, the finest thing he left behind, will always be his daughters, Shelby and Jenna Van Allen."

He stepped back as the crowd applauded and the band struck up the school fight song again. The principal nodded to a student stationed at the scoreboard and the white sheet fell away to reveal the words Van Allen Stadium inscribed across the top. Gabe studied it for a moment, then turned to find Kendall behind him.

She embraced him with a fierce hug and kiss. "Thank you," she murmured, holding his shoulders. "You gave all of us something positive to remember about Carter. Something good."

Then the superintendent touched her arm, and she turned to him with a smile. Gabe stood on the stage, looking at the students milling around on the grass and thought he saw Carter's ghost, galloping down the sidelines with a football under his arm. As he reached the goal line, he slowed and looked over his shoulder, to share the moment with Gabe. Like he'd always done during games.

Gabe couldn't see his face, but he knew Carter would be smiling.

He'd stepped off the stage to wait for Kendall, when Dylan Smith sauntered over. "Quite the turnout for the hometown hero," he said.

"Smith." Gabe looked at the reporter. "Did you get what you needed for your story?"

"It was a nice speech. Any of it true?"

Gabe refused to be baited. "You tell me. Or didn't you do your homework?"

"Oh, I did my homework. I have all kinds of information."

"So this is goodbye, I guess. You came here for the story about the stadium dedication. That means you're leaving today, right?"

"Maybe not," the reporter said, his voice breezy. "I might stick around a while longer."

"What for?" Gabe held his gaze. "Or maybe you didn't come here to cover the stadium dedication at all."

The reporter stilled. "What's that supposed to mean?"

Gabe gave him a cool smile. "I talked to your editor at the *Green Bay News-Gazette.* He said you were on a leave of absence. To work on something personal."

The reporter studied him for a long moment, then shrugged. "I never tell my editor what I'm working on. It's none of your business, either."

"I'm making it my business. You're staying in Kendall's home. You humiliated her by digging personal information out of her garbage. You're nosing around her employees." He took a step closer to Smith and was reluctantly impressed when the man didn't back away. "Stay away from her."

The reporter gave him a knowing grin. "I was right. There *is* something going on between the two of you."

"That's none of *your* business. Why are you here? What are you looking for?"

Smith straightened. "I'm not going to hurt Kendall or her daughters. What I want has nothing to do with them."

"No? So you rummage in people's garbage for sport? Looking for tidbits you can use later?"

"I already apologized for that."

"Then all you have left to do is leave." Gabe crossed his arms as he studied the reporter. "I want you out of her house. Today."

Smith raised his eyebrows. "Are you sure that's what Kendall wants? I saw her bills, remember. I'm guessing *she* wants me to stay."

"She doesn't need your money," Gabe snarled.

"But I need to stay at her place," Smith retorted. "If Kendall wants me to leave, she's going to have to tell me herself."

Gabe rocked back on his heels. "What's going on?" he asked, trying to keep the antagonism out of his voice. "What are you doing here? What do you want, Smith?"

The reporter studied him, then shrugged. "I'm getting tired of having you on my back, Townsend. I'll tell you what I want. I'm looking for my father. I think he was from Sturgeon Falls."

As Gabe stared at Smith, Kendall stepped up beside him. "Hi, Dylan. Did you get all the information you needed?"

The reporter looked away from Gabe, but the shadows of old ghosts lingered in his eyes. "I'm still working on it. But I'll say this—I've learned a lot in Sturgeon Falls."

"What do you mean?"

Smith gave Kendall a weary smile. "Your ceremony reinforced all my reasons for being here. It reminded me that the past shapes the present. You can't move forward until you deal with the baggage that was left behind."

As he walked away, Kendall looked at Gabe. "What was that supposed to mean?"

"Apparently, Smith has a lot more baggage than we thought. He told me why he's in Sturgeon Falls. He's looking for his father."

Kendall watched the reporter walk out of the stadium. "He thinks his father is from Sturgeon Falls?"

"Sounds like it. I guess it explains a lot." Gabe slipped his arm around her shoulders and gave her a quick hug. "I can't believe I'm agreeing with Smith, but he's right about dealing with old baggage."

Kendall moved away from him. "I'm working on it, Gabe. Okay?"

Shelby yanked on her arm. "What about our pictures, Mom?"

"We'll come back for them tomorrow," she said easily. "Right now we need to get home. Uncle George and Amy and Tommy are coming over and we're going to have a picnic."

"Is Uncle George bringing his crab cakes for dinner?" Jenna asked hopefully.

"I don't think he's had time to make them, Jen."

"Tommy Mitchell is coming to our house?" Shelby said with the particular scorn she reserved for all boys. "He's a dweeb."

"He's not a dweeb," Jenna protested. "He was in my class last year and he's okay. For a boy."

"Uncle George is going to marry Amy. So Tommy will be your cousin."

Gabe was sure the girls hadn't noticed her slight hesitation before "cousin."

"Cousins can be lots of fun," he said. "Give Tommy a chance."

"Maybe he knows how to play soccer," Shelby said grudgingly. "He can play with me and Jenna and Elena."

KENDALL SAT on the back porch of her house, watching everyone. Shelby, Jenna and Tommy had found Elena playing with the soccer ball Gabe bought her, and the four of them were now playing together. Elena kept glancing toward the porch, where she'd carefully set the Harry Potter book she'd gotten from the library that morning.

And despite Shelby's "dweeb" remark about Tommy, all four kids looked as if they were having a great time. How would the girls react when she told them Tommy was really their half brother?

She glanced at Amy, who was standing next to Gabe at the grill, cooking the chicken. She and Amy would have to talk about the best way to break the news to all the kids.

"What are you thinking so hard about?" George asked as he dropped onto the step next to her.

"The future," she told him. "Wondering how the girls are going to feel about having a brother."

"Thank you for what you said to Amy today," he said, wrapping his arm around her shoulders and pulling her close. "That was really big of you, Kenny. It meant a lot to her. Of course," he said, his eyes twinkling, "I had to tell Amy not to get so starry-eyed over you. I told her you were usually mean as a snake."

"Poor Amy. You're going to scare her so much she won't want anything to do with me."

"Nah. She punched me when I said it."

"Good for her," Kendall said, grinning. "Everyone knows I'm perfect."

She leaned against him companionably for a moment, watching everyone in her backyard. "My family has suddenly gotten a lot bigger," she said. "That feels good."

"So, is Townsend sticking around?" George asked, trying to sound casual.

"He'd like to." Kendall let her gaze drift over to Gabe, laughing with Amy at the grill. "But I'm not sure."

"Why the heck not? The guy is crazy about you." He turned to look at her. "And I think you're crazy about him, too."

"It's not that simple, George. There are a lot of issues to work through. Because of Carter."

"I know about the party the night Carter died. How Townsend kissed you, and how he and Carter had a fight. Is that what this is about?"

"Partly."

"Carter thought you and Townsend were having an affair, right?"

"Yes."

"Of course he did. Of course he thought you'd betray him. Because he betrayed you."

"He was my husband, George. I shouldn't have been kissing Gabe."

"So that's what this is about. You're going to deny yourself happiness now because you think you screwed up back then."

She shrugged, uncomfortable with George's bluntness.

"Carter is dead, Kenny. Has been for seven years. How long are you going to do penance because you love Gabe more than you loved Carter?"

She *did* love Gabe more than she'd loved Carter. The rows of trees in the orchard blurred as she stared at them. "I'm not doing penance," she whispered.

"No? Then what do you call it?" He took her chin and turned her to face him. "I told Amy you weren't Saint Kendall. Maybe I was wrong."

"Stop it, George." She jerked away. "You don't understand."

"Don't I?" He nodded toward Amy, laughing with Gabe near the grill. "You've forgiven Amy, haven't you?"

"What happened with Amy was just as much Carter's fault. More, because he was older than Amy."

"What about Townsend? Have you forgiven him his part in Carter's death?"

"Of course," she said quietly. "It was an accident." She'd even forgiven his deception.

"So you've forgiven everyone else. Why haven't you forgiven yourself?"

"It's complicated."

"The hell it is. You're scared. Afraid to take a chance. You and Carter screwed up, and you're afraid to get involved again. Afraid to take the risk. It's easier just to hide in this big house, hide behind your daughters, your work."

"That's not true!"

"Isn't it?"

Gripping the railing, she jumped up and glared at her brother. "If you're so smart, how come you walked out on Amy? How come you wouldn't forgive her?"

"It took me two days to come to my senses," he pointed out. "Not seven years."

Before she could answer him, Jenna screamed. "Mom! Mom! Come quick. Elena's in the lake. She's drowning."

CHAPTER TWENTY-TWO

Wednesday afternoon

KENDALL RAN TOWARD the beach, with George right behind her. Amy and Gabe dropped their spatulas and raced for the water, too. By the time Kendall reached the waterfront, Elena was thrashing in water that was clearly over her head. Her face was contorted in panic, and her scream ended in a gurgle as she inhaled water.

Shelby, who had charged into the lake, was in water up to her chest. "Elena," she cried. Water frothed around her small body as she splashed farther out. Deeper. "I'm here. Grab my hand."

As Elena reached out for Shelby, she slipped below the surface. Shelby let out a high, keening cry and lunged toward her.

"Shelby! No!" Tommy cried, running into the lake after her.

Everything slowed as Kendall ran toward the water. Her legs pumped but she seemed to make no progress. Elena was underwater. Shelby was frantically searching for her. And the water was creeping up Tommy's chest.

Finally, Kendall reached the water. "Amy!" she shouted without turning around. "Grab Jenna. Hold on to her."

The pain from the cold water shocked Kendall breathless, then her legs went numb. Charging forward, she snagged an already-struggling Tommy around the waist and dragged him backward as Gabe and George ran past her.

"Get Shelby, Krippner," Gabe called. "I've got Elena."

Kendall gathered the shivering Tommy close to her as she waded back to the beach. Holding Jenna, Amy waited on the sand. When Kendall stumbled out of the water, she handed Tommy to his mother and grabbed Jenna.

"Elena drowned," Jenna said, sobbing. "She drowned. Is Shelby going to drown, too?"

"Of course not, Jen," Kendall said, hugging her daughter tightly. "Look, Uncle George has Shelby." She turned Jenna around so she could see. "And she's fine."

Shelby was clinging to her uncle with both arms and legs, her face buried in his shoulder. But she was moving.

"And Gabe has Elena," Kendall added. "See?"

"She's not moving," Jenna said in a small voice as Gabe waded ashore with Elena's limp body. "Is she dead?"

"I don't think so," Kendall answered, praying it was true. "She was only under the water for a few seconds."

"I'll call 911," Amy said, running toward the house. Kendall reached out and took Tommy's hand. He held it tightly and stared at Elena.

Gabe laid Elena's still body on the ground and began mouth-to-mouth resuscitation. No one moved or spoke. Suddenly Elena gagged, and Gabe lifted her and turned her head as water poured from her mouth. Coughs racked her thin body, and Gabe eased her back to the ground.

Finally, she opened her eyes and stared at Gabe, confusion on her face. "What's wrong?" she asked, struggling to sit up, her voice hoarse.

"Nothing's wrong, Elena," he said, brushing her wet hair away from her face. "You tried to go for a swim, and it's a little cold for that."

"My ball," she said, looking back at the lake.

Kendall saw a soccer ball floating next to the string of yellow buoys she'd set out a couple of days ago. "Don't worry about the ball, Elena. We'll get it later."

The girl struggled to her feet. "I don't want it to float away."

"It won't, honey." Kendall pointed to the yellow buoys. "Those will keep it where we can get it."

"Will you feel better if I get it now?" Gabe asked Elena. When she nodded, he ran back into the water, swam out to the buoys and grabbed the ball. He tossed it onto the beach, then waded back to the sand.

"We all need to get in the house," Gabe said. "We'd better get the kids out of their wet clothes."

Gabe carried Elena, holding her close. As they walked across the grass, Shelby slipped her hand into Kendall's. "It's my fault, Mom," she said, sobbing. "Elena almost drowned, and it's my fault."

"Why is it your fault?" Kendall pulled Shelby close.

"I was trying to do a flip throw with her ball, and I threw it into the water. I thought I knew how to do those throws, but I don't."

"Oh, Shel," Kendall said, hugging her daughter. "It's not your fault. It was an accident, okay?"

"Elena's going to be mad at me," she said in a small voice.

"Elena won't be mad," Kendall said. "She's your friend. She'll forgive you."

"Yeah?"

"Of course. That's what friends do."

As they reached the kitchen door, Gabe set Elena down. "Thank you," she said. "For rescuing me. And my ball."

"You're welcome," Gabe said. "Now you need to get into some dry clothes."

"You, too, Shelby," Kendall said. "Why don't you take Elena upstairs and find something warm and dry for both of you?"

"Okay. Come on, Elena."

Shelby charged out of the room, followed by Elena, moving more slowly. Then Kendall turned to Tommy.

"We need to find something for you to wear, too," she said. When she saw Tommy's look of horror, she grinned. "Not girlie clothes," she said. "I think I can find something manly."

"I'll go get Elena's parents," Gabe said quietly. He slipped out the door as Kendall led Amy and Tommy up to her room on the third floor.

As Kendall grabbed a pair of old jogging shorts out of her drawer and handed them to Amy, she realized she had one thing that would be perfect. She reached far back on the closet shelf and pulled out a red shirt. "This is for Tommy," Kendall said quietly. "For him to keep."

Amy opened the shirt and stared at it for a long moment. It was a Sturgeon Falls High School football jersey bearing the number 12. When she looked at Kendall, her eyes were watery. "Thank you," she said.

Kendall smiled as she touched Tommy's hair. "Who else would I give it to?"

The paramedics arrived at the same time as Elena's parents. The Montoyas clung to each other, terrified, and watched while the paramedics examined Elena. As soon as the EMTs stepped back and nodded to them, smiling, they rushed to their daughter.

Everyone crowded onto the back porch to wave goodbye and watch the family walk through the orchard. As they were heading back into the house, a burnt smell reached them.

Amy looked over at the grill. "The chicken," she yelled, running down the steps.

It was charred black, so Gabe drove into town and picked up pizzas. Shelby, Jenna and Tommy sprawled on the living-room floor, watching a movie while they ate, and the adults relaxed in the dining room.

Kendall pushed her plate away and took a drink of iced tea, gazing around the table. George and Amy were laughing about something Tommy had done earlier that day, and Gabe had just finished telling everyone about Jenna's tennis lessons. Everyone looked comfortable. At home. Relaxed.

They looked like a family.

Finally, when the kids' movie was over, Amy stood up. "I don't want to break up the party, but we should get going. George and I both have to work tomorrow."

While George found Tommy's still-damp clothes, Amy drew Kendall aside. "Gabe is a good man," she said. "He deserves the best." She gave Kendall a steady look. "And so do you. Be happy, Kendall. Make Gabe happy."

She reached for Tommy's hand and they headed out into the evening. Kendall turned to Shelby and Jenna. "You guys get ready for bed. I'll be up in a few minutes."

With the girls heading up the stairs behind her, Kendall watched the headlights of George's car disappear into the trees.

"You okay?" Gabe said, touching her face.

"I'm fine." She turned into his hand. "But it was a long day."

"No kidding."

"Thank you for running into the lake to get Elena."

"Everyone was in the water. I was just the one who got to her first."

She smiled and leaned into him. "I guess no one in this family has sense enough to stay out of the lake in June."

"That's what families do," he said, smoothing his hand down her side. "They jump in without thinking twice."

"Thank goodness everyone was here," she murmured.

Gabe stroked her side with a hypnotic rhythm. "You made Amy feel like a part of this family today."

"That's because she is. She's marrying George."

"And she has Carter's son," he said.

"That, too."

"Have you forgiven her, Kenny?"

"I have." She sighed and moved away from him. "I don't want to hold on to bitterness and anger. I don't want it to poison me or the girls. Or anyone else. It happened a long time ago and Amy's paid for her mistake many times over. And to tell the truth, I blame Carter more than Amy."

"Amy has always taken responsibility for what she did."

"That's more than I can say for myself, isn't it?"

He turned her to face him. "What's that supposed to mean?"

"I was as much at fault in our marriage as Carter was," she said. "Maybe more. I didn't love him, Gabe. And he knew it. That's why I've always felt so guilty."

"And now?" He held her gaze until she looked away.

"Now?" Kendall twisted the loose spindle on the stairs. "I realized I've been using my guilt to protect myself. To avoid making a commitment, avoid letting someone down again. I couldn't face that until tonight."

"Yeah? And tonight the blindfold fell off and you realized I was the man of your dreams?"

"Tonight I realized that life is precious and fragile. That it can disappear in the time it takes to look away from a child on the beach. That sometimes you don't get a chance to correct your mistakes."

"Carter wasn't a mistake. He was a lot of things, but he was also my friend and your husband. I'll never call him a mistake."

"Neither will I. He gave me Shelby and Jenna. I shouldn't have married him, but he'll always be my children's father." She reached for his hands. "But I don't want to let my bad judgment get in the way of the rest of my life. And that's what I've been doing."

"So the guilt is gone?" he asked, watching her.

"The guilt will never be completely gone," she said quietly. "Part of it will always be there. I can't change that. But I won't let it ruin the rest of my life."

"Do you love me?"

"Yes, Gabe. I do."

"I need to hear the words, Kenny."

She took his face in her hands. "I love you, Gabe Townsend. I think I always have. I know I always will."

Gabe folded her into his arms and kissed her. When she deepened the kiss, he eased away from her.

"You're trembling," he said.

"I'm nervous."

He kissed her gently. "How come?"

"I'm taking a big step here, Gabe. George pointed out that I've forgiven everyone but myself. He was right. Now I feel like I'm standing here, naked, in front of you."

"Naked would be good." He nuzzled her neck. "Naked would be excellent, in fact. But you need to know I'll never hurt you."

She smiled. "Yes, you will, Gabe. The people we love hurt us all the time. They have the most power to hurt us. I'll hurt you, too. But they'll never be mortal wounds."

"Will you take a chance, Kenny? On us?"

"I don't take chances," she answered with a slow smile. "I only bet on sure things."

"How's this for a sure thing?" He kissed her again, backing her up until she was pressed against the wall, until she could think of nothing but Gabe.

"Works for me," she said, winding herself around him.

"I'm not going to settle for less than everything," he warned, his breath stirring the hair on her neck. "I want a family. You, Jenna, Shelby. And more kids, I hope. I want to be here for them every morning and every night."

"A family? More kids? Every day and night?" She leaned back and traced his mouth with her finger. "Are you suggesting that we live in sin, Gabe Townsend?"

"I'm suggesting that we get married. As soon as possible."

"I can get behind that idea. After George gets married, of course. He got engaged first."

"I'm not sure I like that part," he said.

"Mmm. I liked the part about the nights," she murmured. "Can they start now?"

"I think we need to wait until we're married," he said, his eyes twinkling. "To set the right example for the girls."

She leaned back, laughing. "Slick, Gabe. Very

slick. Maybe we can compromise. Marriage is all about compromising."

"Yeah?" He nuzzled her ear, and her legs went weak. "I'm open to negotiations. What did you have in mind?"

"Maybe we don't have to wait until George gets married."

"How long?" He pressed closer to her.

"How about tomorrow?"

He rolled his hips against her. "That works for me."

She pulled Gabe's head to hers and kissed him again, losing herself in him.

Finally, he pulled away and cupped her face in his hands. "I'd marry you tomorrow in a heartbeat, but I'm not going to rush you into anything, Kendall. I want you to be very sure."

"I am sure. But are you? Do you know what you're getting into?"

"What's that supposed to mean? Are there deep, dark secrets you haven't told me?" he asked, nuzzling her neck.

"You're not just getting me," she said, grabbing his hands. "You're taking on two children. This house. The orchard. You're marrying a lot more than me."

"And I can't wait. For any of it."

"What about your business? It's in Milwaukee."

"I'll move the business here. And if my employees don't want to move, I'll put my assistant in charge of that office and open another one in Sturgeon Falls. I can commute for a while, too, if I have to." He kissed her slowly, letting his mouth linger on hers. "It sounds like you're trying to scare me off."

"I'm guessing you're not easily scared. I'm just trying to be practical."

"I don't want practical, Kenny," he murmured against her lips. "I want you. Kids, house, messy life and all."

"And I want you. And that's not going to change, no matter how long we wait."

He kissed her hands, then held them between their bodies. "It's only been a week since I showed up at your door. Take your time, Kenny." He brushed his mouth over hers.

"I don't need time. I've already wasted too much of it." She grabbed his shirt in her fists. "Carter is part of the past. He's not going to haunt our marriage."

"Are you sure?"

"Yes." She leaned forward, and with her mouth hovering over his, she said, "There's only you, Gabe. It's always been you."

Her skin heated and desire raced through her as she joined her mouth to his. Needing to touch him, she slid her hands beneath his shirt and clutched his back. He groaned and fumbled with the hem of her shirt.

"Mom, we're ready for bed." Jenna's voice floated down the stairs, and Kendall drew away from Gabe reluctantly. "Will you come and read to us?"

"We'll be right up, honey," Kendall called. Lacing her arms around Gabe's neck, she leaned back until she could see his face. "So much for wild sex on the stairs," she murmured, smiling.

"I know all about delayed gratification," he murmured. "Anticipation is half the fun."

"Then anticipate while we read to the girls." Kendall tugged him toward the stairs. "Come on, Townsend. Our kids are waiting."

He cupped her head and kissed her. "I love you, Kendall."

"I love you, too."

"Mom! Come on!"

Kendall smiled up at him. "Welcome to the family, Gabe."

Set in darkness beyond the ordinary world.
Passionate tales of life and death.
With characters' lives ruled by laws the everyday
world can't begin to imagine.

Introducing NOCTURNE, a spine-tingling
new line from Silhouette Books.

The thrills and chills begin with
UNFORGIVEN by Lindsay McKenna

Plucked from the depths of hell, former military sharp-shooter Reno Manchahi was hired by the government to kill a thief, but he had a mission of his own. Descended from a family of shape-shifters, Reno vowed to get the revenge he'd thirsted for all these years. But his mission went awry when his target turned out to be a powerful seductress, Magdalena Calen Hernandez, who risked everything to battle a potent evil. Suddenly, Reno had to transform himself into a true hero and fight the enemy that threatened them all. He had to become a Warrior for the Light....

Turn the page for a sneak preview of
UNFORGIVEN by Lindsay McKenna.
On sale September 26, wherever books are sold.

Chapter 1

One shot...one kill.

The sixteen-pound sledgehammer came down with such fierce power that the granite boulder shattered instantly. A spray of glittering mica exploded into the air and sparkled momentarily around the man who wielded the tool as if it were a weapon. Sweat ran in rivulets down Reno Manchahi's drawn, intense face. Naked from the waist up, the hot July sun beating down on his back, he hefted the sledgehammer skyward once more. Muscles in his thick forearms leaped and biceps bulged. Even his breath was focused on the boulder. In his mind's eye, he pictured Army General Robert Hampton's fleshy, arrogant fifty-year-old features on the rock's surface. Air exploded from between his lips as he brought the avenging hammer down. The boulder pulverized beneath his funneled hatred.

One shot...one kill...

Nostrils flaring, he inhaled the dank, humid heat and drew it deep into his massive lungs. Revenge allowed Reno to endure his imprisonment at a U.S. Navy brig near San Diego, California. Drops of sweat were flung in all directions as the crack of his sledge-hammer claimed a third stone victim. Mouth taut, Reno moved to the next boulder.

The other prisoners in the stone yard gave him a wide berth. They always did. They instinctively felt his simmering hatred, the palpable revenge in his cinnamon-colored eyes, was more than skin-deep.

And they whispered he was different.

Reno enjoyed being a loner for good reason. He came from a medicine family of shape-shifters. But even this secret power had not protected him—or his family. His wife, Ilona, and his three-year-old daughter, Sarah, were dead. Murdered by Army General Hampton in their former home on USMC base in Camp Pendleton, California. Bitterness thrummed through Reno as he savagely pushed the toe of his scarred leather boot against several smaller pieces of gray granite that were in his way.

The sun beat down upon Manchahi's naked shoulders, grown dark red over time, shouting his half-Apache heritage. With his straight black hair grazing his thick shoulders, copper skin and broad face with high cheekbones, everyone knew he was Indian. When he'd first arrived at the brig, some of the prisoners taunted him and called him Geronimo. Something strange happened to Reno during his fight with the name-calling prisoners. Leaning down after he'd won the scuffle, he'd snarled into each of their bloodied faces that if they were going to call him anything, they would call him *gan,* which was the Apache word for *devil.*

His attackers had been shocked by the wounds on their faces, the deep claw marks. Reno recalled doubling his fist as they'd attacked him en masse. In that split second, he'd gone into an altered state of consciousness. In times of danger, he transformed into a jaguar. A deep, growling sound had emitted from his throat as he defended himself in the three-against-one fracas. It all happened so fast that he thought he had imagined it. He'd seen his hands morph into a forearm and paw, claws extended. The slashes left on the three men's faces after the fight told him he'd begun to shapeshift. A fist made bruises and swelling; not four perfect, deep claw marks. Stunned and anxious, he hid the knowledge of what else he was from these prisoners. Reno's only defense was to make all the prisoners so damned scared of him and remain a loner.

Alone. Yeah, he was alone, all right. The steel hammer swept downward with hellish ferocity. As the granite groaned in protest, Reno shut his eyes for just a moment. Sweat dripped off his nose and square chin.

Straightening, he wiped his furrowed, wet brow and looked into the pale blue sky. What got his attention was the startling cry of a red-tailed hawk as it flew over the brig yard. Squinting, he watched the bird. Reno could make out the rust-colored tail on the hawk. As a kid growing up on the Apache reservation in Arizona, Reno knew that all animals that appeared before him were messengers.

Brother, what message do you bring me? Reno knew one had to ask in order to receive. Allowing the sledgehammer to drop to his side, he concentrated on the hawk who wheeled in tightening circles above him.

Freedom! the hawk cried in return.

Reno shook his head, his black hair moving against his broad, thickset shoulders. *Freedom? No way, Brother. No way.* Figuring that he was making up the hawk's shrill message, Reno turned away. Back to his rocks. Back to picturing Hampton's smug face.

Freedom!

* * * * *

Look for UNFORGIVEN by Lindsay McKenna,
the spine-tingling launch title from
Silhouette Nocturne ™.
Available September 26, wherever books are sold.

Introducing...

nocturne

a spine-tingling new line
from Silhouette Books.

These paranormal romances will
seduce you with dark, passionate tales
that stretch the boundaries of conflict,
desire, and life and death, weaving
a tapestry of sensual thrills and chills!

Don't miss the first book...

UNFORGIVEN

by *USA TODAY* bestselling author

LINDSAY
M^cKENNA

*Launching October 2006,
wherever books are sold.*

THE DIAMOND SECRET

by Ruth WIND

THIS DIAMOND WASN'T A GIRL'S BEST FRIEND...

When a bag switch at a Scottish airport left her in possession of a stolen medieval diamond, gemologist Sylvie Montague had to escape being the fall guy—fast. But soon Sylvie had to protect against another grand larceny—the theft of her heart by the man behind the heist....

Available March 2006

SAVE UP TO $30! SIGN UP TODAY!

INSIDE *Romance*

The complete guide to your favorite
Harlequin®, Silhouette® and Love Inspired® books.

✓ Newsletter ABSOLUTELY FREE! No purchase necessary.

✓ Valuable coupons for future purchases of Harlequin,
  Silhouette and Love Inspired books in every issue!

✓ Special excerpts & previews in each issue. Learn about all
  the hottest titles before they arrive in stores.

✓ No hassle—mailed directly to your door!

✓ Comes complete with a handy shopping checklist
  so you won't miss out on any titles.

- -

SIGN ME UP TO RECEIVE INSIDE ROMANCE
ABSOLUTELY FREE

(Please print clearly)

_____
Name

_____
Address

_____
City/Town   State/Province   Zip/Postal Code

(098 KKM EJL9)

Please mail this form to:
In the U.S.A.: Inside Romance, P.O. Box 9057, Buffalo, NY 14269-9057
In Canada: Inside Romance, P.O. Box 622, Fort Erie, ON L2A 5X3
OR visit http://www.eHarlequin.com/insideromance

IRNBPA06R   ® and ™ are trademarks owned and used by the trademark owner and/or its licensee.

HARLEQUIN *Blaze*

Those sexy Irishmen are back!

Bestselling author

Kate Hoffmann

is joining the Harlequin Blaze line—and she's
brought her bestselling Temptation miniseries,
THE MIGHTY QUINNS, with her.
Because these guys are definitely Blaze-worthy….

All Quinn males, past and present, know the legend
of the first Mighty Quinn. And they've all been
warned about the family curse—that the only thing
capable of bringing down a Quinn is a woman.
Still, the last three Quinn brothers never guess
that lying low could be so sensually satisfying….

The Mighty Quinns: Marcus, on sale October 2006
The Mighty Quinns: Ian, on sale November 2006
The Mighty Quinns: Declan, on sale December 2006

Don't miss it!

Available wherever Harlequin books are sold.

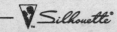

SPECIAL EDITION™

Experience the "magic" of falling in love at Halloween with a new *Holiday Hearts* story!

UNDER HIS SPELL

by KRISTIN HARDY

October 2006

Bad-boy ski racer J. J. Cooper can get any woman he wants—except Lainie Trask. Lainie's grown up with him and vows that nothing he says or does will change her mind. But J.J.'s got his eye on Lainie, and when he moves into her neighborhood and into her life, she finds herself falling under his spell....

THE PART-TIME WIFE

by *USA TODAY* bestselling author

Maureen Child

Abby Talbot was the belle of Eastwick society;
the perfect hostess and wife. If only her
husband were more attentiive. But when
she sets out to teach him a lesson and files
for divorce, Abby quickly learns her husband's
true identity...and exposes them to scandals
and drama galore!

On sale October 2006 from Silhouette Desire!

*Available wherever books are sold,
including most bookstores, supermarkets,
discount stores and drug stores.*